WILDFIRE UNICORN

FIRE & RESCUE SHIFTERS: WILDFIRE CREW, BOOK 2

ZOE CHANT

Copyright © 2019 by Zoe Chant

All rights reserved.

No part of this book may be reproduced in any form or by any electronic or mechanical means, including information storage and retrieval systems, without written permission from the author, except for the use of brief quotations in a book review.

Cover designed by Augusta Scarlett

❦ Created with Vellum

AUTHOR'S NOTE

This book is a complete romance without cliffhangers. However, the *Wildfire Crew* series is intended to be read in order.

Each book in the series features a different couple, but characters reoccur throughout, and events from earlier books are referenced in later ones. There is an overarching plot that is gradually revealed over the course of the entire series.

Wildfire Unicorn follows immediately on from the end of *Wildfire Griffin*. Please read that book first!

If you need a reminder of where the previous book finished…the Thunder Mountain Hotshots are currently battling an enormous wildfire in northern California. And they've just discovered something *very* unexpected hiding under a bush…

CHAPTER 1

Wystan Silver knew exactly how many unicorns there were in the world.

Two.

Well, technically three. If he included himself.

His grandfather and father had both been happily mated for decades. He was absolutely certain that neither of them could be hiding a shameful secret. And as for himself...

It was physically impossible for him to have left a surprise baby behind *anywhere*. Let alone in the middle of the north Californian wilderness, a place where he'd never been before.

Which left him completely unable to explain the tiny unicorn hiding in the bushes.

Rory, his firefighter squad leader, cocked a tawny eyebrow at him. "Something you want to tell us, Wys?"

The rest of the hotshot crew were also staring at him with a combination of astonishment and expectation. Wystan pushed down a surge of irritation. They'd all grown up together. They knew the unfortunate, unique difficulties that unmated unicorn shifters faced. Did they *really* think this could have anything to do with him?

"I'm afraid that I'm at as much a loss as you are," he said. Long habit made it easy to maintain a light, pleasant tone, not letting any of his true emotions show in his face or voice. "But in any event, an explanation isn't our most pressing concern."

"No kidding." Joe cast a worried glance over his massive shoulder at the other fire crews working a little way off. He moved so that his towering bulk blocked the baby unicorn from the humans' view. "Try to look casual everyone."

The rest of the squad—Edith, Callum, and Blaise—closed ranks around Joe, forming a wall of yellow safety jackets. Wystan crouched down in their shadow, trying to get a better look at the creature trembling in the tangled thicket of thorns.

"I can't see any obvious injuries from here, but at the very least it's in shock," he said to Rory, who was also down on his hands and knees in the ash-flecked dirt. "Can you use your power to make it come out fully?"

The griffin shifter shook his head. "It's clearly scared. I don't want to force it with the alpha voice unless we really have to. See if you can persuade it. You're both the same kind of shifter, after all."

That was debatable, but Wystan didn't have a better idea. He stripped off his thick work gloves.

"It's all right, little one." He extended a bare hand toward the baby unicorn so that it could get his scent. "I'm here to help."

The unicorn backed away further, even though the sharp points of the thorns pressed cruelly into its shivering flanks. It was so *tiny*, about the size of a newborn fawn. Its blunt, stubby horn was shorter than his thumb. Had he ever been that small?

No, his unicorn whispered. *Something is wrong here.*

Wystan hardly needed his inner animal to tell him *that*. Even if unicorns had been a dime a dozen, no infant shifter should be found alone and scared on the edge of a raging wildfire. The haze of smoke in the air was getting thicker. They didn't have much time to get the baby to safety.

Which left him with only one option.

Wystan grimaced. "A little space please, everyone."

Bowing his head, he closed his eyes…and shifted.

Grace and strength filled him. As always, the illusion of power stabbed his heart. Even after a lifetime of bitter disappointment, some tiny part of him couldn't help hoping.

Maybe this time...

He opened his eyes to find the baby unicorn staring up at him. The radiance from his horn bathed them both in silver light.

He dipped his head. Tentatively, the other unicorn crept forward. It stretched out its own head, touching its stubby horn to his.

Its mind brushed against his own, light as butterfly wings. No words; just a confused, flickering jumble of emotion and pictures. Fire, dark, fear, pain—and through the chaos, a rising hope. A mental image of something huge and protective, bright as the full moon, crowned with blazing power...

It took him a moment to realize it was himself. Or at least, how the baby saw him.

His heart twisted again. *If only.*

Nonetheless, he sent back telepathic warmth and reassurance. *That's right, little one. You're safe now. I'll protect you.*

The baby gazed up at him with trusting lavender eyes.

Then it collapsed.

Rory was faster than he was. The griffin shifter lunged to catch the unicorn as its frail legs buckled. The tiny creature lay in his big hands, limp as a scarf.

"Unconscious." Rory looked more like a man holding a live bomb than a live baby. "It must have breathed in a lot of smoke while it was hiding from the fire. It needs help. Wystan, given the circumstances, perhaps if you try really hard..."

Wystan was already reaching deep into his soul for his unicorn's power. His horn glowed even brighter as he concentrated. Closing his eyes, he touched the tip to the baby's ash-streaked flank.

You feel what needs fixing, his father had always tried to explain. *You gather your strength, your will. And then you just...send it out.*

He could see his own silver light even through his closed eyelids. He drew on every scrap of will he possessed, jaw clenching so tight his head hurt. Silently, he begged whatever force might be listening for a miracle.

Please. Just once. Just once, let me be able to heal...

Nothing.

Rory cleared his throat after a moment. "Never mind, Wys. Shouldn't have asked. I think your hands would be more useful than your horn right now."

Wystan deflated like a punctured balloon, bright power leaking away. He let go of his own disappointment as well, bottling up the familiar bitter feeling of uselessness. There would be time to brood on his own inadequacies later.

Right now, the baby needed his help. In whatever small way he could provide.

He shrank back into his human form. "Right," he said briskly, stripping off his protective jacket and spreading it out to cushion the ground. "Lay it down here so I can take a look."

"Her," Edith corrected. She always noticed small details that others missed, one of the benefits of her autism. Her hands fluttered in the air, signaling her worry. "She's a girl. Is she going to be okay, Wystan?"

Wystan had never performed triage on an animal before—let alone a unicorn—but he did his best. "Her pulse and breathing are stable. But I think she's gone into shock."

Rory's eyebrows knotted. "In that case, shouldn't she have shifted back?"

Wystan had been wondering about that too. Young shifters usually reverted to human form if they lost consciousness.

"Perhaps she can't," he said, his mind racing. "Her telepathic contact was unlike anything I've ever encountered. She didn't have any language at all."

"Well, she is just a baby," Blaise pointed out.

Wystan shook his head, still busy checking the unicorn for any injuries. "It was more than that. There was an alien flavor to her thoughts. Sentient and intelligent, but not even remotely human. This is going to sound ridiculous, but I don't think she's a shifter at all. I think she's a genuine unicorn."

Edith's eyes widened. She looked like a kid who'd come downstairs on Christmas Day to discover that Santa had delivered a real live pony. "There are actual unicorns?"

Rory looked more like the *parent* of a kid who had unexpectedly been given a pony. "First I've heard of it."

Joe shrugged. "There are weirder things in the sea, bro. And I've seen—I've heard about this sort of thing. Even ordinary humans have urban legends about fabulous creatures hiding in the wild."

Rory blew out his breath, looking unhappily down at the unicorn. "So if she isn't a shifter…what are we supposed to do with her?"

Callum abruptly stiffened, his head turning. "Someone's coming."

Normally mythic shifters were invisible to ordinary humans when they were shifted…but there was no guarantee that the unicorn could do that trick. Especially not in her current state.

Wystan ripped off his crew t-shirt, hastily casting it over the tiny unicorn. He was only just in time. Boots crunched through the leaf litter as the leader of the other firefighting squad joined them.

"Hey guys, what's taking so long—" The human woman broke off, staring at him.

Wystan's pulse spiked. He glanced down…but the baby unicorn was completely hidden, just an anonymous lump under the soft black fabric.

Nonetheless, the female squad boss appeared to have completely lost her train of thought. And the ability to speak.

Rory rose to his feet, oh-so-casually blocking the woman's view. "We're just about finished here. Where do you need us next?"

"Guh." The woman swallowed hard. "Over on the chest. I mean the line! We need your help on the line!"

"Of course." Rory put a hand on her shoulder. "Show me where you want us to clear fuel. The rest of my squad will be along in a second."

The woman resisted his attempt to steer her away, her head swiveling around like an owl's. Belatedly, Wystan realized that he *was* standing in the middle of a forest fire with no shirt on.

He had to be breaking at least a dozen health and safety regulations.

Fortunately, Rory had realized the problem too. He dropped into the deep, rumbling tones of the alpha voice, focusing his power on the gawping woman. *"Everything's fine here. Nothing to see. Fighting the wildfire is more important."*

The woman blinked at last. "Right. Yes. It's certainly getting…hot."

Blaise smothered a snicker.

"The fire's not *that* close," Edith said, sounding puzzled.

"Well, we need to get on with fighting it before it gets any closer," Rory said firmly. "But there's something else that needs our attention too. We found the animal that you heard earlier."

The woman shook herself as though waking up from a dream. "Oh, the one that was stuck in the thorns? What was it?"

"Baby deer," Rory said without the slightest trace of hesitation. "Our paramedic's going to get it to safety. He'll take care of it."

"Rory, I'm going to need more than my emergency kit." Wystan scooped up the unicorn, being careful to keep it safely hidden in his shirt. "The, ah, fawn needs proper care and attention. Food, medicines, somewhere warm and safe to recover. This is going to require proper facilities, not a tent in the middle of nowhere."

"There's an animal rescue unit deployed back at the main fire camp. They've got trailers set up for this kind of thing." The woman frowned in concern. "But that's hours from here by foot. And I don't think Control will dispatch a rescue helicopter for a deer."

"No need." Wystan caught Callum's eye. The pegasus shifter nodded slightly. "We'll manage."

"Right. See what you can do. We'll meet you back at camp later." Rory managed to draw the other squad boss away at last. "Now, let's work out how we're going to stop this fire…"

Edith lowered her voice as the two leaders moved off. "Wystan, what are you going to tell the animal rescue officer?"

The baby unicorn was a soft, warm bundle in his arms. Its silky mane tickled his bare chest.

"I," Wystan said, "have absolutely no idea."

CHAPTER 2

"People," Candice Ayres announced to the world in general, "suck."

"A strange sentiment." Her colleague Bethany didn't look up from examining their patient. "Coming from someone who's currently being savaged by a rat."

"It's not *savaging* me."

"You're bleeding," Bethany pointed out.

Candice looks down at the thin line of red trickling out from under her glove. "Eh. I've had worse. Remember the goat?"

"I try very hard to forget the goat. Lift it up a bit so I can listen to its heart."

Candice raised her arm higher, the rat dangling from her wrist like a particularly Goth bracelet, so that Bethany could get at the rodent's chest. She hid her wince as the chisel-like teeth bit down even harder.

She was used to pain. At least this was in a good cause.

"It's all right, sweetie," she crooned to the animal. "We just want to check that you're okay. We're going to take care of you. Not like the horrible owner who left you to burn to death."

Bethany shot her an exasperated look over her stethoscope. "You always have to think the worst of people. Maybe they were out at work and couldn't get back home when the evacuation order went out."

Candice curled her lip. "You didn't see the house. Someone had enough time to take their flat screen tv and game consoles, but they left this cutie behind."

"Can't imagine why," Bethany muttered, now struggling to get a finger between the rat's clamped jaws. "Get *off*, you scrawny terror."

"It's not his fault. You'd bite too, if someone snatched you out of your peaceful home and shoved a thermometer up your butt." Candice scooped up the rat with her free hand, protecting the sleek black creature from the vet. "Stop pawing at him, you're just upsetting him further. Let him calm down in his own time."

"It's got its *teeth* in your *wrist*."

"He'll let go when he's ready." Candice shrugged. "If nothing else, he has to get hungry eventually."

Bethany sighed, giving up. "Is there *any* creature you don't unconditionally love?"

"I will admit that I find it difficult to appreciate mosquitoes."

"I'm pretty sure you'd still try to nurse one back to health." Bethany dropped the stethoscope back into her medical kit. "Well, it's your arm. I'll go get a cage ready in the small animal tent for when the little demon decides it's feasted on enough human flesh for one day."

Cuddling the rat in the crook of her arm, Candice leaned back against the examination table to let the other woman past. The rescue trailer was forty feet long, but so packed with equipment that moving around inside required balletic coordination. It was basically an entire veterinary surgery on wheels.

Bethany wove around the neatly-labelled stacks of supply crates and cages with the ease of long practice, snagging a blanket and a bag of rodent chow along the way. As she shouldered open the trailer door, a flurry of ash scudded in, along with a swirl of noise—men's shouts, the thudding roar of a passing helicopter, the ever-present rumble of trucks carrying firefighters to the front lines.

The rat tensed, ears flattening. Four sets of pinpoint, needle-sharp claws joined the teeth digging into her flesh.

Candice grimaced. Still, at least it was her right arm. The rat was mostly latched onto scar tissue. It didn't hurt *too* badly.

Cradling the rat as best she could, she awkwardly swept the ash out with the side of her boot, adding it to the growing drifts mounded outside. It was impossible to maintain a surgically clean environment in the midst of fire camp. The hubbub from the surrounding trailers and tents dropped back into a dull murmur of background noise as she kicked the door closed again.

"It's okay, little guy." She sat down on an empty dog cage, stroking the rat with her free hand. "There, see? It's quieter now. You're safe here."

Slowly, the rat's knotted muscles relaxed. Its jaw relaxed a tiny fraction. Whiskers wriggled as it tested the air.

Thankfully, all it would be able to scent was disinfectant and laundry soap. The most recent batch of injured animals had been transferred to proper medical facilities this morning, for better treatment than the emergency rescue team could provide. She was glad that all the critical-care cages were empty. The last thing the poor rat needed at the moment was a distressed, whimpering dog or complaining cat in the background.

"Nothing to be scared of, sweetie." She kept her voice soft and low. Claw by claw, the rat relaxed. "No predators or nasty humans here. Just you and me—"

Someone knocked on the trailer door.

The rat promptly redoubled its death grip on her arm.

Candice very much felt like biting too. Preferably the idiot who had just ignored the DO NOT DISTURB - INJURED ANIMALS sign prominently posted outside the trailer.

Sheltering the rat in the crook of her arm, she flung open the door. "This had better be an emergency—*whoa*."

The man on her doorstep was the most beautiful person of any gender she'd ever seen. If he hadn't been standing right in front of her, she would have sworn he had to be Photoshopped.

His short, spiky hair was a startling platinum blond, moonlight touched with the faintest hint of gold. No question of it not being his natural color—his eyebrows and eyelashes were the same ethereal shade. A streak of ash on the side of his face only emphasized the perfection of his razor-sharp cheekbones.

Even dressed in soot-stained, bulky turn outs, he looked like he'd stepped off the cover of GQ. He should have been plastered across twenty-foot billboards advertising exorbitantly expensive men's cologne—*Wildfire, by Chanel*—not standing in the middle of a disaster zone.

"I'm terribly sorry to bother you," he started. Even his accent was ravishing. He sounded as though he'd grown up in a Jane Austen novel, all cultured English courtesy. "But I—"

Their eyes met.

"I," he stuttered. "You."

Familiar irritation swamped attraction. She heaved a sigh.

"Let's get this over with." Deliberately, she turned her head so that he could get a good look at the full extent of her scars. "It was a fire, it was a long time ago, yes, I know plastic surgeons can do amazing things these days. No, I can't afford it. Yes, I know about crowdfunding, and I haven't the slightest interest—I'd much rather people donated money to animal rescue charities. If that covers all your questions, can we move on?"

Normally that was enough to make people blush and look away, mumbling apologies. He, however, just kept on staring at her.

"Hello?" She snapped her fingers in front of his face. "Earth to whoever you are?"

He blinked at last, jerking back. As well he might, given that she'd just brandished a rat at him.

"Oh no." She withdrew her arm hastily. "I'm so sorry!"

"I, ah." The man's throat worked. He was *still* staring at her. "That's quite all right."

"I wasn't talking to you." She cuddled the rat back against her chest, dropping her voice into a soothing croon. "Poor little guy, I forgot you were there. I'm sorry I flung you about like that."

The firefighter's eyes flickered from her face at last, dropping to the rat attached to her arm. His whole body tensed.

She shot him a death glare. "Shut up and stay still," she said, still in sing-song baby tones. "I need to calm him down before I can help you."

The man jerked his chin in the direction of the rat. He seemed to have his own hands full as well—his arms were wrapped around his torso, supporting something bundled under his jacket. "But it's hurting you."

"Not really," Candice lied. "He barely got through my glove. I'm fine."

"I'm a paramedic." The man shifted his hidden bundle, freeing up one arm. "Please, let me help."

"Stop it," Candice hissed, trying to shelter the rat. "You'll only upset him—"

The words died on her tongue. The rat's ears were up, whiskers bristling in the man's direction. As he reached for the rodent, it gladly relinquished its grip on her arm, swarming up his instead.

The man chirruped at the rat, his supermodel features softening into a gentle, genuine smile. "There's a fine fellow. Where would you like me to put him?"

The sight of him cuddling a fluffy animal had melted her higher brain functions. And her ovaries as well.

Candice firmly reminded herself that he was almost certainly an asshole. Good-looking guys never had to work on developing a winning personality.

"Uh." She managed to drag her attention away from those strong, sensitive hands and back onto more important matters. "We don't have any rodent cages in here—this trailer is our examination and treatment center. I'll need to take him over to the tent where we're keeping the smaller animals until we can get them taken to a local shelter."

"I'll just pop him up here for now, then." He lifted the animal to his shoulder. It snuggled against his neck, pink tail curling around the pale, smooth column of his throat.

Candice had never been jealous of a rat before.

The man ducked his head, looking at her sidelong. It was a curiously shy, endearing expression, as though he wasn't quite sure of his welcome.

Which was nonsense. A man who looked like he did would be welcome *anywhere*, anytime. Even with a rat on his shoulder.

He would definitely be welcome in her bed tonight, for example. Or on the examination table, or up against the nearest wall, right here and now...

Candice gave herself a mental slap. He was eying her like that because of her scars, obviously. The livid burn marks stretching over the right side of her face always made people nervous. They never knew where to look.

The man held out a now rat-free hand. "Allow me to introduce myself. Wystan Silver, at your service. I'm with the Thunder Mountain Hotshots."

Looked like a Greek god, sounded like a Regency aristocrat, good with animals *and* he was an elite wildland firefighter?

Clearly the man was an axe murderer in his spare time. No one was that perfect unless they were hiding something.

"Candice Ayres." She pulled off her glove to give him a firm handshake. A strange electric jolt shot through her as their palms met. "I'm the senior Animal Control officer here."

She started to let go again, but Wystan's fingers tightened, stopping her. He turned her hand over, revealing the neat puncture marks in the side of her wrist.

She caught her breath as he brushed his thumb lightly over her skin. Not from pain—he was being careful not to touch the wound itself—but from the sheer awareness of his presence. Just that tiny amount of contact had every nerve in her body sparking.

She had got to get a grip on her hormones.

Wystan frowned, bending down to inspect the bite more closely. "This needs medical attention."

"I won't say no, if you're offering." Candice raised an eyebrow at him. "But haven't you got something else you need to give me first?"

"Oh," he breathed, lifting his head. "Yes."

His eyes were startlingly green, the color of new spring leaves.

This close, she could see shadows in them, and secrets. She felt like she'd stumbled into a hidden forest glade, lush and wild, where no one had ever set foot before.

Right. She definitely needed to get laid.

She cleared her throat, jerking her chin at the wriggling lump under his jacket. "I meant, whatever animal you've got hidden under there. Assuming that *is* an animal, and not an alarming mobile stomach tumor."

A faint flush crept over those sculpted cheekbones. He straightened quickly, releasing her hand. "Er. Yes. But it's a bit…unusual."

"Buddy, a nice little old lady once asked us to visit her house because she was worried her 'babies' would be lonely while she was in hospital. Turned out she was keeping fourteen fully-grown alligators in her basement." Candice shrugged. "Trust me, I've seen it all in this job."

"Ah." Wystan's arms curved protectively around his abdomen, like a pregnant woman cradling her bump. "I am fairly certain you won't have seen this before. Perhaps you should sit down."

Oh. *There* was the flaw. He was a patronizing ass.

Pity.

Still a piece of man-candy she could lick for hours, mind.

"Don't tell me how to do my job." She grabbed the dangling tag of his jacket zipper. "Nothing you've got under there could possibly surprise me."

CHAPTER 3

He was so caught up in the wondrous beauty of his mate's eyes, he didn't register what her hands were doing until it was too late.

With a firm jerk, she pulled his zip down. His jacket fell open, revealing everything.

He froze.

Candice froze.

The baby unicorn popped up like an adorable, fluffy version of the chest-bursting monster from *Alien*.

Her body was still swathed in his t-shirt, but her incriminating head was on full display. She'd woken up when Callum had dropped them off at the edge of the camp, and had been increasingly wriggly ever since. There was nothing quite like trying to do a nonchalant walk through a crowd of mundanes while you were being repeatedly head butted in the chest by an annoyed unicorn.

Now her pointed ears pricked up, swiveling in Candice's direction. The firefly glow of her tiny horn brightened.

"Er," Wystan said, as Candice's jaw dropped. "I can explain."

"Okay, I admit, I wasn't prepared for this," Candice said faintly. "I think I'm going to need a minute here."

He wondered how he could possibly catch her if she swooned, given that his arms were fully occupied with what was now an unhelpfully enthusiastic unicorn. If the worst came to the worst, he'd just have to try to dive to the ground ahead of her in order to cushion her fall.

"Take deep breaths," he urged, watching her pupils for any sign that she was going into shock. "In through your nose. Hold. Out through your mouth. Sit down if you feel light-headed."

His effort to calm her succeeded, albeit in an unexpected way. Her dazed expression sharpened into annoyance.

"Oh, get over yourself." Suddenly all business, she plucked the bundle of unicorn from his arms. "You aren't *that* dazzling. Now let's see what we've got here. Hi, baby. Aren't you a cutie?"

She plopped the baby unicorn down onto the examination table. All brisk efficiency, she unwrapped his shirt from the gleaming white body. Without a trace of surprise, she began to palpitate the foal's abdomen.

Wystan was left with both his jacket and his mouth gaping open.

"You're taking this very well," he said after a moment.

Candice didn't look up as from her examination. "I've treated animals while literal wildfire swept toward me. You aren't the hottest thing I've ever had to work near."

...What?

Our mate is not easily impressed, his unicorn informed him. *We need to remove more clothing.*

He was so addled, he actually found himself reaching for his belt buckle. Candice shot him a startled look. He hastily drew his jacket back together instead.

"I, ah, I think there's some confusion here," he said, clutching at the fire-resistant fabric as though it was a string of pearls.

Candice snorted. "Well, either I'm unknowingly starring in a very bizarre porno, or you breathed in a whole lot of fumes out on the line. I know which option I'm picking. Just sit down there a minute, okay? I'll take you over to the first aid tents as soon as I can, but this fawn needs attention first."

"Fawn," Wystan repeated blankly. *"Fawn?"*

"You must be a city boy. What did you think she was, a goat?" Candice's sharp voice softened into a maternal coo. "She's the sweetest little baby albino deer, aren't you cutie?"

Wystan sank down onto a dog crate, relief washing through him. She only saw a deer. She had no idea that her patient was actually a unicorn.

She had no idea that *he* was a unicorn.

The thought was like a bucket of ice water dumped over his head. Dismay swamped relief.

How on earth was he supposed to open *this* conversation?

Actually, that isn't a fawn, he pictured himself saying. *She's a unicorn. I'm one too. Also, by the way, you're my one true mate and I am irrevocably, permanently, madly in love with you.*

Forget taking him to the first aid facilities. She'd be calling for some large, burly orderlies to gently escort him away in a straitjacket.

"Poor baby. You've been through a rough time, haven't you?" Candice said to the unicorn. "What shall we call you? Snowflake?"

The baby unicorn did not look at all impressed with this suggestion. She caught Wystan's eye, and a confused jumble of colors flashed through his head. The telepathic images were too foreign to parse, but the overall emotion was clear.

"You know," he said cautiously. "I'm not sure she looks like a Snowflake. She may be small, but she doesn't strike me as delicate or fragile."

Golden approval shimmered through his head. Candice gave him a startled look, which turned more thoughtful as she looked down at the baby.

"Actually, you're right. She's a little fighter, this one." She pursed her lips. "So what would you name her?"

Wystan frowned, focusing. He leaned forward to put one hand on the baby's soft hide. The closer contact allowed him to see her telepathic message more clearly.

"Something fierce and bright and fast," he said slowly. "Like... Lightning? Or Comet?"

No, that isn't quite right. The mental picture the unicorn was insistently sending was more abstract. A concept rather than an actual thing…

He smiled, getting it at last. "Flash. That's her name."

"Flash," Candice said, as though tasting the word. The baby gave a happy neigh, ears pricking up. "Huh. She seems to like it. You've got a good eye. Flash it is, then." She straightened from her examination. "Warmth and fluids are what she needs now. Wystan, can you pass me one of those heat pads?"

Wystan twisted around to find a stack of self-heating chemical packs neatly stacked on the shelf behind him. He cracked one between his hands to activate it, then tossed it to Candice.

"So you think she'll be all right?" he asked.

Candice swaddled the heat pad in a fuzzy blanket, making up a bed in a wire-framed cage. "I'll monitor her round the clock just to be safe, but I'm confident she'll make a full recovery. The biggest challenge will be finding somewhere to take her."

His stomach lurched. In the rush to see to the baby's immediate needs, he hadn't stopped to consider the future.

"All of the rescue shelters around here are only able to house domestic animals," Candice continued, looking as concerned as he felt. "Deer are outside their remit, unfortunately. I'll have to make some calls."

"Actually, I can help with that," he said, improvising at top speed. "I have some friends who work very closely with wild animals. They'd be glad to help."

"Are you sure?" Candice sounded doubtful. "It'll be a long-term commitment. She's not going to be able to be released back into the wild, not standing out the way she does. Albino animals don't tend to last long."

"It won't be a problem," he said firmly. "I'll make sure she has a forever home."

He was determined to do everything in his power to reunite the baby with her family. But if that turned out not to be possible…he'd take care of her himself.

Oh good. This hypothetical future conversation with Candice was getting better and better. *Hello, I'm a unicorn, your mate, and as of today I'm also unexpectedly a single dad to a four-footed daughter. Marry me?*

It was probably a bit much.

He pushed that problem aside for now. "It might take me a little while to make arrangements. Would you mind looking after her here for a few days? I'm happy to pay for her upkeep, of course."

Candice broke into a smile that warmed every inch of his body. "Well, I never turn down a donation. Now, let me just get Flash here settled, and then I'll take that rat off your shoulder. If I can. He certainly seems to have taken a shine to you."

He'd almost forgotten the rodent was there. The rat had dozed off, curled trustingly into the hollow of his neck.

"Animals tend to like me." He patted the rat absently. It made a whuffling, snuffly noise in its sleep, whiskers tickling his skin. "Runs in the family, actually. Many creatures seem to be attracted to us."

Candice was bustling around the trailer, gathering cartons and supplies from the shelves. She stretched over him to fetch a bottle, treating him to an exceptionally fine view between the straining buttons of her flannel shirt. As he sat in riveted attention, she flashed him a sly sideways look.

"Mmm." She leaned even closer, inhaling deeply through her nose. "Well, you do smell good."

Was she…*flirting* with him?

His unicorn stamped a hoof in exasperation. *She is doing everything short of turning around and lifting her tail. Of course she wants us to mount her! Right now!*

His unicorn, like all stallions, tended to have a somewhat over-inflated opinion of itself.

She's literally only known us for ten minutes, he silently reminded his egotistic beast. *And for at least eight of those, we've been acting like a raving lunatic. I highly doubt that she's overcome with lust* just *yet.*

Unlike himself, unfortunately.

He tamped his animal urges down as best he could. This was difficult, given the limited floor space in the trailer. Candice kept brushing against him—no doubt inadvertently—as she went about the task of preparing a bed and bottle for the unicorn.

Much as he tried to control himself, he couldn't tear his gaze away from her. He had never seen anything as perfect as the curve of her waist, or as graceful as the deft sway of her hips. He longed to press his lips to the tender nape of her neck, enticingly exposed by her short, boyish haircut.

The haircut exposed her scars, too. He'd noticed that she made no attempt to minimize or hide the pink, shiny burn marks that ran down the right side of her face and neck. Her bold assurance was utterly intoxicating.

He watched as her swift, capable hands settled the baby unicorn into a cozy nest. He couldn't help imagining what it would be like to have that confident, sure touch exploring his own body…

Wystan shifted position, surreptitiously tugging his jacket further down. There was a child present, after all.

"There, that's better, isn't it?" Candice cooed to the unicorn as the baby began sucking eagerly on a propped-up bottle. "You just fill that little belly, then you can have a nice long sleep. I'll be right here if you need anything. Now," her tone turned more business-like as she turned back to him. "Time to see about that rat."

He caught her wrist as she reached for the rodent. "No. First, we need to take care of you. Or had you forgotten your injury?"

From the dismissive glance she cast the bite mark on her arm, she had. "Eh. It's fine. You don't need to fuss over me."

"Actually I do," he said firmly, standing up so that they could trade positions. "It's my job."

She made a face, but took a seat on the dog crate. "Oh, right. You mentioned that you're a paramedic."

"Among other things." He unclipped his emergency medical kit from his belt and crouched down.

Candice scrutinized him as he pulled on a pair of sterile surgical gloves. "Wystan, are you sure *you* don't need treatment? You're still looking a little dazed."

"Truly, I'm perfectly well." He essayed a wry smile up at her. "It's just turning out to be rather an eventful day."

"Heh. I bet." Candice held out her arm, allowing him to inspect the bite. "Where did you find Flash, anyway? Somewhere out on the front lines?"

"Yes. My crew are deployed on the east advance today. Area 15B."

Candice's eyebrows shot up. "That's a long way out. How did you manage to sweet-talk someone into air-rescuing a deer? Flash your abs at them?"

He chuckled, thinking of Callum. "Actually I did, though I highly doubt that influenced him. I have a friend who has a softer heart than he cares to admit. He gave me a lift. Now, my apologies, but this may sting a bit."

Candice's breath hissed between her teeth as he dabbed the bite with an antiseptic wipe. "How come no doctor will ever just flat-out admit that something is going to hurt like hell?"

Wystan clenched his jaw, wrestling his protective instincts. He *had* to cause his mate discomfort if he was to properly treat her injury.

Settle down, he snapped at his furious unicorn. *I don't like it any more than you do. If you don't want me to hurt her, you* heal her.

His unicorn bared its teeth, but grudgingly subsided.

Well, that settled *that* question for once and for all. If even an injury to his mate didn't unlock his theoretical healing ability, nothing ever would.

So what did he have to offer her?

"Oh, what the heck," Candice muttered while he was still brooding over that one. "Wystan, sorry if I've misread things, but if I don't at least ask, I'm going to be kicking myself for the rest of the week. If you aren't working tonight, do you want to come back here?"

His glum mood lifted at the prospect of being able to do something for her. "Of course. I'd be delighted. I can watch over the baby while you rest."

Candice gave him a level look. One that clearly said she was once again wondering whether all his brain cells had fallen out his ears.

"No, Wystan," she said, enunciating very slowly and clearly. "I'm asking if you'd like to have sex with me."

CHAPTER 4

Oh, balls.

From the expression on Wystan's face, she *had* misread the situation. He couldn't have looked more stunned if she'd proposed a threesome with the rat.

Embarrassment flooded through her, quickly followed by irritation. If he hadn't actually meant to flirt with her, he could have had the courtesy to keep his eyes on her face rather than her butt. And fastened his damn jacket.

The faded yellow material was still hanging open, displaying a mouth-watering slice of his perfect torso. With an effort, she yanked her eyes away from his chiseled muscles.

"Never mind." She pulled her arm out of his slack hands, standing up. "Thanks for the bandage. You should probably get going now."

"No, wait!" He shot to his own feet, waking up the rat on his shoulder. The rodent squeaked in displeasure, scrabbling to maintain its perch. "I'm sorry, I'm not quite sure I—are you asking if I'd like to go on a date with you?"

Wow. No wonder he looked so spooked. Candice wasn't quite sure how he'd managed to misinterpret her *that* badly, but at least it meant she still had a chance.

"Not at all." She faced him head-on, raising her chin. It was something of a struggle to keep her own attention above the level of his clavicle. "Look, I say what I want and mean exactly what I say. I've got no interest in relationships or any of that commitment crap. One night stands suit me just fine. I'm thirsty, you're a hot snack, and I would like to take you back to my tent and bang you like a drum. After that we can happily go our separate ways. No strings, no catches. So what do you say?"

His eyes had gone darker throughout her speech, alarmed confusion giving way to something more feral. For a moment, he was absolutely still, all his attention focused on her as if no one else existed in the whole world.

Then he moved, with the lightning speed of a pouncing cat. Before she quite knew what was happening, he had her pinned against the examination table, his hard body pressed against hers.

Her ovaries were A-OK with this development.

She could hear the ragged edge to his breath, and see his pulse leaping in the hollow of his throat. The heat in his gaze stripped her to her core.

Hot damn, she thought inanely. *It takes real talent to look that sexy while wearing a rat.*

"I do not," he growled, "do one-night stands."

"Well," she said, rather breathlessly. "We should all try new experiences sometimes."

An electric thrill ran over her as his eyes darkened even further. His hands were braced against the table, his rigid arms bracketing her. He leaned in closer, his breath warm against her lips—

"I hate to interrupt," Bethany said from the door, "but I really need a pack of feline worming tablets."

Candice yelped, shoving hard at Wystan's chest, which had no effect whatsoever. For all his prettiness, the man was built like a solid brick wall.

Wystan had a rather dazed expression, as though he'd just woken up from a drunken coma and was still trying to remember who he was and how legs worked. He glanced around at Bethany, and abruptly leaped backward, disengaging himself from Candice.

"Er." Wystan cleared his throat. "Hello. I was just, ah..."

"Yes, I can see that. And with a rat, too. Kinky." Smirking from ear to ear, Bethany reached past him to grab a packet from the shelves. "Don't mind me. Just passing through. I'll let you get back to...what you were doing."

Wystan went a spectacular red from throat to forehead. "I wasn't—we weren't—"

"Then I'm highly disappointed," Bethany informed him. She plucked the rat off his shoulder on her way back out the door. "That woman needs more fun in her life. Don't forget to wipe the examination table down with the antiseptic spray afterward, Candice."

Bethany left with a cheery wave. Wystan stared after her, his face frozen in an expression of mute horror.

"She's going to be teasing me about this for *years*." Candice sighed, then shrugged. "Still, given that she already assumes that we're screwing like bunnies at this very second, we can't do any more damage to my reputation. Where were we?"

She reached for Wystan, but he stepped out of reach. He scrubbed his hands across his face as though to wipe away his blush.

"Not like this," he muttered, expression hidden. "It shouldn't be like this."

Need still beat between her thighs, but Candice had to admit that he had a point. The cramped space wasn't exactly ideal for the sort of acrobatics she had in mind.

Not to mention the audience. The baby deer was watching them both with interest, sucking on her bottle with the air of someone munching through a bucket of popcorn.

Candice's hormones put up a valiant fight, and lost. Sanity reasserted itself.

"Yeah, this isn't the time or the place." With an effort, she pulled herself back together. "Sorry, but I've got to get back to work. I guess you've got to get back to your crew too."

Wystan dropped his hands with a sigh. He was still rather pink around the ears, but he'd reassembled his air of self-controlled, untouchable courtesy. His green eyes were steady, revealing nothing of the thoughts behind them.

"Actually, I'm at a bit of a loose end," he said. "My crew are still out on the fire line. My lift has already headed back that way, so I don't have transport. If I set out now on foot, by the time I catch up with them they'll already be returning to camp. Perhaps there's something I could do to help here?"

There were always more jobs than volunteers. Candice started to say an automatic *Yes*—and hesitated. She was abruptly aware of just how much she *would* like him to be hanging around the trailer the rest of the afternoon.

"Thanks, but no." She picked up a clipboard, pretending to be deeply engrossed in an inventory of dog food. "You go enjoy an afternoon off."

Even without looking at him, she could feel his gaze lingering on her. "Are you certain there's nothing I can do for you?"

Oh, she could definitely think of a few things. More than a few things.

Down, girl, she told herself firmly. Deliberately, she looked at her own reflection in the polished steel surface of the examination table. The scar across her face was better than a bucket of ice cold water. *Keep your distance. You know better than to get too involved.*

"I appreciate the offer, but I don't sleep with volunteer charity workers or colleagues," she said honestly. "Too much potential to get weird. Let's keep business and pleasure separate, okay? Assuming you're still interested."

She jumped as his hand touched her shoulder. She looked up into his face, and the magnetic depths of his eyes. Her pulse stuttered at the wicked, dangerous curve of his mouth.

"Oh," he breathed. "Yes."

CHAPTER 5

My mate. I've met my mate.

The thought echoed endlessly through his head all afternoon. Wystan mechanically bandaged minor burns and treated sunstroke at the first aid tent, lending a hand wherever he could. He smiled and soothed and made his patients feel better, and no one ever guessed that his mind was miles away.

Or, more precisely, about two hundred yards away.

My mate. She's my mate.

It was sheer torture to be separated from her even by a few rows of tents. Her absence was like an amputated limb. His skin felt raw, every touch that wasn't hers painful. The constant noise and bustle of fire camp grated on his senses. It seemed unthinkable that everyone could be carrying on as normal, when everything had changed.

My mate. I've met my mate.

As the hours dragged on, Wystan seizing on any excuse to walk through the camp, just in the hopes of seeing her. A few times, he was rewarded—catching sight of Candice striding from trailer to the tents enclosing the animal cages; conferring with a local ranger; briskly directing a pack of volunteers. He hoarded each stolen glimpse as greedily as a dragon gloating over gold.

They'd agreed to meet at eight, after Candice had finished her shift. It was too much to think about what might—*would*—happen after that. His unicorn was a frenzy of impatience and longing. It was all Wystan could do to restrain his beast. He fixed his mind on the time, counting down each minute.

Soon, he promised his unicorn. *We've waited a lifetime for this. Just a little longer.*

As dusk fell, he found himself repeatedly looking around, feeling a phantom sensation like a hand tapping on his shoulder. He was so caught up in his inner turmoil, it took him some time to realize Rory was trying to contact him telepathically. Welcoming the distraction, he opened his mind to the griffin shifter.

About time, Rory said in his head. **It isn't usually this hard to get your attention. What's wrong? Is the baby all right?**

She's fine, Wystan replied silently. **She's in good hands. I'd rather discuss it in person, though. Are you on your way back to base?**

*We're at *the base,** Rory said wryly. **I've been yelling at your thick skull for the past half hour, ever since we got back in telepathic range. We're just parking now.**

Wystan hurriedly finished off his paperwork for his last patient, scrawling his signature at the bottom of the forms. "My crew's due back in," he said as he handed it over to the medic in charge of the first aid tent. "My apologies, but I have to go rejoin them."

The woman gave him a grateful, weary smile. "Thanks for helping out this afternoon. Anytime you aren't needed on the line, feel free to drop by. We can always use another pair of hands."

A pair of hands. Wystan maintained his smile, giving no indication of how the words cut. Anyone else with a minimum of medical training could have replaced him today. Lacking unicorn magic, he was simply a moderately useful warm body.

And is that all I am to Candice? he wondered as he left the first aid tent. *A body to warm her bed, hands to give her pleasure for a night?*

She had been alarmingly honest about her desires. He admired that directness, even though it had utterly floored him at the time.

She'd been clear about what she expected from him tonight—a casual encounter, nothing more.

His unicorn flared its nostrils in eagerness at the thought. *Yes. Claim her. Show her how we will fulfil her every need.*

Wystan grimaced as he made his way through the sprawling lines of tents and trailers, heading for the edge of fire camp. He wished he shared his animal's unshakable self-confidence. Given his lack of experience, even satisfying Candice's needs on a purely physical level was far from certain. He was just grateful that at least *she* clearly knew what she was doing.

We will please her, his unicorn insisted. *And sharing our body with her will bring her closer. She will begin to see what we offer. She will desire us for more than a single night.*

He hoped that was true. He *needed* that to be true. He couldn't imagine living without Candice's bright, fierce presence in his life. From the moment he'd first met her eyes, she'd claimed his heart. Even now, he felt off-balance, as though he'd left his center of gravity back in her trailer.

The Thunder Mountain Hotshots had pitched their tents some distance away from the edge of the main encampment, as was their habit on any large job like this. Wystan had sometimes heard the humans in the crew grumbling to about always being last in line for breakfast, but not within earshot of Superintendent Buck. The fire chief picked the camp site, and his word was final.

The human firefighters of B and C squads didn't know that Buck selected the remotest sites out of consideration, not sadism. Big crowds were hard on all kinds of shifter, not just unicorns. Super-human senses made it difficult to sleep in the middle of a sprawling encampment. For all his grumpy, surly manner, Buck always took care of his crew—human and otherwise.

At the moment, a casual observer would have been hard pressed to tell that. As Wystan approached the camp, he could hear that the Superintendent was in full creative flow.

"—Will fashion your fuzzy butts into an attractive quilt for my guest bed, understand? You mouthbreathers get so much as a flicker of a bright idea briefly illuminating the cavernous voids you call skulls, you pick up the motherloving radio and *check with me first*! I decide if and when anyone comes off the line, not you second-rate shaved monkeys!"

Buck's stocky, grey-haired form was pacing up and down in front of a hangdog-looking line of shifters. Rory stood a little in front of the rest of A-squad, his broad shoulders braced as though he could physically shield his squad from the Superintendent's wrath. Behind him, Joe, Blaise, and Edith were wearing varying degrees of guilt. Two figures were notable by their absence.

Where's Callum and Fenrir? Wystan sent silently to Rory.

Rory flicked him a pained glance over Buck's shoulder. *Still out in the woods. I asked them to search for any sign of the baby unicorn's parents.*

Wystan winced as a particularly inventive bit of invective from Buck. The Superintendent had a remarkable ability to blister the air without actually swearing. *And you 'forgot' to clear it with the chief first?*

I thought it would be easier to ask forgiveness than permission. Rory returned to his stoic endurance of Buck's tongue-lashing. *In retrospect, that may have been an error.*

The human firefighters of B and C squads were creeping around in the background, earnestly pretending to be completely engrossed in putting equipment away. No one wanted to catch Buck's eye when he was in this sort of mood. The chief's ire had a tendency spill over onto innocent bystanders.

The Superintendent swung around, fixing Wystan with a ferocious glare. As always, Wystan felt his inner beast back off a little, head bowing in respectful acknowledgement of the man's sheer authority. Although Buck was, as far as Wystan knew, completely human, he exuded enough alpha power to cow a dozen unruly werewolves.

"At least one prodigal son returns," Buck growled. "And what have you got to say for yourself?"

"I met my mate," Wystan blurted out.

There was a beat, in which everyone stared at him.

Then Joe let out a loud, raucous whoop that scared a couple of crows out of the nearest pine tree. "Bronicorn! Congratulations!"

"That's wonderful, Wystan!" Edith's hands flapped, expressing her delight. Words spilled out of her in an enthusiastic torrent. "Who is she? Is she a firefighter? Oooh! Is she going to join the team like I did?"

"That would be awesome," Blaise said before Wystan could so much as open his mouth. She glanced around at the others, raising an eyebrow. "No offence, guys, but we could do with more women to balance out this sausage party."

"No argument from me." Joe stuck one hand straight up in the air. "All in favor of Wystan's mate joining the squad?"

"I swear, it's like herding cats on meth," Buck growled, slapping Joe's arm back down again. "What do you think this is, a democracy? Stop flapping your lips. I'm not done yelling."

Wystan noticed Leto, one of the B-squad firefighters, nudging his husband Tanner with an elbow. Shifter hearing let Wystan overhear Leto's muttered, "Do you have the faintest friggin' clue what's going on?"

Tanner shook his head slowly, his face baffled behind his bushy brown beard. The rest of B and C-squads were also looking back and forth between Wystan and Buck as though watching a particularly perplexing tennis match. Wystan caught Buck's eye, jerking his head to indicate their all-too-human audience.

Buck swept his flame-thrower scowl indiscriminately over the rest of his crew. "And what are you lot all gawping at? Practicing your frog impressions for the next season of *America's Got Talent*? Get those tools properly stowed away before I decide to store them up your lazy butts!"

The crew scattered at his roar, fleeing back to their tasks. Buck crooked a finger, motioning A-squad to follow him. The shifters trailed at his heels as he stomped out of earshot of the rest of the crew.

"Seven billion people on this planet," Buck muttered. He looked physically pained. "Seven *billion*. And yet another of my best team happens to bump into his one true soulmate while he's supposed to have his mind on the job. Do normal statistics not apply to you people? Do you magically screw with probabilities just to annoy me?"

"Er." Wystan wasn't quite sure what to say to that one. "Sorry?"

"And now, I suppose, you're going to turn into another Rory," Buck said gloomily. "Moping around like a scolded puppy, and about as useful on the line."

"I didn't *mope*," Rory protested. His face fell as he looked around at them all, taking in their expressions. "Did I?"

"Bro, you were Mopey McMopeface," Joe said, patting him on the shoulder. "It's a miracle Edith didn't run for the hills."

Edith wound her arm around her crestfallen mate's waist. "I thought you were cute."

"Yeah, but the rest of us were about ready to bash him over the head with a shovel and forcibly gift-wrap him for you," Blaise said, grinning. "Don't worry, chief. Wystan can't possibly be worse."

"That remains to be seen," Wystan muttered.

Buck shook his head. "If I'd known shifters attracted weird crap like cat hair on corduroy, I'd have thought twice about hiring a whole damn squad of you. Fated mates, all that business with that demon-snake thing earlier in the summer…and now, apparently, motherloving *unicorns*. Whose good idea was that?"

"What did you do with the baby, Wys?" Edith asked anxiously. "Is she okay?"

As briefly as he could, Wystan filled them in on the events of the afternoon. At least, he *thought* he was being brief. Halfway through his description of Candice, he became aware that Buck was staring at the sky with the expression of a man longing for the sweet relief of death, while the rest of the crew were all exchanging glances and nudging each other.

He broke off his recital, looking around at them all in confusion. "I'm sorry, is there something wrong?"

"Not at all." The lines around Rory's golden eyes crinkled with amusement. "Just…she really *is* your mate."

"Please make him stop," Buck entreated the heavens. "I think I'm developing diabetes."

"She sounds wonderful, Wys," Blaise said. She was also looking a little glazed. "But maybe leave a few things for us to discover about her for ourselves, okay?"

"I'm just relieved you didn't make her a job offer." Buck folded his arms. "I'm running a hotshot crew, not a lonely hearts club."

"Edith worked out all right," Rory said, with the barest hint of a growl in his tone.

"Edith is one in a million," Buck said matter-of-factly. Edith's cheeks went pink, her hands flurrying in embarrassed pleasure. "Any of your mates turn out the same, I'll gladly take them on. But crew members need to earn their place." He fixed Wystan with a penetrating stare. "Every day. *Are* you going to start pining, Wystan? I've got no place for fools on my crew, and love makes the biggest fools of all."

Wystan straightened his shoulders. "I promise I will continue to fulfil my duties to the best of my abilities, Superintendent. This won't affect the crew. And I'm deeply sorry for returning to base camp without permission today. It won't happen again."

Buck grunted, looking marginally mollified. "Well, it *was* a damned unusual situation. Can't say I would have ordered you to do any differently. Just check with me first before you go haring off in future. I need to know where my crew is at all times."

"Ah." His face heated. "In that case…may I have permission to, er, not be in my own tent tonight?"

Joe let out an impressed whistle. "Damn, bronicorn. You work *fast*."

Coming from Joe—a man who, on average, picked up women in under five minutes—it was quite a compliment. Wystan could feel his ears going beet-red.

Buck pinched the bridge of his nose as though he had a headache. "For the love of fuzzy little squirrel nuts. Let me rephrase. Always check in with me *when you're on duty*. What any of you randy freaks do in your own time in base camp, I actively do not want to know."

"No moping and pining for you, hey Wys?" Rory's tone was teasing, but genuine delight showed in his warm eyes. He held out a hand. "Truly, we're all happy for you."

A sheepish smile spread across his own face in response to his squad's beaming grins. He clasped Rory's hand—and snatched his fingers away again with a gasp.

"Wys?" Rory's amusement fell away in an instant. The griffin shifter automatically reached out to support him, but dropped his hands quickly as Wystan flinched away. "What is it?"

Wystan gripped his own wrist, sparks of agony still stabbing through his fingers from that brief contact. He couldn't suppress a hiss of pain.

No wonder Buck was so angry. Apparently I wasn't the only ones skipping out on cutting line today.

He would never have thought that Rory and Edith would engage in some surreptitious extra-curricular activities out in the woods when on duty. But there was no fooling a unicorn.

His own weak beast was much less sensitive to sexual energy than most. But he still couldn't bear to come into contact with people who had recently been intimate. It wasn't like Rory—his oldest friend—to forget his minor disability.

"Usual problem," he said through gritted teeth. "I'm sure it just slipped your mind in all the excitement, but please try to be more careful in future."

Rory blinked at him. "What?"

He cast a meaningful glance at Edith. "You know there are times when I find touch…difficult."

"But Rory and I haven't had sex today." Edith sounded distinctly disappointed by this fact. She sighed, oblivious to Rory's sudden fit of coughing. "We haven't had sex for *three* days, actually."

"I did not need to know that," Buck muttered.

"That can't be right," Wystan said blankly. Even from several feet away, the sexual energy roiling off of Rory and Edith had his unicorn shying away in distaste. "Are you certain?"

"I think I would know when I've had sex!" Edith said indignantly.

A *powerful* unicorn would flinch back from someone who'd last been intimate days ago. But not *his* pathetic beast.

Unless…

He whirled on Joe. The sea dragon's eyebrows shot up as Wystan threw his arms around him.

"Uh, I love you too, bro," Joe said, returning the embrace with some confusion. "Also, are you feeling okay?"

"No," Wystan gasped, releasing him again. "You're like sandpaper on the inside of my skull. Did you seduce that nice lady crew leader out on the line?"

"While we were *working*?" Joe sounded honestly affronted. "Of course not."

"I thought she invited you back to her tent tonight," Blaise murmured.

"*She* seduced *me*," Joe said with great dignity. "And nothing's happened yet. I have standards. I at least demand a blanket between my backside and the ground."

"You hurt too," Wystan said, grabbing Blaise's wrist. It was a much fainter twinge of pain than that from Rory, Edith or Joe, but it was definitely there. "When did you last…?"

"Hey!" Blaise snatched her hand back. "What is this, some kind of unicorn purity test? Stay out of my sex life."

That left only one.

"Do not," Buck said, in tones of great finality, "even think about it."

"Wys, what's going on?" Rory said, looking concerned. "You're acting very strangely."

"Don't you see?" His heart was pounding almost as much as his head. "It's my unicorn! I'm suddenly more sensitive to sexual energy. A *thousand* times more sensitive!"

Buck's eyebrows drew down. "And what the blazes does that mean, in plain English?"

"It means," Wystan said, "that I need to make a phone call."

CHAPTER 6

This was, Wystan was certain, going to be the most mortifying conversation of his life.

He braced himself, and dialed.

The time difference meant that it was some ungodly hour in the morning at the moment in England. Nonetheless, it only took two rings before the video call connected. A familiar white-haired figure frowned up at him from his phone screen, ice-blue eyes narrowed in concern.

"I take it this is an emergency," his father said.

"I need to ask you about sex," Wystan blurted out.

Hugh stared at him. From his appalled expression, he was clearly now hoping that this was all a terrible nightmare.

"Sorry," Wystan added. "Did I wake you up?"

His father grimaced. "No. I'm on duty—"

"Wystan needs to ask about *what*?" said several overlapping voices in the background.

"And you're on speakerphone," his father finished.

"Out of the way, Hughnicorn!" The image on the screen whirled dizzyingly, showing glimpses of a parked fire engine and a rack of turn out gear before focusing on a wide, wicked grin. "This calls for an expert. Let me explain matters to the boy. You see, Wystan, when a mommy unicorn and a daddy unicorn love each other very much—no, wait, let me correct that. When two unicorns, or indeed more than two unicorns, of any or all genders, love each other very much—"

"*Thank* you, Chase." The screen went black as a hand closed over the camera. "I think I can handle this."

"But you'll do it so badly," Chase's voice said, sounding somewhat muffled. "You'll probably use words like 'secretions' and 'gusset.'"

Not for the first time, Wystan wondered how on earth someone like Callum could have a father like Chase.

From the thumps and scuffles coming down the line, his father was having a hard time reclaiming the phone from the pegasus shifter. "Chase, if you don't drop it *right now* I swear I will break your arm, Hippocratic Oath be damned. Dai, John, stop laughing and come restrain this joker, or you'll both be healing your next injuries the slow and painful way that nature intended."

A last burst of white noise, and the picture returned again. Hugh ran his hand through his now somewhat mussed hair, scowling.

"Right," he said, straightening his uniform shirt. "We're private now, or at least as private as it's going to get in a small fire station filled with nosy shifters. Why were you calling? And please don't tell me it really is about sex."

He was really starting to wish that he'd made this a voice-only call. He wasn't quite able to look his father in the eye. "I'm afraid that it is."

His father looked just as pained as Wystan felt. "Didn't we already have this conversation some time ago?"

As if he could have forgotten *that* childhood experience.

It was, of course, an obligatory rite of passage to have your parents sit you down for 'The Talk.' For most children, it was merely excruciatingly embarrassing.

Sex is a beautiful and natural thing, many parents doubtless told their cringing children.

Wystan suspected that very few followed that up with: *And if you ever do it you'll lose your unicorn.*

His father had—in a horrifying hour that still haunted his nightmares—laid out exactly what was on the line. The old legends associating unicorns with virgins had a kernel of truth. If he engaged in any form of sexual activity, he'd lose his inner animal. He'd never shift again.

He'd told Candice that he didn't do one-night stands. It was absolutely true. He'd had no choice other than to remain untouched.

Until now.

"You explained why I had to wait for my mate," Wystan said. He cleared his throat. "Well. I've met her."

Startled joy wiped away his father's usual cranky expression. "Wystan! Truly?"

"Yes. Just this afternoon." Despite everything, Wystan found himself grinning foolishly. "Her name is Candice. She's an animal rescue officer, and utterly marvelous."

His father suddenly seemed to be needing to blink rather a lot. The video picture lurched as Hugh swiped his sleeve across his eyes.

"Well," Hugh said gruffly, coming back into focus again. "Your mother will be very relieved. As am I. You've never breathed a word of complaint, but I know how difficult it's been for you over the years."

"Oh, it's not so bad," Wystan said lightly, on pure reflex. "Can't miss what you've never had."

His father's penetrating stare cut through his automatic defenses. "Wystan. I *know*. You might be able to smile and wave it off with everyone else, but not me. It's not just about denying yourself the physical pleasures. Having to cut yourself off from closeness, intimacy, all forms of human contact—it leaves a deep wound. I'm the one person who truly understands how much it hurts."

"Which is exactly why I need your advice." Wystan hesitated for a moment, searching for the right words. "When you were explaining things to me all those years ago, there were a few areas you left vague."

Hugh coughed, looking embarrassed. "Well, you were eleven at the time. It seemed inappropriate to tell you in detail about my own sexual experiences."

"Believe me, I am very grateful for that decision," Wystan said fervently. "Unfortunately, I suspect I can no longer remain in blissful ignorance."

His father muttered a swearword, rubbing at his forehead. "Sometimes I really wish we were squirrel shifters. What did you want to know?"

"You said that before you met my mother, you used to get terrible headaches around people who were unchaste, right?"

From his father's blink, whatever he'd been expecting him to ask, it wasn't that. "That's correct. My unicorn was unusually sensitive to sexual energy, even for one of our kind. But why are you asking? You've never been too badly affected by that issue, thankfully."

"I *wasn't*," Wystan corrected. "But suddenly I am. Just standing within three feet of Joe gave me a splitting migraine."

"Oh no." Hugh narrowed his eyes. "Wait. Why do you look downright delighted by this development?"

"Don't you see? At last my useless beast is behaving like a proper unicorn! Do you think it's the influence of my mate? You did say that your own bond made your animal stronger."

Hugh's frown deepened. "Yes, but in my case the effect was that I *stopped* experiencing pain from sexual energy. I became a better healer purely because touching other people no longer felt like laying my hands on hot coals."

"I wouldn't mind enduring a bit of pain if it meant I could finally heal."

"I know. And I also know that it's a much heavier burden than you think. I wish you weren't so eager to shoulder it." Hugh shook his head. "Wystan, I'm concerned. This seems backward. Meeting your mate shouldn't cause you pain. Are you certain Candice was the trigger?"

"Positive. It's like meeting her knocked something loose inside me." He keenly felt Candice's absence, like a hollow in his chest where his heart should be. "Perhaps mating her will finally unlock my powers!"

His father suddenly looked alarmed. "Wystan, you aren't thinking of rushing into anything, are you?"

Damnation, he could see his own face going red in the picture-in-picture display. "Well. Er. My mate is certainly a woman who has no qualms in going after what she wants. And I'm fairly certain she's experiencing the mate attraction, albeit on a subliminal level. We're both consenting adults. What harm could there be?"

"More than you can possibly imagine," his father said, strangely urgent. "Wystan, does she know what you are? And what she is to you?"

"It's not exactly something that's easy to work into casual conversation. I only met her today."

Hugh put a hand over his eyes. "And yet you want to leap into bed with her."

Wystan couldn't help bristling. "She *is* my mate."

"Yes, but that's not a magic Get Out Of Jail Free card!" his father snapped, dropping his hand to fix him with a glare. "*Think*, Wystan. The only sexual energy our unicorns can tolerate is pure, true love, freely given and freely accepted. That takes more than a single moment of eye contact!"

He felt like his father had just whipped the ground out from under his feet. "What are you saying?"

His father sighed, his shoulders slumping. For once, he didn't look self-possessed and sardonic. Every line of his face betrayed his worry.

"I'm saying that you can't charge blindly into a physical relationship," Hugh said heavily. "Not for selfish reasons, with secrets still between you. If you do…it won't matter that she's your mate. You'll lose your unicorn."

CHAPTER 7

*B*ethany poked her head through the flap of the feline rescue tent. "Your fawn is loose."

"Ha ha." Candice didn't pause in shaking kibble into bowls. "Very funny."

"No, seriously." Bethany stepped into the tent, Flash cradled in her arms. "I found her wandering around outside. Again."

This time Candice *did* stop, much to the displeasure of the eight cats waiting for their dinner. She narrowed her eyes at the vet. "Are you messing with me?"

"If I was, I'd pick a more believable way to prank you." Bethany shook her head, looking baffled. "I have no idea how she's getting out. Not only that, she's closing and locking the cage behind her. I checked."

Candice frowned at the fawn, who was now innocently nibbling Bethany's shirt buttons. "Well, she can't be magicking her way out."

"You should have named her Houdini." Bethany freed her blouse from Flash's inquisitive mouth. "Maybe the cage is defective."

Personally, Candice thought it far more likely that Bethany *was* messing with her. Though practical jokes were a bit of a departure from the vet's usual sense of humor, which tended more to sarcastic remarks. It was one of the reasons the two of them got on so well.

The feline chorus of disapproval was reaching deafening levels. She went back to her task, doling out the food bowls as fast as she could.

"I'll take a look at the cage once I've finished here," she said, as meows transformed into munching. She cast another glance at the fawn, her frown deepening. "I wonder why she's so determined to escape, anyway."

"Maybe she's lonely in that big trailer all by herself." Bethany was having a hard time keeping a grip on Flash. "Or she's imprinted on you."

"She's a deer, not a duckling. She probably just associates me with food."

Nonetheless, Flash *did* seem to be straining in her direction. The fawn's strange purple eyes were fixed on her face in a way that Candice would have called adoring, if she was a more sentimental person.

It would take a heart of stone to resist that winsome expression. Candice sighed.

"All right, you can stay here with me," she said to Flash. "But you're going back in the cage later, understand? I draw the line at deer in my bed."

Bethany smirked as she handed her the fawn. "Especially when it's already reserved for a smoking hot firefighter."

Candice wrinkled her nose. "If he actually comes."

"Oh, I think he fully intends to come. Let's hope he's got the skills to make sure you do as well." Bethany's dirty grin widened. "Though from what I saw, there's no worries there. Looked like he was on the verge of managing that through two layers of clothing."

Just the memory of Wystan's hard body pressed against hers was having a certain effect. The man had *better* turn up, or her vibrator was going to be getting one heck of a work out tonight.

"You don't mind doing the night checkups?" Candice asked

Bethany. "I know it's my turn on the rota, but I'll take the next two shifts in return."

"Don't make promises now." Bethany waggled her eyebrows. "You might find yourself wanting to keep all your upcoming nights free, at least while a certain hotshot crew is still in camp."

Candice shook her head firmly. "Not going to happen. I don't do rematches."

"Didn't *he* say he didn't do one night stands?"

"Still not going to happen. Anyway, he was just saying that. It's probably part of his standard script to charm women into bed."

Bethany pursed her lips. "Girl, even I can tell that a man who looks like that doesn't need a script to charm anyone. He seemed pretty serious to me."

"Says the lesbian. Be glad you don't have to deal with all the garbage straight men spout. No doubt he assumed he had to dangle the prospect of a relationship in front of me like a worm on a hook."

"Only you would compare a relationship to worms." Bethany sighed. "Well, I can only hope that the sex is so fabulous you finally break your own rules."

"Gee, thanks. It's so nice to know that my best friend is rooting for me to end up sobbing broken-heartedly into a tub of Chunky Monkey."

Bethany gave her a look. "Not *all* relationships end in tragedy, you realize."

Candice turned her head, showing the right side of her face. Nothing more needed to be said.

Bethany cast her eyes up to the heavens, or at least the canvas ceiling, giving up. "Well, I'm going to go take a shower and get a few hour's sleep. Enjoy your definitely-single-use-only firefighter."

"Oh, shut up." Candice shooed her away.

She put Flash down, keeping a careful eye on her in case she lived up to her name and made a bolt for the great outdoors. The little fawn seemed happy now that she had company, though. She nosed about the big tent, inspecting cat litter bags and catch nets with equal curiosity, as Candice finished settling all the rescued cats in for the night.

She was halfway through updating all the feed times on the clipboards when she became aware of something odd.

Normally, cats rescued from fires were defensive and shy, spending most of their time huddled at the very back of their cages. Now, however, every single cat had its nose right up against the bars. Eight pairs of feline eyes were fixed on Flash.

Her first thought was that the cats were viewing the fawn as a four-footed dessert cart. But there was nothing predatory about their regard--no bristling whiskers or eager butt-wiggling. The cats were simply…watching.

No, not just watching. A faint, soft rumbling vibrated the air, underneath the louder hum of the generator.

They were watching…and purring.

"Okay, that's weird." Candice bent to peer through the bars at a big ginger Persian. He stopped purring to shoot her a disgruntled glare, as though she'd interrupted his favorite TV show. "I know she's cute and all, but you guys are supposed to be indifferent to that sort of thing. What happened to the famous cat superiority?"

Flash, for her part, seemed completely unbothered by the mass feline attention. She sniffed noses with the lowest layer of cats without a trace of fear. Even a feral tomcat that had ripped through four of Candice's catch-nets politely exchanged greetings with the fawn, all the while rumbling like a coffee grinder.

"Huh." Candice shook her head in bemusement. "How about that. You're like an emotional support animal for animals. Want a job as a nurse, Flash?"

The little deer's ears swiveled as though she could tell she was being addressed. She cocked her head to one side, then snorted.

"No, suppose not. It's not practical, anyway." Candice bent to pet the fawn. "Wouldn't be much of a life for you, cooped up in metal trailers, carted from disaster zone to disaster zone."

Candice knew it wasn't sensible to get attached to any one animal.

It was one of the first things she'd learned as an animal rescue officer. You had to care deeply, but lightly. Love, but let go.

Nonetheless, some part of her couldn't help wishing that she *could* keep Flash with her. There was just something about the deer. Her white coat seemed to glow with an inner radiance that made even the dingy, patched tent seem warm and homely. As Candice stroked the fawn, her own shoulders relaxed, releasing a knot of tension she hadn't even known she was carrying.

Flash's broad ears pricked up. The fawn went from relaxed to alert in a heartbeat, tiny hooves twinkling as she pranced to the door flap.

"Guess you're trying to tell me someone is coming." Candice scooped up the excited deer just as a soft cough sounded from outside. "Oof! Stop wiggling!"

With some difficulty, Candice managed to juggle Flash and pull back the tent flap. From the fawn's enthusiasm, she'd already guessed who would be standing on the other side of it.

She had not, however, been expecting Wystan to be holding a bouquet of wildflowers.

For his part, he clearly hadn't been expecting her to be holding a fawn.

Flash took full advantage of their mutual surprise.

"Oops." Candice wrestled the deer back, too late. "Sorry. From her point of view, you were offering her a snack."

Wystan looked down at the now mostly headless bundle of stems in his hand. "Do you always answer the door while carrying wildlife?"

Candice shrugged as Flash munched happily, daisy petals dribbling from her busy jaws. "More often than not."

"Perhaps is just as well I wasn't able to locate two dozen red roses." Wystan shook his head, his mouth curling up as he held out the remains of the bouquet—not to her, but to Flash. "Ah well, at least someone's enjoying them."

No one had ever brought Candice flowers before.

Not that she'd ever *wanted* them. As far as she was concerned, gifts were just a not-so-subtle form of pressure—*look, I bought you a thing, now you have to let me into your panties.*

But as Wystan fed the rest of the stalks into Flash's eager maw, something inside her softened a little. It wasn't that he'd brought her flowers, or at least tried to. It was that slight, rueful smile; his genuine amusement as his attempt at a romantic gesture disappeared down a deer's gullet.

You had to like a man who could laugh at himself.

She could really like *this* man.

Oh no, she thought in dismay.

"All gone, I'm afraid," Wystan said to Flash as the fawn licked at his fingers. "I promise I'll find you some more tomorrow. But not right now."

He started to hold out his hand, then grimaced and swapped it for the hand *not* covered in deer spit. "If you're done here for the day?"

If she was smart, Candice knew, she should claim an unexpected emergency. Some animal in urgent need of treatment. She should run a mile before her traitor heart could melt any further. It was a *bad* idea to sleep with someone she actually liked.

But with Wystan standing there in front of her, the setting sun gilding his white-gold hair, she couldn't say no. He'd changed out of his turn out gear, into slim-fitting black jeans and a figure-hugging T-shirt emblazoned with *THUNDER MOUNTAIN HOTSHOTS* in yellow letters. Even though she'd already seen the full glory of his ripped torso, somehow he was even more enticing covered up, like a glittering Christmas present waiting to be unwrapped.

I'm going to regret this, she thought, and took his hand.

CHAPTER 8

I'm doing something very wrong. Wystan hadn't missed that moment of hesitation. For a heart-stopping second, he'd been convinced Candice had been about to shut the tent flap in his face.

He had no idea what had caused her sudden wariness. Even with her hand warm in his, she felt distant, as though there was some invisible barrier between them.

"I'm nearly done here," Candice said, pulling him in the direction of the big trailer. "Just need to put Flash back in her cage."

The baby unicorn in her arms put her ears back, letting out an indignant huff. Wystan received a very distinct mental picture of sharp hooves stomping a wire cage flat.

"I know you don't like it," Candice told the small animal, as though she too had received the telepathic message. "Tough beans. Two's company, three's a crowd." She cast him a sly sideways look. "And the things I'm planning to do tonight aren't for the eyes of kids."

Oh no. Dismay twisted his stomach, even as the wicked glint in her eyes had an entirely different effect on other parts of his body. *Of course. She's still expecting sex.*

We must give our mate what she wants, his unicorn said promptly. *At length. Repeatedly.*

Are you suicidal? he snapped at his inner beast. *She may find us attractive, but we've hardly given her reason to fall head-over-heels in love with us. You heard my father, it's too soon to risk going to her bed. Do you want to disappear in a puff of sexual ecstasy?*

His unicorn flicked an ear, supremely unconcerned. *It would be worth it.*

"Something wrong?" Candice asked. "You're looking a little pained."

"Er." He groped for an excuse that wasn't: *Sorry, the animal in my head is giving me terrible advice.* "Just a bit of a headache."

"Oh." To his dismay, Candice started to pull her hand out of his. "You know, you don't have to make up excuses. If you've changed your mind—"

"No!" He tightened his grip, catching her fingers before she could slip away. "That's not what I meant. I truly did have a headache. But it's gone now."

It was true, he realized. The oppressive weight that had been smothering him all afternoon had lifted. He could no longer feel the grinding irritation of being surrounded by unchaste people. It was as though Candice was an umbrella, sheltering him from the psychic storm of the crowded fire camp.

In one way, it was a relief. It *had* been a strain, coping with his unicorn's increasing distress. He had a new respect for his own father. He could only imagine how hard it had been for him to live with that level of sensitivity for decades.

But on the other hand…the headache had been a *good* sign. If Candice's presence stopped the pain, was she also stopping his powers from awakening at last?

They'd reached the big trailer. He was forced to relinquish Candice at last so that she could unlock the door. She turned to confront him, one hand resting on the handle.

"Look, bud," she said, lifting her chin. Her burn scars stood out vividly against her tanned skin. "I'm a big girl. You don't need to worry about hurting my feelings. You don't really seem to be into this. Maybe we should just call the whole thing off."

"No!" The word shot out of him with rather more force than he'd intended. It was all he could do not to lunge at her. Every instinct screamed to hold her close and never, ever let her go. "Believe me, I am very into you."

Her penetrating blue eyes searched his features as though measuring his sincerity. "Let's be really clear here, just for the sake of formality. You do want to have sex with me tonight, right?"

If he said no *now*, she'd take it as a sign that he wasn't really interested after all. Saying that he wanted to wait or get to know her better first would just sound like a feeble excuse.

He'd been silent too long. Candice was starting to turn away. He seized her shoulders, stopping her.

"Yes." He would have said anything, promised her anything, to stop her from walking away. "Yes. I want that. I want you."

It was, after all, absolutely true.

Candice hesitated a moment longer, then shook her head.

"I can't make you out at all," she said. Nonetheless, she opened the door. "One moment you seem to be in your own little world, the next you're full-on intense. You can relax, you know. Dial it back a little, okay?"

"I'll try." On impulse, he added, honestly, "I'm just terrified that you'll shut the door in my face if I say the wrong thing."

Her expression finally lightened. She hooked a finger over the top of his jeans, making his breath catch in his throat.

She pulled him inside. "Then don't say anything at all."

At that moment, wild horses couldn't have dragged words out of him. Her light touch against his hip set fire to his entire body, banishing all other thought. Only the fact that she still had the baby unicorn in her arms stopped him from pushing her up against the nearest wall.

Candice glanced up at him, and did a double-take, her eyes widening. Her tongue flicked out, brushing over her lips in a way that made his abdominal muscles clench.

"Holy hotness," she muttered. "I take it back. Be as intense as you want. Hold that thought for two seconds, okay? I just need to put Flash to bed. Then I'm all yours."

His unicorn pranced in his mind, horn blazing in triumph. Distantly, he knew that he had to rein his beast in, but at the moment it was hard to remember why.

Every flex of Candice's body was a new revelation. When she squatted down to put Flash back into the cage, it was all he could do not to groan out loud. The curve of her thighs, the lushness of her hips, the strength in her arms as she dragged heavy boxes around the cage—

Wait, what?

He blinked, the reality of what she was doing finally penetrating his erotic reverie. The baby unicorn was now peering disconsolately out from a veritable fortress of crates, the wire bars of her own cage barely visible. Her lavender eyes fixed on him as if in hope of rescue.

"Is that strictly necessary?" he ventured.

"Yep." With a grunt, Candice hefted a pallet of dog food cans on top of the pile. "Apparently our little Flash is quite the escape artist. Let's see you get out of *that*, baby."

Flash huffed, the glow from her horn brightening. She eyed the crates with the distinct air of a duelist sizing up an opponent.

Worried that Flash might start hurling herself at the walls, Wystan crouched down. "Please, little one, lie down and rest. It's been a long day and you need to recover your strength. I promise, we aren't going far. If you call, I'll come back straight away."

Candice was staring at him. He realized that he was, to her perspective, making an earnest and heartfelt speech to a baby deer.

He cleared his throat, his face heating. "I, ah, was just trying to calm her down. I was worried she might hurt herself on the bars."

Candice didn't *look* like someone who was concerned for his sanity. There was a strange tenderness to her expression, a kind of gentle warmth that he'd previously only seen her direct at creatures with four legs.

"You talk to her like she's a person," she said—and then seemed to shake herself, the wariness hardening in her eyes again. "It's kinda cute. Wystan, I'm really sorry, but I don't think this is a good idea after all. Flash doesn't seem to like being left on her own."

Ah ha. I was right. Wystan couldn't help feeling a little smug. Given Candice's level of devotion to the animals under her care, he'd suspected that she might cancel their date at the last minute, and for this very reason.

Fortunately, he had a secret weapon.

Wystan stood up. "I agree. But I might be able to offer a solution."

He reached out with his mind as he spoke. He'd barely reached the end of the sentence before there was an eager whine from outside the trailer.

Candice whipped around, professional reflexes evidently triggered. "Did you hear that? It sounded like a dog!"

"It was." Smiling, Wystan opened the door. "Candice, allow me to introduce one of my colleagues. This is Fenrir."

Her reaction was everything he'd hoped. Sheer delight glowed from her face. She let out a gasp of pure glee.

"He's a service dog? On your hotshot team?" Her eyes shone as she knelt to fling her arms around Fenrir's shaggy black neck. "Oh, he's *gorgeous!* Who's a good boy? Who's the *best* boy? Yes, it's you! You are!"

The hellhound's pink tongue lolled out. His amused copper eyes met Wystan's over the top of Candice's head.

Has good taste, this one, Fenrir informed him, mental tone dripping with smugness. *Likes me best.*

Perhaps Candice's reaction was a little bit more than he'd hoped.

He wrestled down his unicorn's seething desire to toss the hellhound out the door like a farmer pitching hay. "I thought Fenrir could keep Flash company. He'll let us know if she needs anything."

Candice seemed to come down a bit from her dog-induced high. She sat back on her heels, looking Fenrir over more critically.

"Are you sure?" Somewhat absently, she ran her hands over the hellhound's broad chest and thick legs, as though automatically checking him for injuries. "He's a big boy. I'm sure he means well, but he might scare her."

Wystan tilted his head in the direction of the unicorn, whose ears had pricked up. "Look, she's not in the slightest bit worried. He'll take good care of her. I assure you, he's very well trained."

Fenrir wrinkled his muzzle. *Have you *very well trained, Icehorse.**

I beg you, help me out here, he sent back telepathically. *I'm on thin ice with Candice as it is.*

Good. Fenrir's mental tone was matter-of-fact. *Too much ice around you.*

That was Fenrir. Wystan was never quite sure whether the hellhound took things too literally, or not literally enough. Sometimes he suspected that both were true.

Oh, very well. Will help. With a rather human roll of his eyes, Fenrir got up, casting a glance at Candice as he did so. *Watch, Sun Bitch.*

Sun Bitch? It took all Wystan's control to keep a straight face. He wondered what on earth had prompted the hellhound to come up with *that* nickname. He was also very glad Candice was deaf to the hellhound's telepathy.

Fenrir padded over to Wystan's side. The hellhound gazed up at him with an exaggerated expression of canine adoration. Wystan could only pray that it didn't look as sarcastic to Candice as it did to him.

"Well, he's certainly obedient," Candice said, sounding a little uncertain.

"He's very intelligent," Wystan said, scratching Fenrir behind one ear. "He won't let Flash leave the trailer, and he'll do everything he can to keep her calm. He has excellent judgement."

Candice bit her lip. "I don't know…"

Is you she is not sure about trusting, Icehorse, Fenrir growled in his mind. *Not me. Told you, shouldn't have offered her stupid dead plants. What strength shown by that? Should have caught her a squirrel.*

He had to admit that the hellhound was probably right. Based on the sum total of evidence so far, he was fairly certain Candice *would* have preferred to be presented with a squirrel. As long as it was a live one.

"You can trust him." On pure instinct, he reached out, skimming his fingertips down her spine to settle on the small of her back. He felt her suck in her breath, but she didn't move away. "Trust me. Please."

Fenrir cocked his head, looking at Candice thoughtfully. *Understand your doubt, Sun Bitch. Icehorse is hard to scent, behind his frozen walls. But has good hands. Good heart. Trust him.*

"Okay," Candice said, as though she *had* been able to hear Fenrir's comment. Her tongue darted out, wetting her lips in a way that sent an electric jolt through his blood. "Your tent or mine?"

If only he could. It was torture to keep his touch light on her back rather than pulling her close. All he wanted to do was seize her, bury himself in her, and never, ever let go.

But he couldn't. Not yet. And somehow, he had to find the right way to explain that…without making her think he wasn't interested after all.

Delay. I have to delay her.

"Actually," he said as he steered her out, "I was hoping to take you out to dinner."

CHAPTER 9

Lost in a lust-fueled daze, it took Candice a moment to process his words. "Dinner? You're kidding, right?"

He still had his hand on the small of her back. It was only the lightest touch, but she might as well have been glued to his fingers. Just thinking of pulling away was impossible. She couldn't resist as he guided her away from the trailer.

"When did you last eat?" he asked.

"Uh." Candice had to think about that one. "I had some trail mix for lunch."

Wystan raised an eyebrow at her.

"All right, breakfast," she admitted.

He shook his head, that wicked smile tugging at his mouth once more. "Then, as a medical professional, I prescribe dinner. To be taken immediately. Much as I would like to make you swoon, I'd rather it wasn't from low blood sugar."

"I'm an emergency responder. I can run for days on coffee and adrenaline." Still, now that she'd stopped working, she was aware that she *was* hungry. And Wystan had probably been working all day too. It was only practical to get some food before satisfying other appetites.

It wasn't like it was a *date*, after all.

The animal rescue site was set back a little from the main body of the camp, away from the heavily trafficked areas. No fire camp ever truly slept. With the sun setting behind the smoke-shrouded hills, the towering floodlights were switching on, powered by emergency generators so that people could keep working through the night. Even now, commanders and senior staff would be poring over maps and reports, planning the next battle in the war against the fire.

They had to stop to let a short convoy of trucks rumble past, headlights staring through the dark. A squad of firefighters slumped in the backs of the dirty vehicles, many asleep despite the bone-rattling ride. No doubt they would be up again at dawn, making the long, hard trek back out to the fireline.

Wystan, she realized, didn't have that grimy air of bone-deep exhaustion. "You haven't been on the job long, have you?" she asked him as they picked their way across the rutted dirt track.

He took her arm to steady her, as gallant as if escorting her across a ballroom. His mouth quirked ruefully. "Is it that obvious? No, this is my first season."

"I meant here, actually." She waved a hand at the encampment. "Working this fire."

"Oh." He shook his head. "No, they only started pulling in the interagency crews this week. Up until now it's been local state fire departments handling things, but it just got too big. My squad arrived yesterday. What about you?"

"We've been here since the start. I go to all the big wildfires across the state. Kinda my specialty, especially when there are horses to evacuate. Unfortunately, I've had a lot of practice. Seems like there's more wildfires every year."

His jaw tightened. "Wildfires have been getting worse in a lot of states."

"Climate change, I guess. Lot of dry tinder around these days."

"And lightning," he murmured, strangely. Before she could ask what he meant, he continued, "So this is just a boring typical day at work for you?"

She snorted. "Hardly. This fire is a real monster. They've had to evacuate whole communities for this one. We're working flat-out to save the animals left behind."

He gazed up at the hazy night sky, fogged with reddish smoke even though the fire camp was well back from the front. "I never imagined anything of this scale. This blaze is bigger than my entire home county."

"That's back in England, right? What are you doing all the way out here?" she asked, curious. "No offense, but you aren't exactly the usual sort I meet at these things."

"Ah." He smiled, but it didn't reach his eyes. "I was ambulance crew, back home. To cut a long story short, my meagre skills weren't up to the job. A career change seemed like the best move."

"Taking up firefighting on the other side of the world is a heck of a move. What on earth prompted that?"

His expression shifted, shadows chased away by something else. She shivered as he swept her with that slow, heated look.

"Perhaps it was fate," he said.

The rough catch to his voice was pure liquid sex. She was acutely aware of every point of contact between their bodies.

She rapped her knuckles against his forearm. "Turning it up to eleven again there, bud."

He let out his breath, looking away. "Sorry."

"I'm not exactly complaining. Just that you were the one insisting that we get some food." She bumped her hip against his, shooting him a playful mock-glare. "If we're going to make it as far as the food trucks without me climbing you like a tree, you'll need to take it down a notch."

It was hard to tell in the harsh glare of the floodlights, but she was pretty sure he was blushing. For a man who was a walking incitement to public indecency, he sure was shy about dirty talk. Even the mildest innuendo made his pale skin flush. It was oddly endearing, as well as just plain odd.

Well, he's English, she reminded herself. *Maybe they really are all weird about sex over there.*

They'd reached the dining area—a wide, square clearing set

with ranks of folding tables and chairs and well-lit by floodlights. Enormous catering trailers lined two sides of the square, hatches thrown open for the dinner service. From inside came the clatter and harassed shouts of line cooks feverishly grilling and boiling. A line of firefighters shuffled forward, clutching trays. Most were still in turn out gear, soot streaking their tired faces.

They joined the end of the line, taking trays and cutlery from the stack. The cooks were on fire tonight, dishing out chicken cutlets and fries with machine gun speed. It only took a few minutes to receive their meal.

"Thank you," Wystan said to the server as the stone-faced man dumped a pile of steaming green beans onto his plate. "This looks marvelous. Truly impressive teamwork, to do all this so quickly."

The server grunted noncommittally, but the faintest hint of pleasure tugged at his sour mouth. He added a second scoop of beans to Wystan's plate before passing it over.

"That's more a punishment than a thank you," Candice muttered to Wystan as they headed for a free table. "Those canned beans are awful. Maybe he thought you were being sarcastic."

"I wasn't," Wystan replied, smiling. "As far as I'm concerned, any food that doesn't come out of a self-heating packet is gourmet cuisine. Usually my crew is eating whatever we've managed to carry up to the fireline. Having an actual encampment to return to at night is a luxury for us."

"My tent is going to blow your mind, then," Candice said, returning the grin. "I have a *pillow*. If you're very good, I might even let you sleep on it."

Wystan's expression flickered a little, his gaze sliding away. He held out a chair, which momentarily confused Candice until she realized he was offering it to her. He seated her as if he was a waiter in a fancy restaurant before taking his own place opposite.

Why has he suddenly clammed up? Candice wondered. She shoved chicken in her mouth to fill the weird awkward moment. *What did I say?*

After a second, it came to her. *Crap. I implied that I wanted him to spend the night.*

She swallowed hastily, clearing her mouth. "I mean, you're welcome to crash at my tent overnight if you want to, but it's no big deal. I don't care either way. I meant what I said, earlier. No strings, no expectations." She tried a smile, in an attempt to lighten the mood. "Other than really hot sex, of course."

"Indeed." Wystan cleared his throat. She had the impression his own smile was a bit forced as well. "Moving swiftly to other topics, how is your wrist?"

"My what?" It took her a second to remember the bite. "Oh, that. It's fine. I've had much worse."

His gaze flicked back to her face, and the evidence written there in stark red scars.

"From animals," she clarified, before he could ask her about them. That was definitely not a story she wanted to get into tonight. "Getting bitten is kind of a hazard of the job."

He chuckled under his breath, looking more relaxed. "At least my patients never tried to take a chunk out of me."

"Yeah, but I can put mine in cages when they're rude."

"I have to admit, there have been times in my career when that would have been a tempting prospect."

"Well, there you go." She nudged him under the table with her foot. "You should have trained as a vet, not a paramedic. Humans are awful. Give me animals any day."

He looked sidelong at her, his expression turning more thoughtful. "You must have encountered some of the darker sides of humanity, in your work."

"Oh boy. Could I tell you some horror stories. Not that I'm going to." She wrinkled her nose at him. "How did we get onto this? We're supposed to be having fun, not discussing how much people suck. You don't want to hear all about my job."

"But I do," he said softly. His gaze still held that intent focus, as though she was the most fascinating woman in the world. "I want to know everything about you."

Uh oh. She hoped it was a line, because otherwise she had massive alarm bells going off in her head.

"You've pretty much already seen it all." She deliberately adopted a casual, carefree tone. "I rescue animals from disaster zones. I have a habit of answering the door with wildlife hanging off various parts of my anatomy. I'm here, willing, and available. Nothing more you need to know."

His eyebrows drew down. He looked at her in silence for an unnervingly long moment, fork frozen in midair. He had the expression of a Scrabble player with a handful of Qs, who had just realized there wasn't a single U anywhere on the board.

"For a woman who has invited me into her bed," he said slowly, "you are very determined to keep me at arm's length."

"My bed, my rules, bud." She stabbed at her fries. "We don't need to know each other's life stories to have a good time."

"Wouldn't it make things better if we did, though?"

"As far as I'm concerned, foreplay doesn't involve using your mouth to talk." She waved a fry at him. "Look, you can cut the seduction crap. I hate the whole fake romantic thing, where we pretend that we aren't simply two thirsty grown-ass adults looking to get laid. Let's just eat so we can get down to business, okay?"

Wystan laid his fork down across his barely-touched plate. "I'm not pretending, Candice."

"Oh boy," Candice muttered. By now so many alarm bells were ringing in her mind, she half-expected one of the nearby firefighter squads to leap up and dig a fireline around her. "Wystan. You do realize this is a one night stand, not a date, right?"

His green eyes were shadowed and unreadable. "Does it have to be?"

"Yes," Candice said firmly. "I told you, I don't do relationships."

"In general?" His voice dropped a little. "Or just with me?"

"In general. Though if I *was* on the market, I gotta say your chances would have just gone down the toilet." She put her palms flat on the table, pushing herself up. "Look, bud. I was really clear about what I was offering. You told me that you wanted the same. The one thing I won't stand is dishonesty."

He jolted upright too, every muscle tense as though he was poised to physically tackle her to the ground. "I'm a virgin."

It was so far from anything she'd expected him to say, for a moment she wasn't sure she'd heard him right. "What?"

"I'm a virgin," he repeated. For once he wasn't blushing. He held her gaze steadily. "I wasn't lying. I can't tell you how much I would like to take you to bed. But this is my first time. I need it to mean as much to you as it does to me."

"Are you kidding me?" she said incredulously. "You expect me to believe that…that…*seriously?*"

"I was waiting for the right person," he said quietly. "I was waiting for you."

It was either the most spectacular, bare-faced lie she'd ever heard…or, even worse, it was the truth.

Either way, there was only one thing to do.

"Right." Candice held up her hands. "And we're done here. I'm out."

"Sorry," said a deep, unfamiliar voice from right behind her. "But we can't let you do that."

\

CHAPTER 10

Candice whipped around, and found herself nose-to-nipple with an impressive set of pectorals. The chest barred her way like a solid rock cliff. Yellow letters stretched across the front of a straining black t-shirt: THUNDER MOUNTAIN HOTSHOTS.

The owner of the chest stepped back, his rugged face and broad smile coming into her field of view. He was a big, tough-looking man, with tawny hair and startling amber eyes. He held out a broad, dirt-streaked hand.

"I'm Rory MacCormick, Wystan's squad boss." He had a distinctly Scottish accent, his *rs* rich and rolling. "Sorry for barging in on your date."

Out of sheer reflex, Candice shook his hand. "It's not a date. Don't worry, I was just leaving."

"But you can't!" A tall blonde woman wearing turn out gear elbowed Rory aside. Before Candice quite knew what was happening, the woman had her hand in a two-fisted, bone-crushing grip, and was shaking it vigorously "Hi! I'm Edith. I'm Rory's mate."

Candice blinked at her. She didn't sound Australian.

"Partner," Rory corrected gently, his thick arm settling across

Edith's shoulders in a way that made it clear they didn't run a small business together.

"Right, that's what I meant." Edith leaned against her—boyfriend? Husband?—beaming widely. Her snub nose and freckled cheeks gave her a cute, coltish air, which was entirely belied by the strength of her grasp. Candice was starting to lose feeling in her fingertips. "Anyway, you can't go. We won't let you."

"Uh." Candice managed to extricate her hand at last. "What?"

"You'd be making a terrible mistake." Edith's tone was earnest, but her gaze slid sideways, avoiding meeting Candice's eyes. "You'd be throwing away something wonderful. We can't let you do that to Wystan. Or yourself."

Candice stared left and right. Two more firefighters—a curvy black woman and a glowering red-headed man—had moved to flank Rory and Edith. A grinning black man loomed behind them all, his towering height dwarfing even Rory. They all had their feet set and braced, as though ready to repel a charge.

Candice turned back to Wystan. "What the hell is going on?"

He looked, if anything, even more confused than she was. "I have no idea. Is there some sort of emergency, Rory?"

"Apparently." Rory cocked a tawny eyebrow in Candice's direction. "Since, unless I'm very much mistaken, your m—ah, your date was about to storm off in a huff."

"Still not his date," Candice snapped, bemusement starting to give way to annoyance. "Also, it's none of your business."

"Afraid it is." Rory shrugged one shoulder. "We're a squad. We look out for each other. And right now, it's pretty obvious Wystan is in dire need of help."

Candice's half-formed suspicion that Wystan had put his squad mates up to this withered and died in the face of his obvious alarm. He looked as though *he* was now minded to run away.

"Oh now you don't, bronicorn." The black man barred Wystan's way, grinning like a wolf. He pushed Wystan back down into his seat. "Trust me, you'll thank us for this later."

Wystan had gone even paler than normal. "Please don't take this the wrong way, but I very much doubt that."

"Okay, now this is just getting weird." Candice folded her arms, glaring around at them all. "So, what, you're all Wystan's wingmen? You all going to tell me how great he is, so that I'll swoon into his arms?"

"Nope," said the curvy black woman next to Edith. There was a distinctly wicked gleam in her dark brown eyes. "I'm gonna tell you a story about something he did when he was twelve."

Wystan made a strangled noise of pure horror. "*Blaise.*"

Candice hesitated.

Then she sat down.

"Okay." Whatever Wystan's colleagues had to say, it was clear he very much didn't want her to hear it. That was good enough for her. "I'm listening."

The woman flipped a chair around, straddling it backwards. Rory pulled up two chairs too, holding one out for Edith. The red-haired man remained standing, a few steps from the table as though not really part of the group. He stared into the distance with the air of someone who was trying to block out irrelevant chatter in order to concentrate on something more significant.

"Blaise Swanmay," the woman introduced herself, taking one of Wystan's fries. Licking her fingers, she pointed at the redhead, then at the towering black man still standing behind Wystan. "That's Callum, and over there is Joe. We're all hotshots on A-squad."

Rory also stole a handful of Wystan's fries, passing some to Edith. "Now, the first thing you need to know is that we all grew up together."

"Apart from me," Edith interrupted.

"Yeah, but it feels like you've been part of the family forever," Blaise said to her, wicked grin softening with affection. She turned back to Candice. "But the rest of us really have known each other forever. Our dads are firefighters back in England, on the same engine crew. That kind of thing leaves a close bond. So Wystan's like my brother from another mother. And we're the same age, so we went to school together."

Wystan buried his face in his hands. "Blaise, would it do any good if I begged for mercy?"

"None whatsoever," Blaise informed him. She held up her hands, framing Wystan in a rectangle formed of her forefingers and thumbs. "So, let me set the scene. Picture Wystan, age twelve. Hasn't hit his growth spurt yet, mop of white hair falling into those huge green eyes, totally adorable."

"Bambi in human form," Joe put in.

Wystan raised his head to shoot his squadmate a pained look. "Thank you for that marvelously manly comparison, Joe."

Blaise continued, "Now not only does he look like he stepped off a Christmas card, he's a total teacher's pet. Straight A's, volunteers for everything, always polite. Literally, the school poster child—his angelic little face is plastered all over the front cover of the brochure. You get the idea."

"Huh." Fascinated, Candice examined Wystan, trying to see the kid he must have been. "How the heck did you survive to adulthood? I'm amazed you weren't beaten to a pulp within two weeks."

"Oh, the bullies tried." Rory's white teeth flashed in a rather feral smile. "Once. Go on, Blaise."

"Please don't," came Wystan's heartfelt plea.

"So there's Wystan." Blaise turned her hand to point at herself. "And then there's me. Early bloomer. Busting out everywhere, zits all over my face, just a wrecking ball of hormones. Complete ugly duckling, right?"

"I'll have to take your word for it." Candice couldn't imagine Blaise as anything other than totally at home in her body. The hotshot exuded confidence. "Since you evidently turned into a swan at some point."

Blaise's smile flickered, just for a second. "Not quite. Well, anyway, you know how kids are. So I'm going around swathed in five layers of sweaters trying to pretend none of this is happening. Which of course makes me a prime target for our resident school assholes, despite Rory's best efforts. The mean kids are circling around me like sharks scenting blood. And then one day in the middle of English class there's *literally* blood. All over the seat of my pants."

Candice winced in feminine empathy. "Oh man. That happened to me once or twice in high school. Our resident assholes were utter jerks about it too."

Edith's hands fluttered through the air in an odd gesture, as though even the thought of such an embarrassing nightmare made her shake with nerves. Evidently this story was new to her, too. "What did you do, Blaise?"

"Nothing," Blaise said. "I *couldn't*. I just sat there, paralyzed with humiliation, feeling this damp spot spreading out underneath me. I knew what it was, and I knew that as soon as I stood up, everyone would see. Even if I managed to be the last one out of the classroom, there was no way I was going to be able to make it all the way to the bathroom without someone noticing, and then it would be all over the whole school. So I just sat there in silence, wishing the ground would swallow me up. And Wystan, who was sitting next to me, noticed. And he asked me what was wrong."

Wystan appeared to be trying to slide under the table. Joe, standing behind his chair like a police escort, fished him out again by the scruff of his neck.

Blaise raised her eyebrows at Candice. "Imagine that one of your best friends has just confessed that she's got her period in the middle of class. Imagine that you're twelve. Imagine that you're a twelve year old *boy*, teacher's pet, star student. What do you think you'd do?"

Candice shrugged. "Blurt it out to the teacher?"

"Wystan," Blaise paused dramatically, "took off his shoes."

Candice blinked. "What?"

"He took off his shoes," Blaise repeated, drawing out the moment. "And undid his belt, and all his zips and buttons, so quietly that even I didn't realize what he was doing. Until he abruptly threw off all his clothes and jumped onto the desk butt naked."

"*Wystan?*" Candice and Edith said together.

Wystan looked like he was earnestly wishing a naked distraction would appear *now*. "I was twelve. I panicked."

"Utter. Pandemonium," Blaise said with relish, while both Rory and Joe chuckled. "Wystan raced around the room, little white buns twinkling, all the while yelling stuff like 'I am not a number! For the rebellion! Carpe diem!' and evading all attempts to catch him. Then he streaked out the door, teacher in hot pursuit, and naturally the entire class pelted after them because this was some class-A entertainment. Half the boys were throwing off their own clothes too, just for the sheer hell of it."

A slow grin spread over Candice's face. "And in the meantime, you…"

"Wrapped Wystan's discarded shirt around my waist, borrowed his trousers, and got myself cleaned up in the bathroom without anyone the wiser," Blaise said with great satisfaction. "And *that's* how Wystan mooned the entire school."

"And ended up with a suspension and four months of compulsory therapy," Wystan said, now face-planted onto the tabletop. "Thank you so much for telling that story. It was certainly the most critical thing Candice needed to know about me at this point in time."

"Yes, it was." Blaise pointed at him, angling her head to catch Candice's eye. "By nature, this man is the most polite, proper, modest guy you will ever meet. And when someone he cares about is in trouble, he'll do literally anything to make it better."

"Without a second of hesitation," Joe added.

"And, most importantly," Rory finished, one big hand settling on Wystan's shoulder, "in the most complicated, self-sacrificing, and above all *idiotic* way possible."

Candice looked at the cringing Wystan in bemusement. "If these are your friends, I'd hate to meet your enemies."

"They mean well." Wystan looked around at his squad, his expression caught somewhere between fondness and utter mortification. "I think. Callum at least has my sincere thanks."

Candice glanced up at the red-headed man, who had yet to say a word. "You aren't joining in this roast, or intervention, or whatever the heck this is?"

Callum raised one shoulder in the tiniest of shrugs. His handsome face still wore that abstracted frown, as though he was trying to listen to something none of the rest of them could hear.

"Just give Wystan a chance." For someone who evidently didn't talk much, Callum had an unexpectedly gorgeous voice—deep and mellow, with the faintest trace of a lilting Irish accent. "He'll surprise you. Rory."

Callum didn't say anything more, but Rory's back stiffened. Candice's skin prickled as the squad's relaxed attitude evaporated, every one of them suddenly focused and alert. It was like sitting in the middle of a wolf pack that had just scented a stranger approaching.

Edith slapped Rory's upper arm, frowning at him. "Don't do that. It's rude."

"Do what?" Candice asked, confused.

"Sorry." Rory grimaced at her apologetically, though she still had no idea why. "Squad thing. Like we said, we've known each other a long time. Sometimes we don't need to use words. Cal, are you sure?"

Cal's chin jerked down in a curt nod. For no apparent reason, his expression had shifted from preoccupied to downright grim.

Rory blew out his breath. He reached for the radio clipped to his belt. "Then I'm sorry, Candice, but I need to steal Wystan from you for a moment. We have a problem."

CHAPTER 11

Wystan was already was on his feet, along with the rest of the squad. Their collective tension thrummed in his mind down the pack-bond that they all shared.

"What's going on?" Candice had seemed to be loosening up throughout Blaise's appalling anecdote, but now her shoulders tensed again. "Wystan?"

"My apologies," he said, distracted. Rory was already striding away, murmuring into the radio. The rest of the squad had fallen into step around him, huddling around to catch Buck's words. "There may be an emergency. Please, promise me you won't go anywhere for a minute?"

He'd braced himself for an annoyed retort—*no promises, bud*—but to his surprise Candice regarded him in silence for a long moment. There was something new in her sharp eyes, a kind of thoughtfulness that hadn't been there before the squad's intervention. He couldn't interpret her expression.

"Okay," she said at last. She toyed with her drink, swirling the water around the plastic cup. "I'll wait."

He hesitated, nonplussed. "If Blaise's tale somehow caused this change of heart, I'd like to inform you that I have dozens of equally embarrassing childhood incidents."

The corner of her mouth twitched up. "I'll bet. Go on. I'll be here."

Rory and the others had moved far enough away to be out of earshot from Candice or any of the other humans in the immediate area. Wystan hurried after them, though he made sure to keep Candice in view out of the corner of his eye.

"*...Callum's sure?*" Buck was saying over the radio as Wystan joined them.

"Positive," Rory said. "It's the Thunderbird. It's right on the limit of his range at the moment."

"Not anymore," Callum added. He was staring off into the distance, his eyes unfocused as he concentrated on his pegasus talent for sensing living creatures. "It's coming in fast. Heading straight for us."

"*Well, isn't that just the cherry on this cow pie,*" Buck growled. "*Never seen our feathered friend this far from its home territory before. If that cursed thing started this fire in the first place, I swear I will serve it up for Thanksgiving dinner with a side of motherloving mashed potatoes. Well. Time for you to get to work, A-squad. We can't have that thing hammering any lightning down into this dry tinderbox of a fire camp.*"

"We're on it," Rory said, his jaw setting. "We'll get in the air, meet it head-on. We won't let it start any fires."

"*Do better than that,*" Buck said, sounding grim. "*Take it out for good this time. Buck out.*"

"I thought that thing only hung around Montana," Blaise said as Rory clicked the radio off. "What the hell is it doing all the way out here in California?"

Everyone else looked stumped, but Wystan's mind was racing. "Every time we've seen the Thunderbird, it was hunting that demonic snake creature. That might be why it's here now."

"You think there might be *more* of those monsters?" Joe said. "Oh, joy."

"Callum, can you sense anything?" Rory asked the pegasus shifter.

Callum shook his head. The pegasus shifter's expression was as cool as always, but his jaw clenched, betraying his frustration. "Just the Thunderbird. I think. Hard to tell through all these people."

"That doesn't mean anything, though," Blaise said. "When that creature was possessing animals, it just seemed like a normal rabbit or hawk to your senses, didn't it Cal?"

Callum nodded, looking unhappy. "I couldn't even tell when it was possessing Rory."

"If there *is* one of those monsters around," Joe said, "I bet I know what it's after."

They all exchanged glances.

"The baby unicorn," Edith said, voicing what they were all thinking. "It's too much of a coincidence."

"The demon went after me because it wanted my powers," Rory said. He'd gone a little pale under his tan, the traumatic experience clearly still fresh in his mind. Edith took his hand, squeezing it. "When it was in me, I could feel how hungry it was, how delicious our souls seemed to it. A real unicorn would be irresistible to one of those creatures."

"I agree, but let's not ignore the possibility that the *Thunderbird* could be after the unicorn," Blaise said. "Maybe it doesn't like any supernatural creatures. It certainly doesn't like *us*. Remember how it tried to roast us all?"

Rory shook himself free from his memories, squaring his shoulders. "No matter the Thunderbird's motives, we can't let it start any fires. Joe, Blaise, Cal, with me. We're going to intercept it."

"I'm coming too," Edith said firmly. "You needed me last time."

Rory touched her face, his golden eyes warm. "I always need you." His tone turned business-like again. "Wystan, you and Fenrir stay here. Guard the unicorn."

And our mate, his own unicorn put in. It was agitated, pacing back and forth in his mind, horn lowered and ready.

"Of course," Wystan said, to both Rory and his own animal. "I'll shift and guard the trailer in unicorn form. That way no one will see me and ask awkward questions about why I'm hanging around."

"Good plan." Rory gave him a distracted smile. "Tell Fenrir what's going on, and stay alert. Let's go, team."

The squad followed Rory, heading for a shadowed, private area behind a nearby supply trailer in order to shift. Ordinary humans couldn't see mythic shifters in their animal forms, but they *did* tend to notice when people vanished into thin air.

Candice was still sitting at the table, watching him across the dining area with that impenetrable expression. He hadn't the faintest idea what she was making of all of this, but he had a sinking suspicion that it wasn't helping his case.

"Are you being called away?" she asked as he returned.

"There's a bit of a situation," he replied, wishing he didn't have to be evasive. "Our Superintendent needs the squad to check something out."

As he spoke, Rory's golden, broad-winged form swept over their heads. Callum followed on the griffin's tail, a black shadow against the clouded sky. Even burdened with riders, both shifters were swift fliers. In a few breaths, they'd disappeared into the night.

Candice, of course, was oblivious to it all. Although she was his mate, they weren't yet mated. The subliminal connection between them might let her see a mythic shifter if she was in immediate danger from one, but she wouldn't be fully immune to invisibility tricks until they were fully bonded.

If we're ever bonded. His current rate of progress on that front was not encouraging.

"I understand. Work has to come first." Candice drained her water and stood up. She hesitated, then shook her head as though thinking better of whatever she'd been about to say. "Well. I guess this is goodbye, then."

"Candice." He caught her elbow as she turned away. "It isn't."

"Oh, it isn't, is it?" Despite the challenging words, she didn't try to pull free. "I thought we'd established that we had wildly different ideas about where this was going."

"I know, and I'm truly sorry that I led you on." He turned her to face him. "You were right to be angry with me. It was unconscionable for me to falsely offer you something I had no intention of delivering, as a means to my own ends."

That startled a snort of laughter out of her. "You do realize that most guys promise a relationship as a way of getting sex, right? Not the other way around."

"I'm not exactly like most men," he said. "Candice, I do desire you. I can't tell you how much. But I want you for more than a single night. I need this to be more than a casual fling."

"Why?" She sounded honestly baffled. "Why are you so set on me?"

"Because you," he said, simply.

Candice sighed. "Wystan, I gotta admit, you seem like a great guy. But we've only just met. I don't really know you, and you sure as hell don't know me if you've built up some romantic idea that I'm some kind of once-in-a-lifetime soulmate that you can't live without."

"I know that you take care of a lost fawn as if she was a lost child. I know that a rat can be chewing your hand off, and your primary concern will be its health. And I know…" he hesitated, then plunged on. "I know that you have been hurt."

Her arms tensed under his hands. She gave him a withering look, turning her head to show her scars. "Well, duh."

"I don't mean there." He tapped his own chest, over his heart. "I mean here. I know that you must have good reasons to want to keep me at a distance. I know that you don't want to risk getting hurt again. But I also know that something else, some strange impulse that you don't fully understand, is stopping you from just walking away without a backward glance right now."

The defensive scorn on her face flickered, just a bit. Her eyes searched his face. She was still listening.

"I know that you desire me. I know that you will always be honest with me. I know that you don't suffer fools gladly." He let out his breath, his mouth quirking ruefully. "Which is somewhat of a pity. As my friends told you, I can be exceptionally foolish."

Her own mouth twitched in response. "I believe *idiotic* was the word they used."

"They know me exceedingly well."

She was smiling properly now, truly smiling. It was like the sun coming up. It dazzled him.

"Everything I know about you so far makes me yearn to know more." He took both her hands in his. "Give me time to show you who *I* am. I know you don't have any reason to want me the way that I want you. Not yet. But please, give me a chance."

She considered this for a moment that stretched into an agonizing eternity.

"I'll think about it, she said at last. "On one condition."

His heart moved sideways in his chest, leaving him breathless with hope.

"Anything," he managed to get out.

She stepped closer. All he could feel were her hands, sliding around his waist. All he could see was her face, turning up to his.

"Kiss me," Candice commanded.

He couldn't have *not* kissed her. A force stronger than gravity had him in its grip, molding his body to hers. Without thought, without hesitation, he bent to her lips.

He'd entirely forgotten the existence of noses.

"Ow." Candice pulled back before he could make a second attempt. "Okay. Now I believe you."

Need beat through him. He could barely form words. "About what?"

"You really are a virgin." She put her head to one side, her eyes widening. "Wystan, is this your first kiss?"

"Yes," he growled, and claimed her mouth at last.

It was awkward. It was clumsy.

It was utterly glorious.

And it was interrupted by an explosion.

CHAPTER 12

Wow, Candice thought dazedly. *Talk about fireworks.*

Then, as Wystan jerked back from that brain-melting kiss, she realized that the explosive blast had not, in fact, been entirely in her own head. All around, people were looking around in alarm. A nearby group of firefighters leaped up from their half-finished meals, automatically grabbing for their turn out jackets as they tried to locate the source of the sound.

"Fenrir," Wystan breathed.

Before she knew what was going on, he'd whisked her off her feet. Literally—one moment her boots were firmly on the ground, then next he'd thrown her over his shoulder and was sprinting flat out. Her startled squeak was left behind in the dust. Trailers and tents whirled past in a blur.

I'm in shock, decided the small part of her brain that was wasn't reeling in confusion, trying to catch up with her body. *That's why time is moving strangely. No one can run* this *fast.*

It couldn't *really* have been mere seconds before they'd reached the edge of camp, but it certainly seemed like it. Wystan released his hold on her, letting her slide down his body.

Still in a daze, she stared up at him. The look in his green eyes sent a shiver down her spine. All his old-fashioned English courtesy had dropped away, revealing something more dangerous and primal beneath. A flickering orange glow painted his face, highlighting his sharp cheekbones and the grim set of his jaw.

Where's that light coming from?

She turned, and the breath froze in her throat.

Her trailer was on fire.

Darkness encroached on the edges of her vision. Her world narrowed to those hungry flames. Even though they were still distant, she felt them gnawing at her skin. She was helpless, her body paralyzed, unable to flee—

Strong arms wrapped around her, pulling her out of her flashback. Wystan's reassuring warmth banished the terrible heat burned into her memory. She gasped for breath, clinging onto his forearms as though he was a life buoy.

Panic receded, allowing her to take in the scene properly. It wasn't the trailer itself that was on fire, but rather the dry grass behind it. The blaze was spreading through the bone-dry stalks like water. The trailer was a black silhouette against the rising flames, thick smoke swirling around the vehicle.

She could hear shouts coming from the main camp, but they were distant. Wystan really *had* gotten them here before anyone else had even had time to react. Now the alarm was being raised…but at the rate the fire was sweeping through the grass, it would engulf the trailer and tents before help could arrive.

"The animals," Candice gasped. "Flash!"

"I'll get them." Wystan thrust her away from the flames. "Stay here!"

"Screw *that*," Candice snarled, and pelted after him.

He was a lot faster than she was. He'd disappeared around the trailer before she'd taken three steps. A cloud of smoke blew into her face, making her cough.

"Wystan!" She pulled her t-shirt up over her nose and mouth. Eyes watering, half-blind, she staggered through the thickening smoke. "You idiot, you haven't got the trailer key! *Wystan!*"

She found the trailer by running head-first into it, hard enough to see stars. She groped her way to the door, the metal already alarmingly warm under her palms. There was no sign of Wystan.

Her hands were shaking so badly that it took her three attempts to unlock the door. She got it open at last, half-falling into the trailer. The smoke was even thicker in here.

Seeking cleaner air, she dropped to the ground. Through the haze, she glimpsed a gaping rent in the side of the trailer. The metal walls were splayed inward like flower petals, as though someone had shot a cannonball at the trailer. Smoke poured in through the jagged hole.

What did that?

No time to worry about that now. Holding her breath, she crawled on hands and knees through split-open bags of kibble and smashed feed bowls. Bits of burning paper swirled over her head. Her heart thumped an erratic, panicked rhythm.

Flash. She held onto the thought, fighting against the rising darkness trying to suck her down. Her head felt light as a balloon. *Got to get to Flash.*

She sobbed with relief as her fingers found the wire front of the cage, still locked and barred. The poor fawn must be going mad with panic. No chance of unlocking the padlocks and bolts with her numb fingers. She'd have to carry the whole thing.

"Sorry baby," she croaked. "Gonna get you out. Just hang on!"

She grabbed hold of the bars, hauling with all her strength—and fell flat on her butt as the cage shot forward without resistance.

It was empty.

Dull-witted from lack of air, she stared blankly at the empty nest of blankets inside the cage, struggling to make sense of what she saw. She shook the cage, rattling the lock. "Flash?"

"Candice!"

Strong hands seized her under the arms. She fought and kicked, but she might as well have been a newborn kitten dangling from Wystan's grasp.

"Let me go!" she cried as he hauled her out of the burning trailer. "I have to find Flash!"

"Candice, it's all right, she's not in there!" Wystan held her wrists, stopping her from clawing at his face. "I found her. She's fine."

He'd carried her upwind of the grass fire, where the air was clearer. Sanity returned along with oxygen. "She's okay?"

"She's with Fenrir." Wystan jerked his chin in the direction of the woods that bordered the fire camp. "They're over there, under the trees."

Candice squinted, and just about made out a tiny white smudge in the night. "Oh, he's a *good* boy. He got her to safety."

"Yes, but he's not in good shape." Wystan's fists clenched, as though he longed to punch the fire for hurting his dog. "He's unconscious. Can you see if there's anything you can do for him while I get the other animals out?"

"Of course." She caught at his t-shirt as he turned back to the fire. "Wait! There are eight cats in the first tent, a rat and two hamsters in the second, and four dogs in the third. And be careful. You aren't wearing your turn out gear."

"I'll manage without it," he said, though his clothes were already pocked with singe-marks. Strangely, her own were still immaculate, despite the embers that had whirled around her as she'd crawled through the trailer. "I'll be fine. Take care of Fenrir and the baby until I get back."

She knew he was an elite firefighter, but she still flinched from the thought of him going back into those flames. She had a sudden mad impulse to throw her arms around him.

She stepped back instead, giving him a firm, professional nod. "Right. Good luck."

He touched her face; a brief, reassuring caress. Then he was gone, dodging through clumps of burning grass in the direction of the animal tents. More firefighters were arriving now, struggling into turn out jackets as they ran to help. Wystan's voice rang out above the crackle of the flames, giving orders in calm, clear tones.

He'll be fine, she told herself, making herself turn away.

The rising hubbub faded behind her as she hurried toward Flash. It was further than she'd thought, well out of range of the light from either the fire or the camp. She had to slow down, her eyes struggling to adjust to the night. If it wasn't for Flash's white hide, she'd never have been able to find the fawn at all.

How did Wystan spot them so fast? She tripped over a tree root, only just managing to catch herself on a sapling. *Maybe Fenrir's trained to always carry wounded in a specific direction. Poor Flash, getting hauled out all this way…it's a miracle she didn't bolt into the woods as soon as he dropped her. She must be paralyzed with fear.*

As she got closer, she saw that Flash was nosing at a big black heap on the ground. She lifted her head as Candice approached, ears swiveling.

Candice blinked. For a second, Flash didn't look like a deer at all. Her muzzle was too long, her ears too pointed. And her forehead… her forehead…

Must be a trick of the light. Or smoke still in my eyes. Candice shook her head, scrubbing a hand across her face. When she looked again, the ethereal white shape had resolved back into the familiar shape of the fawn.

"It's okay, baby." Candice approached at a crouch, keeping her movements gentle. "I'm here to help you."

To her relief, the fawn didn't seem alarmed by her appearance, making no move to bound away. Flash lowered her head, once more nudging at the furry heap. The fawn made a soft, plaintive noise that sounded more like someone playing a mournful trill on a flute than an animal in distress.

"I know, baby. I'm gonna help him too." Candice went to her knees next to Fenrir, her heart in her mouth. "Oh, poor boy, good boy, please be okay…"

He didn't stir as she touched him. She let out her breath as her searching fingers found his pulse. It was thin and weak, but at least it was *there*.

Flash hovered anxiously at her side as she checked Fenrir for injuries. The fawn licked at the big dog's ear as though urging him to get up. She made a questioning sound.

"I don't know, baby. I can't find anything wrong." She'd assumed that Fenrir must have collapsed from smoke inhalation, but his breathing sounded clear. She couldn't find a scratch on him...yet there he lay, unconscious, tongue hanging limp from his mouth.

When she put her hand flat on his shoulder, she could feel strange twitches spasming through the muscles. It was as though he'd been zapped by a Taser, but that was patently ludicrous.

Could he have had a stroke?

Flash's head snapped up, making Candice jump. The fawn sprang away from Fenrir, standing stiff-legged, staring into the dark woods. She stretched out her neck, making the flute-whistle call again.

And something answered.

The dry, hissing noise sounded like autumn leaves blowing over ice, like claws scraping against glass. It crawled over Candice's skin like a snake, making every hair stand on end in pure monkey-instinct terror.

She found herself on her feet, snatching at Flash. The fawn bleated and struggled, but Candice had a lot of experience restraining animals. She clamped the deer's kicking legs under one arm, wrapping her free hand around Flash's muzzle to silence her.

Whatever was out there in the dark, it was alive.

It was angry.

And it was *hunting*.

Something moved under the trees. Not coming out of the dark—it *was* the dark. Shadows ran together, coalescing into solid form.

Long, delicate legs. A slender body, rake-thin, every bone visible through the stretched, pitch-black hide. Mane and tail flowing like fog, ethereal wisps tumbling to the ground in ever-shifting, silent motion.

The apparition stalked delicately forward on hooves like knife blades, impossibly balanced on razor-sharp points. For all its predatory grace, its head hung low, swaying with every step.

Candice had seen that blank, numb look on rescued horses, sometimes. The ones that she couldn't save.

Then its eyes met hers, and any nascent pity within her withered and died.

Red, blood red, without pupil or white. There was hatred there, and intelligence, and above all, a burning madness.

That cold crimson stare swept over her as though she was nothing more than an ant. Then it fixed on the fawn in her arms.

The creature made the death-rattle sound again. It took a single step forward.

She couldn't run. Even her feet hadn't been rooted to the ground in frozen horror, she couldn't abandon the animals to this nightmare.

"No." Her voice came out as a squeak. She swallowed, and tried again, clutching Flash to her chest protectively. "Not for you. Go on, get! Shoo!"

It lifted its head, slowly, as though it took immense effort. The skeletal neck didn't seem strong enough to support the twisted black horns crowning its skull. Two curved above its ears like goat horns, short but wickedly sharp.

The third, lancing out from its forehead like a spear, pointed straight for her heart.

CHAPTER 13

*L*ight exploded in her face. The pure white radiance blinded her, wiping out the world.

Oh, Candice thought with the numb, detached clarity of utter shock. *I'm dead.*

The light, however, refused to resolve into anything as cliché as a glowing white tunnel. Belatedly, she realized that she could still feel Flash struggling in her arms. She'd always assumed animals went to Heaven, but she was pretty certain they didn't kick you in the ribs while you were carrying them there.

Apparently they hadn't just been blasted into atoms after all.

Her eyes watered in the fierce glare. She blinked rapidly, squinting. Grudgingly, her vision adapted, making sense of the scene.

Or…not.

A gleaming white creature stood protectively in front of her, barring the monster's way. Her disbelieving gaze tracked up from braced silver hooves, along the powerful line of its body. She followed the elegantly arched neck to the bright light burning on its forehead—at which point her mind simply gave up, flatly refusing to even attempt rational thought any longer.

It's a unicorn. She'd run out of disbelief, and was left with the simple evidence of her eyes. *There's a unicorn standing in front of me.*

It towered over her, tall as a racehorse, but even the finest Thoroughbred would have looked like a waddling pug next to that sleek, swift form. The light from its horn banished the night, burning away shadows—except where the nightmare stood.

Darkness still oozed around the monster's skeletal, spiked form. Blue sparks hissed and snapped where its shadowy veil intersected the unicorn's glowing aura. The two creatures faced off horn-to-horn, eyes locked, neither moving a muscle. They stood poised like sword fighters about to duel, an invisible conflict of wills shivering in the air between them.

It struck Candice that they were perfect mirror images of each other—light against dark, grace against horror. The monster was like a twisted, distorted shadow of the unicorn, a perverted mockery of its heart-stopping perfection. Even their eyes were opposites. The unicorn's were a deep, brilliant emerald, uncompromising and steady, while the monster's crimson stare seethed with frustrated hatred.

The monster made a lightning-fast feint, scuttling sideways like a spider on the knife-points of its hooves. The unicorn flowed like water, matching the movement. Its burning horn stayed fixed on the monster's heart. The light intensified, pushing the nightmare back two stabbing steps.

The monster's red eyes flicked from the unicorn to Candice. Its lips drew back in a snarl, showing long, needle-like fangs.

Foreign emotions washed over her like a foul, grease-slick wave. For a second, she *felt* the creature's emotions: churning rage, bleak despair, and an empty, bottomless hunger.

The creature retreated, fading backward into the shadows of the trees. A final hiss, a ripple in the night—and it was gone.

The unicorn held still for a long moment, still poised for a fight. Then it raised its head, some of the tension draining out of its taut body. Light drained out of its horn too, leaving only a gentle moonlight glimmer.

The unicorn turned to face her, long silver mane flowing like water over its neck. It eyed her sidelong from those emerald eyes, for the first time seeming less than certain of itself. It took a single tentative step toward her, and stopped.

She didn't realize she'd been holding her breath until all the air rushed out of her lungs. Her knees gave way, so abruptly that she very nearly sat on poor Fenrir. Flash twisted out of her slack hands at last, making another of those odd musical chirps as she bounded free.

The fawn pranced over to the unicorn. She was ridiculously dwarfed by its powerful form, but she stretched her tiny muzzle up in greeting without the slightest trace of fear. Solemnly, the unicorn bowed its head, touching horns with her in greeting.

...Wait.

Horns?

A hysterical giggle burst from her lips. Both animals jerked their heads up, staring at her in alarm.

"Sorry." Candice scrubbed her hands across her face, and looked again. Nothing had changed. "Okay. Right. I give up. Of course you're both unicorns. Why not?"

The two unicorns exchanged glances with each other. Two sets of pointed ears drooped. They both looked remarkably guilty.

"Well, at least that explains why you turned up," Candice said to the big one. It was, she noted, very definitely a stallion. "I guess you must be Flash's dad."

Flash snorted. The stallion shook his head, mane rippling.

"And you can clearly understand me." At this point, Candice would not have been surprised if the unicorn had opened his mouth and belted out a flawless rendition of 'Shake It Off'. "Okay. Cool. Do you talk too?"

Flash snorted again, but the stallion hesitated. He eyed her warily, as though he was torn between coming closer or running away. One of his back hooves stamped at the ground.

"No, please, don't go!" She dug reflexively in her pockets, sorting by feel through the animal treats she always carried. "I'm sorry, I don't have any sugar lumps. Uh...dog biscuit?"

The stallion's green eyes softened. He nickered in an amused equine chuckle.

"No, I suppose not." The dog biscuit made her remember Fenrir, and she caught her breath as a piece of unicorn mythology surfaced from her memory.

"Unicorns can heal people, right?" She scrambled to her feet, moving aside to show the stallion the collapsed dog. "Fenrir's hurt. Please, can you help him?"

The stallion's horn dulled to a faint starlight gleam. His great head drooped low. Her heart twisted at his clear sorrow.

"That's just a myth, huh?" He was standing close enough to touch. Greatly daring, she put her hand against his luminous hide. His fur was cloud-soft, far finer than any horse's. "Hey buddy, don't look like that. It's okay. You've already saved all our lives. That's more than enough."

The unicorn rested his chin on her shoulder, just the lightest pressure. She closed her eyes, breathing in his scent: Lilacs and spring rain, forest leaves and the faintest hint of smoke. It was a unique, wild fragrance, and yet somehow curiously familiar...

Fenrir stirred behind her, letting out a deep noise that sounded more like a man groaning in pain than a dog's whimper. With a twinge of regret, she released the unicorn, turning back to the dog.

"Don't worry, I'll take care of him," she said over her shoulder to the watching unicorns. "You guys had better get going before someone sees you."

Though maybe, she belatedly realized, people couldn't. Flash had seemed like a perfectly normal deer to her, even when she'd been touching the fawn. Still, an enormous white stag was hardly inconspicuous.

"No, I mean it, scram," she insisted, when neither unicorn showed the slightest inclination to move. "Wystan will be here any second. It's going to be hard enough keeping my mouth shut about all of this. If he sees you and starts asking questions, I'm not going to lie to him."

She cast a glance back at the distant camp, frowning. Smoke swirled around her trailer, but she couldn't see any orange glow. The firefighters must have smothered the flames. There was still a great crowd of people swarming the site, but their movements were brisk and purposeful rather than panicked. The situation was clearly under control.

So what was keeping Wystan?

Fenrir stirred groggily, making that strangely human moan again. Although he seemed to be recovering, she didn't want to leave him alone in the dark while she ran to get help. She propped his head up in her lap to make sure his windpipe was clear.

"It's okay, good boy. I know I'm not your human, but he'll be here soon. Just stay still until he gets here." She rubbed reassuringly behind his pointed ears, shooting a glare at the distant, anonymous figures milling around her trailer. "Come *on*, Wystan. Where the heck are you?"

With a snort, Flash rounded on the bigger unicorn. She jabbed at his knees with her tiny horn, one front foot pawing at the ground angrily. Candice had the distinct impression that the foal was scolding the towering stallion.

The stallion hesitated. Then he took a step forward, his horn brightening. The light ran down to outline his entire body, his form wavering and shifting...

The silver glow faded.

"Candice," Wystan said, holding out his hands. "It's me."

CHAPTER 14

By now, he knew Candice better than to expect her to faint. Sure enough, she just blinked at him, once, her expression barely flickering.

"Okay," was all she said. She scrambled to her feet, gesturing down at Fenrir. "Can you carry him?"

"It'll be awkward." The hellhound was big enough to be a challenge even with shifter strength. "I'm worried about jostling him, but I don't think we have any choice. We have to get him to safety."

Flash nipped at his leg as he started to bend down. He winced—not from her teeth, but from the bright, urgent flurry of images that streamed into his head. It was difficult to interpret her wordless manner of communicating, but the underlying emotion was clear. She was worried about the hellhound too.

"We're going to help him, little one," he answered her out loud, accompanying the words with a mental picture of himself tending to Fenrir in the first aid tent. "We just have to get him back to camp."

Flash cocked her head to one side. She jabbed at him with her small horn, forcing him to take a step back toward Candice.

"What's she doing?" Candice asked, as Flash herded them all

together like a very small and determined sheepdog with a very stupid flock.

"I have no idea," Wystan replied, busy trying not to step on Fenrir's paws. "I think something must have gotten lost in translation."

Flash gave him a rather exasperated look. A single, very clear picture filled his head: Candice and himself, both with a hand flat against the baby unicorn's flank.

Flash's mental tone was so firm, he found himself reaching out before he knew what he was doing. Candice did as well, as though she too had heard that telepathic order. Their hands touched Flash's white coat simultaneously.

Light flared.

White filled his vision, rippling gently. It took him a second to realize that it was the wall of a tent. He met Candice's startled eyes, their hands still side-by-side on Flash's fur.

"Did she just *teleport* us all?" Candice said.

Someone yelped from behind them. They both spun around. A middle-aged woman was staring at them as though they'd just materialized from thin air.

Which, perhaps, they had.

"Candice!" The woman seized Candice, pulling her into a bear hug. Wystan recognized her as Candice's colleague, the one who'd walked in on their first meeting. "You're okay!"

"I'm fine, Bethany." Candice returned the woman's embrace, then held her out at arm's-length to inspect her critically. "You didn't get caught in the fire?"

"No, I was just on my way back from the showers when I saw the commotion." Bethany's eyes narrowed as she took in Candice's state. "Clearly you *did* get caught in it, though. Or, more likely, threw yourself into the flames in order to rescue the animals."

"Are they all okay?" Candice asked anxiously.

Bethany waved a hand, indicating their surroundings. "They're fine. We've got permission to keep them here for now, until we can assess how much damage has been done to our own camp."

Looking around, Wystan realized that they were in one of the first aid storage tents. Boxes of medical supplies had been hurriedly shunted aside to make room for animal cages. Discontented mews and squeaks rose from them, along with the pungent aroma of cats who had elected to relieve their feelings by copiously relieving their bladders.

"The fawn was the only one we couldn't find, and I see you've got her," Bethany said, nodding down at Flash. She did a double-take at Fenrir. "Good grief, are you rescuing *bears* now?"

"This is Fenrir." Candice moved aside to give her colleague access to the hellhound. "We left him watching over Flash, and he…got hurt. He's Wystan's dog."

Not dog. The mental voice was the barest whisper in the back of Wystan's mind. *And not Icehorse's.*

"Fenrir!" Relief surged through him. Heedless of Bethany's perplexed look, he crouched down next to the hellhound.

Icehorse. Fenrir's muzzle lifted a little. His copper eyes were unfocused and dazed, but his muscles tensed, his paws scrabbling weakly at the ground. *Icehorse! The night mare—we must protect the pack!*

"Hush, it's all right, everyone is safe now." Wystan put a hand on the hellhound's shoulder, pushing him back down as he tried to rise. "What happened?"

Now both Bethany *and* Candice were staring at him—the former in increasing bafflement, the latter in slow-dawning realization. Candice's gaze flicked from him to Fenrir. No doubt it was obvious to her by now that he was no ordinary dog.

Was with the cub when attack came. Fenrir's telepathic voice was slurred and weak. *No warning. One moment wall, next no wall, and Night Mare filling the void. Barked fire at her.*

Fenrir's memory flickered in his mind's eye like a bootleg movie. He saw how the metal wall of the trailer had exploded inward, crates shattering under a blast of black energy. He felt how flames had boiled from Fenrir's throat in instinctive reflex as he sprang to meet the threat.

Well, that explained the fire. Hellhound flames were as destructive as dragonbreath. They were unlucky the monster had managed to leap out of the way in time. As it was, Fenrir's fireball had instantly torched the camp rather than his opponent.

Night Mare flung shadow in return, Fenrir continued. A pulse of remembered pain echoed down the telepathic connection, making Wystan's own chest ache in sympathy. *Then, darkness. Next thing, was here.*

You can thank Flash for that, Wystan replied telepathically, though it was probably too late to avoid appearing like a madman to Bethany. *She appears to have unusual talents.*

He cast a glance at the baby unicorn. She was swaying on her hooves, head hanging. Whatever she'd done to transport them here, it seemed to have exhausted her strength.

He'd assumed that Fenrir had carried her to safety from the trailer, but now he suspected it had been the other way around. The little unicorn must have teleported herself and the hellhound to safety… only to have the creature catch up with them while Flash was still recovering her energy. It was apparent she couldn't pull her trick twice in quick succession.

And how does *she do it, anyway?*

He set aside that mystery to ponder later. *In any case, we're safe now,* he sent to Fenrir. *The creature fled. I think it sensed the others were returning. They'll be here soon.*

He could feel the rest of the squad shimmering on the edge of his awareness. Rory and the others were still too distant to be able to join in the telepathic conversation, but they were on their way back as fast as their wings could carry them.

Pack, Fenrir said, also hearing that distant call. The hellhound dropped his head back to the floor, eyes closing in exhaustion. *Good.*

"You just rest," Wystan said out loud. He smoothed the hellhound's fur, silently sending his gratitude. "Bethany here will take care of you."

Bethany eyed the hellhound's massive bulk with wary respect. "Well, I will if your dog promises not to try to take my hand off."

"He's my colleague, not my dog," Wystan replied. Fenrir's tail wagged once, weak but pleased. "And he'll stay still as long as you explain what you're about to do, and ask his permission first. I know it sounds odd, but please, humor me?"

Bethany cocked an eyebrow up at Candice. "I can see why you like this one so much. Besides the obvious." She shrugged. "Okay, sure. Hi Fenrir. I want to listen to your chest and have a look down your throat. Is that okay?"

Fenrir grumbled, but opened his jaws.

"My, grandma, what big teeth you have," Bethany muttered, going rather pale. Nonetheless, her hands were steady as she set to work, pulling out a small penlight and shining it down Fenrir's gaping maw. "I'll take it from here, Candice. You get your butt over to the paramedics, stat."

"I am a paramedic," Wystan interjected. "I'll take care of her."

"I don't need anyone to take care of me." Candice scooped up Flash, who slumped gratefully into her arms. "Flash is the one who needs attention the most. I'll look after her, then check on the other animals."

Wystan caught her elbow, holding her firmly. "You must have inhaled at least a couple of lungfuls of smoke. I'll see to Flash afterward, but I *am* going to take care of you first. Right now."

"Now *I* like him too," Bethany informed Candice.

Wystan was fairly certain that Bethany liked him more than Candice did at the moment. His mate fixed him with a baleful glare. He held her eyes levelly.

It was a fiercer contest of wills than staring down the monster earlier, but Candice looked away first. "Fine," she said grudgingly. "I guess we need to talk, anyway."

She let him steer her out, to the first aid tent. A couple of other casualties were already there, minor burns being treated by medics. The fire in the camp had caught everyone by surprise. Wystan counted himself lucky that he'd managed to escape with only a few minor burns. In the heat of the moment, he'd charged straight through the flames, forgetting all his training in the instinctive need to save his mate.

He dismissed his own injuries, shifter-fast healing already starting to take away the pain. He found an unoccupied camp bed and sat Candice down on it, then fetched a first aid kit. For all her bravado, she was shivering a little, her skin cold to the touch.

"Here." He draped a silver emergency blanket over her shoulders. "You're going into shock."

"Am not," she croaked.

"After what you've seen tonight, it would be bizarre if you *didn't* go into shock," he said firmly. He clipped an oxygen sensor to her fingertip as he spoke. "It's a physical reaction, not a sign of weakness."

"*You* aren't going into shock." She sounded almost accusing.

"This isn't new to me." He lowered his voice, casting a glance around to make sure no one else could overhear them. "I've seen creatures like that before."

Candice cuddled Flash closer, holding her tight as if fearing the apparition might burst into the tent to try to snatch her away. "What—what was that thing?"

Wystan hesitated, debating with himself. But she was his mate. And he'd hidden enough secrets from her already. Keeping her in the dark wouldn't keep her safe.

In fact, it could put her in mortal peril.

He looked down at the baby unicorn in Candice's arms. "I think it was Flash's mother."

CHAPTER 15

"You think it was the baby unicorn's *mother?*" Blaise said incredulously.

From the expressions on his other team-mate's faces, she wasn't the only one wondering whether he'd lost his mind. The flickering campfire illuminated various degrees of skepticism, ranging from Callum's cool reserve to Buck's outright disbelief.

Only Candice seemed to be withholding judgement. She sat on a log a little distance from the rest of them, her expression impassively unreadable. She'd barely said a word since they'd left the first aid tent to rejoin the others back at the crew's camp. Flash was curled up in her lap, sleeping with the limp abandonment of an exhausted child.

"I know it sounds ridiculous, but hear me out." Wystan looked around at the gathered squad: Rory, Edith, Joe, Callum, Blaise, and Buck. Fenrir was still back at the first aid tent, with Bethany watching over him. "Do you remember the hawk? The one that had been possessed by the snake-demon?"

"As if I could forget," Joe said, wrinkling his nose. "I couldn't get the stench of that thing out of my shirt. Ended up burning it."

"When I examined the body, I found that it had strange mutations.

Red eyes, and the beak was misshapen into fangs." Wystan gestured at his own forehead. "And it had horns. Curved ones, somewhat like a goat's, but sharper. Striations suggested that they'd grown very rapidly."

Callum's mouth thinned. "Seth."

"Right," Wystan agreed. "His body had horns too. Smaller than the hawk's, but he wasn't possessed by the demon as long."

"Now I'm really glad we got that thing out of you as fast as we did," Edith murmured to Rory. He nodded, his arm tightening around her.

"The creature that attacked Candice today had *three* horns," Wystan continued. Picking up a stick, he made a rough sketch in the dry, hard-packed dirt. "Two curving back, just like the hawk's did. And one straight forward, right from the center of its forehead. There's only one creature that has a horn like that."

"Well, if anyone can recognize a unicorn's horn, it's you," Blaise conceded. "But why do you think it's Flash's mother? Surely she wouldn't attack her own baby."

"I don't think she was trying to hurt Flash," Wystan said, thinking back over the confrontation. "Just to get to her. She could have zapped all three of us with her death-bolt power, but she didn't. Perhaps the fact that she couldn't shoot Candice or myself without also endangering Flash stopped her."

"You reckon she's just trying to get her baby back?" Joe asked. "But then why would she have abandoned Flash in the first place?"

"Maybe Flash was the one who ran away," Edith said. "Poor baby. Imagine having your mom suddenly turn into a monster. She must have been so scared."

"Actually, she wasn't."

Candice's voice was surprisingly strong, considering her ordeal. He was grateful she didn't seem to have taken any damage from the smoke. He didn't think he would have been able to live with the guilt of not being able to heal her.

"Flash wasn't scared of the creature," Candice continued. "She called out to it. I think she would have gone to meet it, if I hadn't been holding her back."

"That would make sense, if Wystan's right," Blaise said. "She's too little to understand what's happened. All she knows is that she wants her mom."

"And her mother wants her too," Wystan said grimly. "And is willing to kill to get to her. From the extent of the Nightmare's transformation, the demon must have been possessing her for some time. I suspect she's half-mad. She showed no sign of understanding that we were trying to help rather than hurt her baby. She's not capable of looking after Flash while she's possessed."

"Right. She won't have much control over her own actions." Rory looked sickened by the thought of what could happen. "When I was possessed by a demon, it kept grabbing control of my body as if I was a puppet. We can't possibly risk letting the Nightmare and Flash reunite, no matter how much they both want to."

"This is all mighty interesting speculation." Buck folded his arms. "But more importantly, how do we kill this motherloving…mother?"

"We can't!" Edith exclaimed, her hands flurrying in agitation. "She can't help being possessed. There must be a way to help her. Rory got free of his demon, after all."

"Only with your help," Rory said to her. "The demon couldn't tolerate your presence in my soul, the love binding us together. We'd need the unicorn's true mate."

Buck looked as though he'd bitten into a lemon. "What *is* it with you people and true mates? Is that your answer to every problem?"

"Not mine," Joe muttered.

Candice was looking perplexed. "What's a true mate?"

Wystan's stomach lurched. That was not a conversation he wanted to have right now.

"I'll explain later," he said hastily, before anyone else had a chance to speak. "In any case, I'm afraid I can't see that working here. The unicorns aren't shifters, after all. Most animals don't have true mates. Given that there's no sign of a father unicorn, it's possible they aren't even monogamous."

"That's a good point, actually," Blaise said, frowning. "Where *is*

Daddy? Flash here can't have just split off from her mom like an amoeba."

"No other unicorns around," Callum said with great certainty. There was a weary slump to his usually ramrod-straight posture, betraying his exhaustion. The pegasus shifter had spent most of the day in the air. Not only had he searched the area that afternoon and then gone straight out after the Thunderbird with Rory, he'd flown *another* wide sweep straight after the attack, just to confirm that the creature wasn't still lurking near the camp. "I'm certain of that."

Blaise pursed her lips. "Yeah, but you didn't sense the…what did Fenrir call it, Wys?"

"Night Mare," Wystan supplied. "One of his more appropriate nicknames, I feel."

"Certainly more understandable than 'Icehorse', at least." Blaise shrugged. "Okay, let's call it the Nightmare. In any event, you didn't spot it earlier, Cal."

Callum threw her a flat look. "*You* try listening for a whisper in a thunderstorm. I was distracted."

"The Thunderbird distracted all of us." Rory leaned his elbows on his knees, his rugged face serious. "So the question is, was it *trying* to draw us away, or trying to get through?"

"Who cares?" Buck growled. "*That* monster's solution to everything is a great smoking hole in the ground."

"I agree with the chief." Blaise made a face. "Even if it *was* trying to hunt down the Nightmare, in this case the enemy of our enemy is very much not our friend. If we hadn't forced it to turn back, we'd all be sitting in a wildfire right now."

"You weren't able to communicate with the Thunderbird at all?" Wystan asked Rory.

The griffin shifter shook his head. "I think it can hear our telepathy, but it doesn't react. I'm not entirely convinced the Thunderbird can even understand that we're trying to talk to it. It's more like a force of nature than a sentient being."

"Even when the Thunderbird was fighting us this evening, I

somehow got the feeling that it wasn't personal," Joe put in. "We were just in its way."

Blaise sniffed, looking unconvinced. "I take thunderbolts being hurled at my head pretty damn personally."

Wystan steepled his fingers, frowning in thought. "I wish we could get through to it. Whatever the Thunderbird is, it's clearly opposed to these demon-creatures. It seems to be able to sense them. If we could get it on our side-"

"It's a motherfucking monster!" Buck exploded without warning. "Now you fucking want to make *friends* with it?"

Wystan stared at him, along with the rest of the squad. For all the chief's creative language, Wystan had never heard him actually swear before.

Buck paused in the face of their mass astonishment. He cleared his throat, looking uncharacteristically self-conscious.

"That is, that motherlover has torched countless acres over the years," he said, rather more calmly. "It's *killed* people. I hired y'all to kill it, before it could destroy any more lives." He glared around at them all, his face falling back into its usual fierce scowl. "If you aren't going to do that, then you're all fired."

Edith went white, her whole body jerking violently. "No!"

"It's all right, Edith. That's not going to happen," Rory said. His tone was reassuring, but his amber eyes betrayed his anger at Buck for scaring his mate. "Superintendent, there's no need for threats. You know we won't let the Thunderbird hurt anyone. We'll do whatever we have to do."

Buck spat to one side, standing up. "You'd better. And on that note, I'm breaking up this slumber party. No matter what other weird crap rains down on our heads, we've still got the mother of all wildfires breathing down our necks. Everyone needs to get some shut-eye or you're all going to be as much use as day-old kittens out on the line tomorrow."

"Superintendent." Wystan scrambled to his own feet, blocking Buck's path. "I know I promised that meeting my mate wouldn't affect my performance on the crew, but now..." He spread his hands helplessly. "I can't leave her unprotected. Or the baby. Not while the Nightmare is out there."

Buck massaged his forehead. "Motherloving shifters and your motherloving mates. Fine. We'll work something out. At the moment, I would promise you an all-expenses honeymoon on the actual *moon* if that's what it took to get you out of the way so I can go to bed. I'm too old for this crap."

Relieved, Wystan stepped aside. Buck stomped off in the direction of his tent, muttering imprecations under his breath all the way.

"Buck's right," Rory said as he helped Edith up. "The rest of you should get some sleep while you can. I'll stand guard, just in case that thing comes back."

Edith poked her mate in the side, giving him a stern look. "We talked about the overprotective thing, Rory."

He kissed her forehead; a brief, tender gesture. "I know. But I really couldn't sleep, not when I know there's a threat in the area. Don't worry, I know my limits. When I get too tired, I'll call someone else to take over."

"Me," Wystan said, simultaneously with Blaise and Callum.

Joe smirked, standing up and stretching out his long arms to loosen stiff muscles. "Well, since you have no shortage of volunteers… a certain attractive squad boss will be wondering where I've got to. I'd hate to disappoint her."

"Seriously?" Blaise said to him. "*Now?*"

Joe shrugged, cracking his knuckles. "That's the thing about a reputation. Have to maintain it, or it starts to slip. In any case, I have a hunch that neither the Nightmare nor the Thunderbird will be dropping by again tonight." He hesitated, casting a glance at Wystan and Candice. "We should all enjoy the peace while we can. Night, all."

Joe sauntered off, whistling. Blaise shook her head.

"Unbelievable," she muttered. "And that man is meant to be the next Emperor of the Sea, heaven help us all." Her tone turned brisk. "Well, the rest of us will just have to pick up the slack, as usual. You want second watch or third, Wys?"

"Both," he replied firmly. "I was cooling my heels in camp all afternoon while the rest of you were slaving away out on the line. I'm far fresher than any of you. That includes you, Rory. Just let me get Candice settled, and then I'll take over. Medic's orders," he added, as both Rory and Blaise opened their mouths to argue. "I can sign you off as unfit for duty, remember. Don't think I won't."

"I like it when you go all alpha," Edith said in satisfaction. She tugged on Rory's arm. "Come on, you. If you're too wound up to sleep, I'm sure I can find some way to relax you…"

"Not listennnning!" Blaise called after Edith as she dragged Rory away. "At least *try* to help me pretend that my almost-brother is still a sweet, innocent little boy, okay?"

Callum pointedly looked from Blaise to Candice, and back again. He didn't make any further comment.

"Oh, shut up." Blaise rose, dusting off the seat of her pants. She hesitated, eying Candice herself. "Uh, if you want, you're welcome to share my tent. I promise I don't snore."

One of Candice's eyebrow quirked. "Worried I have designs on another almost-brother's virtue?"

"Please don't make me think about that," Blaise said fervently. "As far as I'm concerned, all your future nights with Wystan will be spent playing Go Fish while fully clothed."

At the moment, Wystan would have been quite happy for that to be the case. At least that would mean he *had* future nights with Candice.

"I'm afraid you do need to stay here tonight," he said to his mate. "You *and* Flash. For the safety of both of you. And I very much appreciate the offer, Blaise, but you don't need to share your tent. Candice can have mine."

Blaise threw him a look he couldn't quite decipher before turning back to Candice. "You okay with that? Offer still stands if not."

Candice didn't reply for a moment, twining her fingers into Flash's silky mane. Then she gathered the sleeping baby unicorn into her arms, getting up. She didn't look in his direction.

"I'll stay with Wystan," she said to Blaise. "Thanks, though."

Callum had already silently faded away to his isolated tent, set on the very edge of the camp away from all the others. With a last backward glance, Blaise went off to her own. She crawled into the small pup tent, zipping the flap closed behind her.

"My one is over here," Wystan said to Candice, gesturing across the clearing. "This way."

He wanted to take her elbow to escort her, but after all he'd dropped on her tonight, he couldn't imagine that she'd welcome his touch. She had a blank, withdrawn look that he knew only too well. Car crash victims looked like that, and refugees driven out by fire—people whose lives had changed in an instant, without warning, leaving them lost in uncharted territory.

Every instinct screamed to wrap his arms around her, to comfort his mate. He shoved his hands into his pockets, his fingernails digging into his palms.

Candice trailed a few steps behind as he led the way to his own tent. Like Cal, he preferred to maintain a bit of space between himself and the rest of the crew. Even though his unicorn wasn't very sensitive to the presence of the unchaste—or at least, it *hadn't* been—he still found groups of people draining. Much as he loved his squadmates, by the end of a long, grueling day on the line he always found himself longing for quiet solitude.

"I'm afraid it's hardly palatial," he said, crouching down to undo the tent flap. The small orange tents were just big enough for one person to lie down, or two if they were exceedingly good friends. "I could steal Joe's bedroll for you if you want extra blankets. It doesn't seem like he'll be using it tonight."

"No, it's okay." Candice shuffled in just far enough to deposit the sleeping Flash on the pillow. "This will do."

Wystan hovered awkwardly as she arranged the bedding to make a comfortable nest for the unicorn. She never so much as glanced his way. He couldn't see her face, but the stiff line of her back spoke loudly enough.

He drew in his breath, bracing himself. "You're angry with me."

"Damn straight I am." Candice crawled out of the tent again, standing up. She folded her arms across her chest, facing him squarely. "I am *furious*. How dare you keep this a secret?"

He winced. "I was going to tell you. Truly. I was just...trying to find the right moment."

He'd thought he'd seen the full range of Candice's glares, but *this* one was fierce enough to melt steel. Even Buck would have been impressed. "The right moment was the second I opened the door and found you standing in front of my trailer!"

He'd been fully prepared to grovel to any degree necessary...but this was, he couldn't help feeling, a little unfair. "You think that the first words I ever spoke to you should have been 'Hello, I'm a unicorn?'"

Candice actually stamped one foot. The fine flyaway wisps of her hair trembled with the force of her rage. "No, you irresponsible idiot! Of course you would hardly blurt out your secret to someone you'd just met. I wouldn't expect you to have ever told me that you were a unicorn. But you should have told me that *she* was a unicorn!"

He blinked at her, wrong-footed. "I'm sorry?"

"Yes you damn well should be," Candice said, evidently mistaking incomprehension for an apology. "I was treating her as if she was an ordinary deer! What if, if unicorns had turned out to be allergic to bran? Or need an entirely different dosage for painkillers? I could have *killed* her!"

Oh. His breath caught. *Oh. Just when I thought I couldn't love her any more than I already did.*

"You," he managed to get out, through the emotion choking his throat, "are utterly magnificent."

Now Candice was the one to be caught off-guard. She paused mid-rant, her anger transmuting to bafflement. "What?"

"A creature out of a nightmare attacked you tonight. Your campsite burned down. I dragged you into a whole hidden world you never suspected existed, one filled with danger and terror, and yet..." He gazed at her, humbled and awestruck. "Still your first thought is for the creatures under your care."

"Well, yeah," Candice said, as though this was nothing out of the ordinary. "Of course. Why are you looking at me like I walk on water? You're the magic one here."

"I'm really not." He shook his head, getting a grip on himself again. "In any event, you're completely correct. I *should* have told you what Flash really is, the moment I gave her to you. I put you both at risk by not telling you the truth. I'm sorry."

Candice's body language relaxed a fraction. "Okay. Just don't let it happen again."

"Er." He eyed her cautiously. "Is this a bad moment to tell you that Fenrir is actually a hellhound?"

Candice scrunched her eyes shut for a moment in a pained expression. "Is *anyone* around here what they actually appear to be?"

"Most of the crew, actually," he offered. "It's only A-squad that are shifters. Everyone else is human, I promise."

Candice heaved a long-suffering sigh. "Fine. I don't suppose you have any convenient veterinary textbooks giving standard dosages of common medications for hellhounds, do you?"

"I'm afraid not." He spread his hands. "But I'm confident Fenrir will be perfectly fine under Bethany's care. When I checked with her, she was just giving him fluids and keeping an eye on him. She won't do him any harm by treating him as a large dog. He'll likely be perfectly fine tomorrow, in any event. Shifters heal very fast."

Candice looked alarmed. "He's a shifter? I'm not sure what Bethany would do if she finds a naked man in a dog cage in the morning."

"That won't happen." He decided this wasn't the right time to get into the whole story of Fenrir's inability—or unwillingness—to take human form. "Candice, you need to stop worrying about everyone else and concentrate on taking care of yourself."

"But—" Candice started.

"I promise, I will explain anything and everything to you," he interrupted her. Greatly daring, he took her shoulders, gently rubbing her tense muscles. She didn't pull away. "But in the morning. You need to rest. Please."

She resisted as he tried to steer her back into the tent. "One question. Answer it honestly, or I swear I'll stay out here all night."

He had no doubt that she would. She was the most stubborn, impossible woman in the world, and he adored that about her even as she drove him mad. "Very well. If you promise me that you'll go to bed afterward."

She locked eyes with him. "What's a true mate?"

He hesitated…but he'd promised her the truth.

"It's something that shifters have. One person who is their perfect soulmate, the one person in all the world who is their true match." Though he tried to keep his tone clinical and detached, his heart quickened as he remembered that indescribable jolt of connection he'd felt when he'd first met Candice. "If a shifter is lucky enough to meet their mate, they recognize them on sight. Instantly. And from that moment onward…there's no one else."

Candice had gone very still. "You…when you were talking to Buck, it sounded like you think I'm *your* mate."

"I don't think it," he said softly. "I *know*."

Her eyes were wide and dark. He could spend a lifetime in those depths, and never come up for air. Without meaning to, he'd drawn closer as he spoke, leaning into her warmth. He could feel the soft, startled whisper of her breath against his lips, and hear the rapid beat of her pulse.

Then: "Nope," she announced.

His heart turned to ice. "I know it sounds impossible, but I swear—"

"Nope. Nuh-uh," Candice interrupted. She held up her hands in a T-shape, one on top of the other. "Time out. You win. I have officially reached my weirdness quotient for one day. I'm going to bed."

Yes, our mate must rest, his unicorn said. He could feel it urging him on as though its horn was poking him in the back. *Lie down with her, hold her, keep her safe.*

He'd have to settle for doing one out of three. Reluctantly, he released her, stepping back.

"I'll be right outside," he said as she crawled into the tent. "Call me if you need anything."

"What I need," Candice muttered from behind the tent flap, "is for things to go back to being normal."

That was, he feared, the one thing that he would never be able to provide.

CHAPTER 16

Candice woke up in bed with a unicorn.

For a moment, she just stared blearily at the shining apparition. Flash's wide amethyst eyes gazed innocently back. Little shimmering sparkles danced around her small horn, turning the interior of the tent into a fairy disco.

"Oh, crap. You're not a dream." Candice groaned, letting her head thump back onto the thin pillow. "None of it was a dream."

Flash twitched her nose, and sneezed in Candice's face.

Contrary to popular belief, unicorn spit was not in fact comprised of glitter and rainbows.

"Ew." Candice sat up, wiping her eyes. "All right, all right, I'm up. I guess you must be hungry."

Flash tossed her mane, her small head nodding vigorously.

"You really do understand what I'm saying, don't you?" Candice scratched the unicorn's arched neck. Flash leaned into the touch, eyes half-closing in pleasure. "I wish you could talk, too. I have no idea what constitutes a nutritionally complete diet for a unicorn."

Flash's pointed ears pricked in her direction. She suddenly found herself, for no apparent reason, thinking of a bouquet of daisies, tender green grass, and…oats?

Candice stared at Flash. "Are you doing that? Putting pictures in my head?"

Flash snorted, nodding again. Delighted rainbow butterflies flurried through Candice's mind.

"Huh. That's handy." Candice raked her hand through her hair, trying to flatten what was undoubtedly a terrible case of bedhead. "Let's go find you some breakfast, then."

She'd slept in her clothes, so she didn't have to get dressed. Just as well, given that the pup tent was far too small for her to stand up. Unzipping the front flap, she crawled out—and nearly sprawled face-first over Wystan.

He lay curled right outside the tent flap as though guarding it. He'd gone to sleep right on the bare ground, one arm pillowing his head, the other outflung with his palm upturned. It was odd to see him sprawled and relaxed, all self-awareness abandoned. She hadn't realized before just how rigidly he carried himself when he was awake.

His face was strangely different too. Most people looked more vulnerable when they slept, but Wystan seemed…stronger. His habitual air of diffident reserve had vanished, revealing the true steel beneath. There was something firmer and more certain to the curve of his lips, the line of his brow. His long silver-gold eyelashes and sharp cheekbones gave him the look of a slumbering angel—but one just resting before battle, ready to leap up at any moment brandishing a burning sword.

Candice edged around him, holding her breath. His eyelids flickered fractionally, but he didn't wake up. There were faint blue shadows under his eyes, betraying his exhaustion. He must have been up most of the night guarding the camp as he'd promised. From the careless splay of his limbs, she suspected that he'd teetered and collapsed where he stood when he couldn't stay awake a second longer.

At least someone found him a blanket. The folds of cloth were too neat for Wystan to have pulled it over himself. Candice could picture one of Wystan's squadmates quietly drawing the soft material over him and tiptoeing away. The whole team obviously shared a close bond.

On impulse, she drew the blanket up a little higher, tucking it around him more securely. He let out the faintest sigh, his curled hand relaxing. It might have been her imagination, but she could have sworn his lips shaped her name.

Flash poked her head out of the tent flap. Candice made a frantic *shhhh!* gesture at the baby unicorn. As best she could, she visualized Flash neatly jumping over Wystan's sprawled form without waking him.

Flash cocked her head to one side. The gleam of her horn brightened. In a flash of white light, the baby unicorn vanished.

Candice spent a split-second gaping at the empty space where the unicorn had been, before something hard and pointed poked her in the thigh. She whipped around to find Flash standing behind her, looking like a cat that had gotten not just the cream but an entire dairy herd.

Of course, Flash had teleported them all to the first aid tent last night. "Neat trick. So that's how you kept getting out of your cage. Do all unicorns do that?"

Flash snorted in denial. She pranced on the spot, arcing her neck in obvious pride. Candice received a mental picture of purple flowers and brilliant amethysts, the exact color of Flash's eyes. Somehow, the image dripped with smugness.

"Okay, okay, I get it." Candice booped Flash on the nose, punctuating the little unicorn's over-inflated ego. "You're a child genius. Don't get too full of yourself, kiddo. You still nearly got in trouble over your head last night."

Flash's ears drooped. She gave Candice a mournful look. A ghostly white apparition shimmered through Candice's head, along with a heartbreaking sense of confusion and loneliness.

Wystan was right, Candice realized, recognizing the shape that Flash was trying to convey. *She doesn't think of that creature as a monster. She only sees her mom.*

"It's okay, baby girl." Candice stroked Flash's soft fur, trying very hard to bury her own worries under a surface layer of sunny confidence. She didn't know how much of her own thoughts the baby unicorn could sense. "We're gonna fix everything. You'll see."

Flash perked up again, beaming out a kaleidoscope of rainbow images. Amidst the whirling, dancing impressions, Candice glimpsed Wystan, tall and strong, with herself at his side. A sense of total confidence and trust accompanied the picture.

"I wish I really looked the way you see me," Candice muttered. Through Flash's eyes, she had *great* hair. "I'll do my best to live up to that, kiddo. Now let's go find you some breakfast."

Flash flicked her ears, then bounded away—though not in the direction of the path that led back to the main fire camp, and the remains of the animal rescue tents. Instead, she trotted toward the campfire at the center of the Thunder Mountain Hotshot's encampment.

It wasn't yet fully dawn, but the camp was starting to stir. A few firefighters did double-takes as the unicorn bounced past. Given that they didn't drop everything and scramble for cellphone cameras, Candice assumed that they were seeing Flash as a white fawn—startling, but not front-page news.

"It's okay, she's with me," Candice called out to the confused crew as she hurried after Flash. "Animal Rescue Officer! The situation is completely under control!"

"It's way too early in the morning for that level of optimism," Blaise fell into step at her side, yawning. The short, curvy woman glanced up at her, brown eyes sharp despite her just-woken-up crankiness. "You feeling a bit better, huh?"

"I think I've reached the point of numb acceptance." Candice shrugged. "Since it doesn't look like this crazy train is making any stops, guess there's nothing I can do but ride it to the end. Do you have coffee? Coffee would definitely help."

"We have..." Blaise hesitated in a way that was not entirely reassuring. "Joe coffee."

"The best kind of coffee!" said Joe himself, overhearing. The huge man was hunched over a pot simmering on the fire, stirring it with the intense concentration of an alchemist. "Just a few more minutes. You can't rush perfection."

Candice looked around for Flash, and found her on the other side of the campfire, next to Callum. He was hand-feeding the unicorn long stalks of fresh-cut grass, with a gentleness that belied his cold, closed expression. Flash was chowing down with extreme enthusiasm, stretching out her neck to demand more.

Well, he turns into a pegasus. She remembered Callum's shift animal from the introductions Wystan had rattled off last night. *Guess he would know what tastes good to a fellow equine.*

It was hard not to stare at the shifters, trying to spot the beasts hidden under their skins. Now that she knew their secret, there *was* a strange sort of vibe to them, a sense of raw animal vitality. Callum had something of a hawk's brooding wariness combined with a stallion's restless energy. Even just stirring a pot, Joe moved with a smooth liquid grace of a huge sea creature.

And Blaise...Wystan hadn't said what sort of shifter she was, but she too had that indefinable sense of power. Candice could almost feel it against her skin, hotter than the smoldering campfire.

"Here." Blaise passed her a plastic lunch box. "Joe picked up breakfast on his Walk of Shame back to camp."

"I think you mean Swagger of Glory," Joe said without looking around. "And you should be thanking me for persuading the head cook to whip us up an early batch. She likes me."

"Your indiscriminate conquests are occasionally useful," Blaise conceded.

"I resent that," Joe said indignantly. "I am extremely discriminating. There are just a lot of women in the world."

Candice opened the box to find a steaming pile of pancakes swamped in syrup and butter, with four thick slabs of sausage. Her stomach growled, reminding her that she'd only eaten half of dinner yesterday.

Several busy minutes later, she'd taken the edge off her hunger enough to experience a pang of guilt. Wystan had to be starving as well.

"I should go wake up Wystan," she said, glancing over her shoulder. She could just see his blanket-shrouded form through the scattered rows of tents. "He's missing out."

"Don't worry, we've saved him plenty," said Blaise, gesturing at a waiting stack of boxes. "Let him rest. You'd find it difficult to rouse him, anyway. Rory laid him out with an alpha command."

"A what?" Candice asked.

"It's his special power." Blaise chased a morsel of pancake around the bottom of her own breakfast box, soaking up the last of the syrup. Her tone was as casual as if she was describing Rory's haircut. "Most mythic shifters—people who turn into creatures like dragons and griffins and whatever rather than regular animals—have some kind of innate ability. Rory's is his voice. He can do a sort of hypnotic suggestion thing that's hard to resist."

"Don't worry, he only uses it when he really has to," Joe added. "Like to force Wystan to get some rest. Otherwise the big idiot would have stood guard over you all night."

Candice wasn't keen on the sound of Rory's power, but she had to concede that in this case it had probably been justified. "Huh. Okay. So Rory's got that alpha voice thing, and Flash teleports—"

Callum's head jerked up. "Flash does *what*?"

"Uh." Candice looked around at them. All three shifters were staring at Flash as though she'd sprouted antlers. The little unicorn flicked her tail, unbothered by the attention. "Is that...not normal?"

"No," Blaise said, very definitely. "It really is not. I've never heard of any shifter that can do that. Especially not a unicorn. They're all healers."

"Oh, so that's Wystan's special power?" Candice frowned. "Wait, in that case, why didn't he heal Fenrir?"

From the silence that fell, she'd just put her metaphorical foot into a conversational pothole. Callum's gaze slid away. Joe was abruptly very interested in stirring his coffee, or whatever he was concocting.

Blaise blew out her breath. "Wystan doesn't have any powers. Don't let on we told you. He's...sensitive about it."

"Oh." If the rest of his squadmates had abilities as powerful as

Rory's or Flash's, Candice could see why. "So what do the rest of you do?"

"I sense people and animals," Callum said. "Blaise—"

"I sense fires," Blaise interrupted, throwing Callum a distinctly warning look. "And Fenrir breathes fire, and can phase through solid objects. All pretty standard stuff for a hellhound. The fact that he can also make himself look like an ordinary dog is a bit unusual, though."

"That's the unusual part?" Candice muttered.

Blaise flashed a grin at her. "Choo choo. All aboard the crazy train."

"No kidding." Shaking her head, Candice turned to Joe. "And what about you?"

"Oh, anyone will tell you that I don't have any powers," Joe said easily. "My charm is all natural. If you ask me, shifters without powers are the lucky ones." He handed her a steaming mug, forestalling any further questions. "Here you go. This will pep you right up."

Candice eyed the pitch-black contents with some trepidation. She glanced at Blaise. "Do I want to drink this?"

"Depends." Blaise raised an eyebrow. "Do you want to be very, *very* awake?"

What Candice *wanted* was to sleep for about a week, but that wasn't an option. There was going to be a ton of work sorting out the damage from the attack on the animal tents. And no doubt there would still be call outs to go to, emergencies to handle…not to mention figuring out what the heck to do about Flash and her mother. She was going to need all her wits about her today.

And that meant caffeine. No matter what form it came in.

Well, no point doing things by halves. With a mental shrug, Candice took a large swig of coffee.

And was immediately *extremely* awake.

"Candice!" Wystan barreled into her, sending the coffee mug flying. He seized her, pulling her tight against his chest as though to shield her from a lurking sniper. His head swiveled, scanning the surroundings. "What is it? Where's the danger?"

"Good grief, Joe." Blaise sounded impressed. "Your coffee triggered Wystan's mate-protect instinct."

Joe gazed thoughtfully into the black depths of the pot. "I may have used just a touch too much Tabasco."

"Wystan," Candice wheezed, nose flat against Wystan's pecs. It was a position she would have appreciated, had Joe's so-called coffee not just scorched her throat and sinuses like red-hot paint stripper. "Can't breathe."

He slackened his grip enough for her to turn her head and gulp down air, but his arms stayed locked around her. Both his hair and his eyes were rather wild. "You're all right? You're safe?"

"As safe as I can be, given the circumstances." She coughed, tasting chili-and-caffeine fumes. She suspected they were going to stay with her for some time. "I'm certainly safe from falling asleep anytime within the next seventy-two hours or so."

Wystan looked like he could do with a shot of Joe's concoction. He was still staring owlishly around, as though his brain hadn't yet caught up with his body. Had he *really* gone from sound asleep to full alert just because she'd been startled by terrible coffee?

It's true. The realization hit her like a brick to the back of her head. She would have staggered, if Wystan hadn't been holding her. *What he was saying about shifters and true mates, a fated connection...he wasn't lying. It's all true.*

I'm his mate.

She could tell the moment that Wystan came properly awake, because he glanced down and flushed as he realized how closely they were embracing. He cleared his throat, releasing her at last.

"My apologies." He rubbed at his eyes. "That was not a pleasant way to awaken. I suppose it's too much to hope that there might be tea?"

"Just caffeinated hot sauce, I'm afraid." Blaise handed him a breakfast box. "Joe did get pancakes, though."

Wystan flashed a slight smile at the sea dragon. "In that case, all is forgiven."

Her own box was rather the worse for wear after Wystan's

surprise tackle, but at least it hadn't gone the way of the coffee mug. In the space of time it took her to finish the last of her breakfast, Wystan had wolfed down the entirety of his and was looking more himself again.

Unfortunately. She couldn't help feeling a little regretful as he reassembled that impenetrable wall of reserved courtesy as though putting on a suit of armor. The way he'd leaped to her defense like that, ready to protect her with his life…she was no romantic, but she couldn't deny that it had been just a *little* thrilling.

No risk of him forgetting himself and sweeping her into his arms again, alas. He was keeping a hesitant, uncertain distance from her, as though he'd glimpsed her at a party and was now trying to work out if he'd actually met her before. She felt just as awkward. Knowing that they were soulmates only made things worse.

Seeking an excuse to avoid looking at Wystan, she watched the rest of the hotshot crew as they went about their morning routine. A few firefighters were yawning and grumbling, clearly dragging their feet, but most were moving about with brisk efficiency despite the early hour. She'd seen enough fire crews to be able to tell that this was a well-oiled team. Given the dangerous nature of the work they did, they had to be. Careless hotshots didn't last long…one way or another.

She caught sight of Rory and Edith, loading up a truck with a pile of gear—MacCleods and Pulaskis, the specialist hand tools used to cut back vegetation and scrape fire lines through wilderness. Even amidst the practiced discipline of the rest of the crew, their coordination stood out. Edith tossed tools to Rory without turning around; he caught them without looking, stowing each one in the back of the truck just in time to be ready for the next.

So that's what a real *mated couple looks like.* It was like watching a pair of circus jugglers. They moved like a single pair of hands, in perfect unison. As she watched, Edith stood up, reaching out to load the last tool into the truck herself. Rory caught the MacCleod's long wooden handle, tugging Edith close enough to steal a kiss. Even at a distance, the love between the pair was obvious.

She snuck a sideways glance at Wystan, trying to imagine *them* having that sort of deep, wordless intimacy. He was watching Edith and Rory too, his face in profile to her. It was hard to tell behind his ice-wall reserve, but she thought there was a hint of wistfulness about his eyes.

That's what he wants. She remembered his insistence on more than a one night stand, how hard he'd fought to get through her deflections. Maybe he already *did* feel that way about her.

So how do I feel about him?

"Candice! There you are!"

Bethany hurried up to the group, trailing curious glances from the surrounding hotshot crew. Fenrir paced at her side, his yellow service vest bright against his midnight fur. He was moving a little stiffly, but other than that there was no sign of his ordeal from the night before.

It was a relief to have an excuse to squash her new, messy, and confusing thoughts into a box at the back of her head, where she didn't have to look at them. Here at least was something she understood.

"Hey," Candice greeted Bethany. She went down on one knee, ruffling Fenrir's thick fur. "Hiya, big guy. What are you doing coming into work? Even if you're feeling better, you should take it easy for a few days."

No time, Sun Bitch.

She jumped at the deep, growling voice. She hadn't heard it with her ears. The words were just *there*, in her head, the same way as Flash's pictures.

Sun Bitch always heard me. Just not denying it anymore. Fenrir's copper eyes met hers. She could see amusement in them, as clearly as if he was human. **Have sharp senses, for a two-legs.**

"Sorry. I didn't have much choice but to bring him along." Bethany glared at the hellhound in exasperation. "He's too big for any of the dog cages, and when I tried to put him in the horse trailer he just sat down and refused to move. He's definitely got a mind of his own, this one. I hope he's better behaved when he's at work."

Blaise grinned, her brown eyes sparkling with suppressed laughter. "Not really. Our Superintendent keeps threatening to send him to obedience school."

Fenrir showed what he thought of *that* suggestion by curling his lip just far enough to reveal inch-long fangs.

Giving Fenrir a last pat, Candice straightened up. "Well, time to go to work. No matter what else is going on, someone still has to scoop the kitty litter."

"That wasn't why I came to find you." Bethany thrust a crumpled sheet of paper at her. With a familiar jolt of adrenaline, Candice recognized it as a call out notice. "We've got an emergency."

CHAPTER 17

There were few things, Wystan was discovering, more excruciatingly awkward than being stuck in a vehicle with someone to whom you had recently made a passionate declaration of eternal devotion.

Uncomfortable silence filled Candice's Jeep, thicker than the smoke outside. A double horse trailer rattled behind the vehicle, jouncing over the rutted backcountry roads. The bulky yellow shape of A-squad's transport led the way. Wystan had no doubt that the rest of his squad were enjoying a much more comfortable journey—and not just because of the crew vehicle's superior suspension.

Candice kept her eyes on the tail lights as though she was navigating New York rush hour. Wystan tried to pretend equally intense interest in the passing scenery, but he kept finding his gaze drifting back to her. With the scarred side of her face toward him, it was impossible to judge her expression.

Flash had grudgingly allowed herself to be put in a blanket-padded animal cage for the journey. There had been no question about leaving her behind. No matter how dangerous the wildfire to which they were headed, Flash was infinitely safer with the whole squad rather than left behind at camp.

Now her horn prodded him in the back of his neck through the wire partition separating the front cab from the rear of the vehicle. An impatient flurry of yellow sparkles swirled through his mind.

Candice's mouth twitched, suggesting that Flash had sent her the same image too. "I'm pretty sure that was the telepathic equivalent of 'Are we there yet?'"

"Some things are the same no matter what species." Wystan twisted around in his seat to address the unicorn. "Soon, little one. Please be patient a while longer."

Flash snorted, but settled down again. One ear swiveled from Wystan to Candice and back again. She sent a peculiar image of a wall of ice running down the center of the vehicle, himself on one side, Candice on the other. A wave of worry and fear accompanied the picture.

"We're not fighting," he found himself saying simultaneously with Candice. She caught his eye, her reserve finally cracking to reveal a glimpse of humor beneath.

"I feel we've skipped several important steps in this relationship," she said. "We seem to have jumped straight to agreeing to stay together for the sake of the kids."

His heart gave a great leap, but he managed to keep control of his expression. "I...did not want to presume that this was a relationship. Given the events of last night."

"Yeah, that whole saving my life thing was a real turn-off," she agreed, deadpan. "And you only turn into a unicorn. Now if you'd turned into something *sexy*, like a skunk or a mudskipper..." She waggled her eyebrows at him suggestively.

A laugh burst from him, along with, "I love you."

He hadn't meant to say it. He froze.

"Yeah," Candice returned her eyes to the road, but there was a new kind of thoughtfulness to her face. "I'm beginning to get that. Crazy as it seems."

His shoulders relaxed a fraction. He still felt as though he was picking his way through bear-traps, but now at least there was the faintest glimmer of hope lighting his path.

"You constantly surprise me," he said.

"Ha. Look who's talking." Candice drove in silence for a few moments. "You know, in a way I'm relieved to find out about the whole one-true-mate thing. At least it explains why you were so weirdly into me right from the start. Now I can stop waiting for the other shoe to drop."

"You kissed me before you knew, though. Surely you didn't still suspect that I harbored some nefarious agenda at that point?"

"*Nefarious agenda?*" Candice repeated in an incredulous tone. "Okay, now I'm beginning to think this soulmate thing must be based purely on hormones. No dating app in the world would have matched the two of us up."

"But fate did. And I for one am very glad of it."

She huffed, but the hint of a smile tugged at her mouth. "You big romantic. Well, I guess opposites really do attract."

"Apparently," he said, gazing at the strong, confident, extraordinary woman next to him. "Allow me to rephrase. Did you truly fear I was trying to, er, swindle you in some way?"

Candice shrugged. She rubbed at her right wrist, above the bandaged rat bite. He had the impression it was a habitual gesture, and one that she wasn't even aware of doing.

"Let's just say life has left me with a healthy sense of caution," she said. "If something looks too good to be true, it is."

He watched her fingers trace the rough burn scars running up her arm. "And how does you and me look?"

She shot him a troubled glance. "Perfect."

Before he could think of an answer to *that* one, she spun the steering wheel, turning onto a narrow dirt track. "This is it, according to the emergency call. Helping Hooves Pony Camp."

Wystan peered through the windscreen. Flecks of ash fell like light snow, dusting the low dormitories and rail fences of the summer camp. A thick pall of smoke hung over the scene, turning what should have been bright mid-morning to a dim, ominous twilight. He couldn't yet see the approaching wildfire through the forest, but it had to be close.

Blaise had already parked the hotshot crew vehicle outside a long building that had to be the stable block. As soon as Candice brought the Jeep to a halt, Wystan jumped out, fast enough to get around and hold her door open for her. She shot him another of those cynical looks—*Really?*—but accepted a hand down. Flash needed no assistance, teleporting to his side in a flare of white light.

The rest of the squad was gathered around Rory, who was talking into his radio. As Wystan and Candice approached, Rory clicked the device off.

"Well, there's good news and bad news," Rory said, clipping the radio back to his belt. "Good news is that the local sheriffs confirm they've got all the people out. All the staff and kids are safe, so we don't have to go looking for any stragglers."

"What's the bad news?" Candice asked.

Rory grimaced. "The spotter helicopter says the fire is bearing down on us fast. They're advising that we abandon the rescue and retreat now. Blaise?"

Blaise had the tight, fixed expression she always wore when they were this close to live wildfire. Someone who didn't know her might have mistaken it for nerves. Wystan knew better. She was fighting to control her inner animal, holding it in check with iron discipline as she drew on its power just enough to be able to sense the oncoming flames.

"It'll be tight," she reported. "But I think we've got time to complete a line to protect this area."

Rory nodded. "I'm not going to risk our lives, but if there's a chance we can save the main buildings, I want to try for it. According to the info, this charity helps a lot of kids. Losing their main facilities would devastate them."

Joe clapped him on the shoulder. "We got this, bro. No problem."

"Assuming no interruptions," Callum added, looking even grimmer than usual.

"I'm relying on you for that, Cal." Rory turned to Candice, his jaw set and serious. "This fire is too far from the main blaze to have been started by an unlucky gust of wind. Looking at the location and timing, I'm pretty certain this is the Thunderbird's work. It was heading this way after we drove it off last night. If it really is hunting the Nightmare, they could both still be in the area. If I give the order to clear out, *move*. Even if that means abandoning the horses."

Candice folded her arms across her chest. "You do your job. I'll do mine."

I'll make sure she's safe, Wystan sent to Rory privately. *If I have to hoist her on my horn and carry her out.*

Rory pressed his lips together, clearly fighting down a smile at the mental image. "All right then," he said out loud. "Wys, you're with Candice. Everyone else on me. Let's get this done, A-squad style."

Wystan grabbed his own gear out of the crew vehicle while the others jogged toward the tree line. As he shrugged into his backpack, he noticed Candice staring after the squad, a worried frown creasing her forehead.

She dropped her voice as though worried they might overhear her. "Are they really gonna be able to get a fire line all the way around these buildings in time?"

"Yes," Wystan said, simply.

Candice looked less than convinced. "I know they're magic and all, but they're still just one squad."

"In this situation, the rest of the crew would just slow us down. On our own, we don't have to hide our abilities." Wystan jerked his head in the direction of the squad, who'd now reached the edge of the ranch clearing, where long dry grass gave way to scraggly pines. "Which means we can do *this*."

CHAPTER 18

*D*ragons, it turned out, were *big*.

Candice's jaw dropped as she stared up at the creature that had, until a second ago, been Joe. His horned head towered above the roofs of the buildings, midnight blue scales glittering like thousands of star sapphires. His sleek, serpentine body was longer than a school bus—and that wasn't even including his tail.

She would have thought that a creature so vast, so clearly adapted for the sea, would have flopped like a beached whale on land. But Joe moved with surprising grace, flowing forward on four sturdy legs. His huge webbed feet dug into the ground, uprooting an entire pine tree. With a casual flick, the sea dragon tossed the trunk aside.

"Okay," Candice said, over the splintering sounds of Joe going through the edge of the forest like a wrecking ball. "I change my question. Why did the *rest* of you bother to come along?"

Wystan chuckled under his breath as he held open the stable yard gate for her. "Joe's as effective as a bulldozer—but only as effective as a bulldozer. There's a reason we have hotshots and other hand crews, you know. To make a barrier the fire can't cross, one has to dig down to bare soil. That's what the rest of the squad will be doing now."

A flicker of orange light made her heart stop in her chest. She grabbed at Wystan's arm, dragging him off balance. "Fire! Wystan, we have to run, Blaise was wrong and it's here already!"

Wystan patted her hand, not looking in the least alarmed. "That's just Fenrir. Like I said, they have to clear the vegetation down to bare soil. Sometimes, the fastest way to fight fire is with fire."

Pulse thudding, Candice stared through a gap between buildings. She caught a glimpse of a black-furred shape trotting along the trail of devastation left by the sea dragon. It looked like a dog…but one with flaming eyes and jaws that glowed like the entrance to hell itself.

"And to think I tickled his tummy," she said weakly, as the creature breathed out a white-hot jet of fire that instantly turned grass and snapped branches to ash. "Uh. Is it just me, or is he a lot…bigger?"

"That's his true form. We're fortunate he can tone it down somewhat. It was hard enough working out a plausible breed to put on his dog license." Wystan tapped her lightly on her shoulder. "Candice. Let Rory and the others deal with the fire. We have other concerns."

The gentle reminder snapped her out of her awestruck trance. She shook herself, turning back to the business at hand. "Right. Let's see what we've got."

Frantic whinnies and neighs came from the barn, along with the crash of hooves kicking at stall doors. Whether it was the smoke in the air or the legendary creatures outside, the horses were on the edge of panic.

Candice hurried to the nearest stall, which was occupied by a small dapple-gray mare with a pale, silky mane. A polished brass plate on her stall door read: *Princess.* From the loving crayon drawings covering the wall nearby, the mare was obviously a favorite with the kids.

Right now, Princess looked more like a wild mustang than a placid and much-loved pet. Foam flecked her lips, the whites showing all round her dark eyes as her hooves hammered at her stall.

"Shh, shh." Candice clucked her tongue soothingly, reaching up to grab a handful of the mare's mane. With the other, she fumbled in a pocket for a syringe containing a mild equine sedative. "There's a brave girl. Everything's going to be all right. We're going to get you all out."

To Candice's surprise, the mare settled before she'd even gotten lid off the syringe, let alone stuck it into the mare's neck. The mare stopped kicking at the door, although her hooves still stamped nervously. All her attention seemed to be fixed on Candice's knees.

Bemused, Candice followed the line of the horse's stare, and found herself looking down at Flash. The little unicorn pressed close against her leg, ears flicking constantly in the direction of the open barn door. Despite Flash's obvious agitation, she seemed to be having a calming effect on the mare.

Like on the cats back at the animal rescue camp, Candice realized, remembering how the little unicorn had captured their attention as well. *Animals are smarter than people, they see what she really is. And they trust her...*

Wystan had moved deeper into the barn, scanning the line of stalls. In his wake, the thuds and neighs fell silent. Black and bay and white faces appeared over doors, every pair of ears fixing in his direction.

"I count all ten present," Wystan said, apparently oblivious to the effect he was having on the animals. "But we're not going to be able to make multiple trips to ferry them out to the safe point two at a time like we planned. What do we do with the rest? I'm confident Rory and the others will hold the fire off, but I'm worried the horses will injure themselves in a panic. Should we sedate them?"

"I've got a better idea," Candice said. "Uh, you don't need a full moon or anything like that to transform, do you?"

He flashed her a somewhat puzzled look. "Very little about werewolf legends is accurate. I could shift, but..." He hesitated, then continued, with a catch in his voice. "I'm not sure what good I could do. I—I'm not like Rory and the others. I don't have any powers."

"Wake *up*, Wystan." Candice jerked a thumb at the fascinated horses. "Look at them!"

Wystan blinked around as though only just noticing his audience. "Well, yes. Animals like me. That's nothing special."

"Oh, stop your pity party. You're a unicorn, not a lame donkey."

Candice strode past him, making a rapid assessment of the horses. She picked out two small Shetland ponies whose stubby legs would have trouble keeping up with the rest of the herd. "This one and this one. They'll come with me in the trailer. You lead the rest of them."

Wystan's mouth hung open for a moment. "You think they'll follow me? But—"

"You. Are. A. *Unicorn*," Candice repeated, punctuating each word by jabbing her finger into his chest. "Now shift your ass!"

For a moment she thought he would argue further. Then he nodded, squaring his shoulders. "It's worth a try. I'll do my best."

A star sparked to life on his forehead. The glow rapidly spread over his whole body, silver radiance illuminating his skin from within. No groaning or writhing, like werewolves in horror movies--without moving a muscle, he abruptly blazed as bright as crystal, his silhouette lost in dazzling rainbow-edged light. She had to fling up a hand to shield her eyes.

When she could look again, there was the unicorn.

She'd seen him before, of course, but she'd been nearly out of her mind with terror and shock at the time, and half convinced that she was simply having a psychotic breakdown. Now she knew that he was *real*.

A lump formed in her throat at his shining beauty. He filled the barn with soft, rippling light, like the moon reflecting from water. All the crashing and noise from the hotshot crew working outside the barn abruptly seemed very far away. She could have sworn that even the smoke in the air thinned, purified by his mere presence.

Every horse in the barn had gone absolutely still. Pulling herself together, Candice hurried down the row of stalls, opening each door in turn. She'd been braced for a mass stampede—but the horses still didn't move. They made her think of shy teenagers hesitating around a dance floor, everyone waiting for someone else to go first.

Wystan looked just as uncomfortable in the spotlight of their attention. He shifted his weight, one silver hoof stamping uncertainly. Then, just as he'd squared his shoulders before, he seemed to steel himself. He moved to Princess's stall, lowering his great head to touch his velvet nose gently to hers. The moonlight glow from his horn brightened.

The grey mare whickered, greeting him as if he was a long-lost friend. When he backed up, she followed willingly, her hooves clicking on the concrete floor.

"That's it, brave heart. Out you come." Swiftly, Candice got a halter on the mare, attaching a tag with the animal rescue phone number just in case she got separated from the rest of the herd on the journey out. The mare held steady as a rock, her attention fixed on Wystan.

"That's one." Candice gave the mare a last pat, then stroked Wystan's gleaming fur. "See? Easy. You're doing great."

The towering unicorn shot her a very Wystan wry look: *I have no idea what I'm doing.* Nonetheless, he paced down the row of stalls, coaxing each horse out in turn. Candice haltered and tagged as fast as she could, all the time aware of the ticking clock. They had to get the horses out before the wildfire cut off the escape route.

She attached lead ropes to the halters of the two Shetland ponies, tugging them out of their stalls. The pair snorted and resisted, shaking their heads as she tried to lead them out of the barn. Flash, who'd been trotting at her heels as she gathered up the horses, darted around to touch noses with them in miniature imitation of Wystan. The ponies settled instantly, following along as tamely as working dogs.

This is the weirdest rescue I have ever done. A mad giggle rose in her throat as she led the whole bizarre parade—two ponies, eight horses, and a mismatched pair of unicorns—out to the waiting trailer. In the distance, she caught sight of Rory and the others grimly scratching out the fire line with superhuman speed. They'd already covered half the distance needed to protect the ranch buildings, but the smoke was thickening fast. Time was running out.

Candice waved at Rory, trying to attract his attention. The big man flashed her a thumbs-up sign, his cutting tool never breaking rhythm.

A hand fell on her shoulder, making her jump. Wystan had shifted back to human form, the horses still clustered behind him.

"Rory says to go," Wystan reported. From the slightly abstracted look in his green eyes, she guessed he was in telepathic communication with his squad boss. "They'll catch us up once they're finished here."

"No sign of the Nightmare or the Thunderbird?" Candice asked as she led the ponies up the ramp and into the trailer.

"Not yet. I'm worried that Callum's not at his best, though. He tends to picks up the emotions of the living creatures around him." Wystan indicated the small herd of horses, who were starting to look more agitated now that they were out of the barn. "He hasn't said anything, but I can tell this is a strain for him. It must be the equivalent of trying to listen out for approaching footsteps while someone screams in your ear."

"Let's get them clear, then, so he can concentrate." Candice stuck each pony with a half-dose of sedative, just to make sure they didn't panic once the trailer started moving. She climbed down, fastening the back doors securely. "I'm going to take it slow and steady. If you're having trouble keeping up, just…neigh or something."

"We might be able to do somewhat better than that, actually. Er." Wystan held out a hand, for all the world as if he was inviting her to dance. "May I kiss you?"

She raised her eyebrows at him. "Is this really the time?"

"It's purely in the interests of effective communication, I assure you." He hesitated, his mouth crooking a little in that devastating, wicked smile. "Well. Mostly."

The heated look in his eyes kindled answering warmth low in her belly. She found that she'd stepped closer to him without thought, drawn by that magnetic pull. A tingle shot through her as his hand slid around the back of her neck.

His lips brushed hers—not fierce and demanding, like their first kiss, but soft, gentle, wordlessly asking permission. She opened to him without hesitation, her eyes fluttering closed to better savor the sweetness of his mouth. Slowly, he deepened the kiss, tasting and taking and giving, until her whole body was alive with sensation, with *him*.

And in the midst of the rising pleasure, his voice spoke in her head: *Can you hear me?*

She yelped, jerking back. It was one thing to have Flash or Fenrir touch her mind. It was quite another to have a *human being* in there.

Wystan winced, gingerly touching his mouth where she'd bitten him. "I'll take that as a yes. My apologies. I should have been clearer about what I intended."

Heart hammering, she stared at him. Somehow she could *feel* a thread of connection between the two of them, fragile as a spiderweb. "Yeah, bud. What the hell did you do, give me some kind of mystic STD?"

He looked pained, and not due to her teeth. "I didn't give you anything that wasn't already there. True mates can talk to each other telepathically once they're bonded."

Her voice shot up an octave. "We're *married* now?"

"No!" he exclaimed, to her relief. "The full link wouldn't activate unless we went through, ah…certain formalities, shall we say. But there *is* a subliminal connection between us. Physical closeness makes it a little less subliminal. Since you seem unusually sensitive to telepathic communication, I thought we might be able to reach each other's minds even without the full mate bond. I believe it worked. Can you reach me?"

She looked him straight in the eye, and silently told him exactly what she thought of him.

He winced again. "I deserved that. I promise, I cannot hear anything that you don't deliberately send me. Your thoughts are still private."

Deliberately, she brought to mind how fabulous his tongue had felt, and how much other parts of her were now panting to receive more of him. Since his pale skin didn't flame instantly red, it seemed he was telling the truth. There was no way Wystan would have been able to maintain his composure if he could see what she was doing to him in her imagination.

With a sigh, she released both her indignation and her ill-timed lust. "All right. I guess the telepathy thing could come in handy. Just don't spring any more surprises on me, okay?"

Wystan grimaced. "We need to have a very long conversation in the very near future."

"No kidding. But not now." Candice boosted Flash into the back of the Jeep. "Let's get this circus on the road."

Wystan shimmered back into unicorn form, rounding up the horses as she started up the Jeep. She rolled out as slowly as she could, keeping one eye on the wing mirror. To her relief, the herd followed in an uneven bunch. Wystan's white form patrolled the edges, gently encouraging stragglers to catch up with the group.

"Well, we aren't wining any blue ribbons at the rodeo with this, but at least we've got them moving," she muttered to herself. She hadn't realized she'd sent the words telepathically as well until she felt a wave of wry acknowledgement in answer. She scrunched up her nose, concentrating on the weird echoing feeling of broadcasting her thoughts beyond her own skull. *All okay back there?*

Yes. Speed up. Wystan's mental voice was different to his real one—stronger and more direct. She was struck by the odd thought that he sounded like he'd looked when he was sleeping. *The herd can tell that the fire is getting close, and they want to run. We'll get them to safety faster if we work with their natural instincts rather than trying to hold them back.*

Candice had been holding the Jeep to a crawl, out of fear of a horse stumbling and breaking a leg, but she trusted Wystan's judgement. She shifted gear, accelerating. A storm of hoofbeats thudded over the rattle of the trailer as Wystan urged the herd into a rolling trot.

Candice led the ragged procession away from the ranch, her heart in her mouth. In short order, they'd left the dirt track behind and were out onto what passed for a main road in this neck of the woods. She was grateful that the local sheriffs had cordoned off the area as part of the emergency evacuation. At least she didn't have to worry about any other traffic.

She could only catch the occasional glimpse of Wystan in the mirror, but she could feel him through that strange, tenuous link. She sensed him darting around the herd, coaxing and cajoling the horses to stay together. It was clearly hard work to keep them all moving in the same direction.

A sudden ear-splitting whinny behind her ear nearly made her swerve into the ditch. Cursing, she wrestled the unwieldy vehicle back onto the road. She risked a glance over her shoulder, fearing to discover that one of the Shetland ponies had emerged early from sedation and was now trying to kick its way out of the trailer—but they both still seemed calm.

Flash screeched again, the sound high and unearthly. Candice jumped again as the little unicorn teleported out of the cage, reappearing on the passenger seat in a flash of white light. Flash's hooves scrabbled at the door of the car as though she was trying to paw it open.

"Whoa!" Candice grabbed at Flash's mane before the unicorn stuck her horn through the window. "What is it, baby? What's wrong?"

She didn't sense the slightest hint of a telepathic message from Flash. The unicorn fought her madly, her purple eyes fixed on the trees blurring past outside. Her muscles bunched as though to hurl herself straight through the windscreen. The glow from her horn brightened.

She's going to teleport herself outside the car! High school physics flashed through her head, half-remembered laws about conservation of momentum. She had a horrifying vision of Flash materializing somewhere else while still maintaining the same speed as the car—catapulting herself into the ground at thirty miles per hour.

She couldn't stop without having the whole herd of following horses crash into her bumper. She was left with only one option, no matter how risky. Frantically praying that she wasn't making a terrible mistake, she grabbed for a tranquillizer syringe, jamming it into Flash's shoulder.

She pulled it out again almost immediately, not wanting to risk giving Flash any more than a quarter dose of the drug. It was still enough. Flash squawked, shooting her a look of utter betrayal. Then the little unicorn's eyes rolled up. She collapsed in a limp heap on the seat.

Candice! Wystan's white flank surged next to the driver-side window. *What is it? What's wrong?*

"Flash," she answered, trusting that the words would reach him telepathically if he couldn't hear her over the roar of the engine. She fumbled to lay one hand against Flash's neck, and let out a shaky breath of relief as she found the little unicorn's pulse beating strong and even. "She's okay, but I had to sedate her. She was about to try to teleport out of the car."

What? Wystan ducked his head, one emerald eye peering through the window. *Why?*

"She just suddenly went berserk. I don't know—"

And abruptly, Candice *did* know why.

"Wystan!" she yelled, fear surging through her. "*Duck!*"

CHAPTER 19

Candice's shouted warning nearly came too late. Only his equine peripheral vision saved him, a flicker of black triggering instinctive reflexes. Wystan shied aside, the bolt of energy crackling through the space where his head had just been.

"It's the Nightmare!" Candice yelled, in both his ears and his mind. "Wystan, run!"

He dropped back instead, positioning himself between the Nightmare and Candice. In this form, he could see in a nearly complete circle, allowing him to keep an eye on the black form ghosting through the trees while still running forward himself.

The other horses had caught sight of the unnatural shape too, and had clearly identified it as *predator*. As one, they broke into a full gallop, necks and legs stretching as far as they could. The herd surged around Candice's vehicle in a chaos of rolling eyes and jostling bodies.

Go faster! he sent to Candice urgently. *It's catching up!*

I can't! I'll hit one of them! Candice was having to slow down to avoid the panicked horses. *They're blocking the road!*

Another streak of black flickered behind him. On pure instinct, Wystan wheeled around, horn flaring bright as he leaped to intercept the bolt. The Nightmare's shadowy missile fractured as it hit his radiant aura, sizzling into a shower of sparks.

WYSTAN! Candice screamed.

I'm all right, he managed to send back, through the pain ringing through his skull. Even though his light had seemed to counteract the Nightmare's dark power, he still felt as though someone had whacked his horn with a sledgehammer. It wasn't an experience he was eager to repeat.

He broke into a gallop again, charging toward the Nightmare. The possessed creature scuttled like a hellish spider on its knife-legs, flicking into the cover of the forest. He slowed, hesitating. He didn't dare try to pursue that flickering, elusive shape through the darkness under the trees.

His unicorn reared in his mind, mane tossing. *Our mate! Protect our mate!*

With a jolt of alarm, he realized that the Nightmare was trying to flank him, circling around so that it could get a clear shot at Candice. He stretched his legs to full extension, but the Nightmare was faster.

Candice, BRAKE! he flung frantically into her mind.

The Jeep's red taillights flashed on just as the Nightmare burst from the forest in a curving leap. Its stabbing forelegs missed the skidding vehicle by inches, knifing instead into the road. Then it was tumbling away, knocked head over heels as the Jeep's bumper caught it a glancing blow. Horses screamed, scattering away from its thrashing form.

He gathered himself to impale the monster through the heart…and hesitated.

It wasn't out of pity. The Nightmare was already hissing and lashing out, scythe-like legs cleaving the air as it struggled to regain its feet. Its red eyes were fixed on him…and there was more than hatred there. A greedy, possessive hunger burned in those crimson depths. It *wanted* him to come closer.

Close enough to bite.

If it gets its teeth in me, it's all over. That was how the demons moved from host to host, jumping from one body to another. With a flash of insight, he realized that the monster was playing up its predicament, trying to lure him into a direct attack. Perhaps it was reaching the end of Flash's mother's usefulness, and now sought a fresher body.

The Jeep had slewed to a halt, the trailer teetering precariously behind it. The Shetland ponies neighed from within, alarmed but unharmed by the abrupt stop. In the time it would take Candice to restart the engine, the Nightmare would be back on its feet.

He made a split-second decision, aborting his charge. Instead, he kicked out at the driver-side door, sending it flying off its hinges. *Grab Flash and get on!*

Candice hurled herself onto his back with a speed that would have done credit to a circus acrobat, Flash in her arms. The second her hands clutched his mane he was off, going from a standing start to a full gallop in an instant. Even so, he felt the Nightmare's teeth snap shut just behind his fetlocks, so close it shaved an inch from his silky fur.

Hold on! He jinked aside as another black bolt crackled harmlessly past his shoulder. Then he was *running*, harder than he ever had in his life, back the way they'd come.

"The horses!" Candice screamed in his ear. She was flat against his neck, holding on to both him and the unconscious Flash for dear life. "We can't leave them!"

It's not them the Nightmare wants. Sure enough, the monster was racing after them, flicking in and out of his peripheral vision. *They'll be safer without us.*

He felt Candice twist around, risking a backward glance. Her knees clenched on his laboring sides. "It's catching up!"

He was grimly aware of that fact. Although it was smaller than him, the Nightmare was faster. Not by much—but enough. Inch by inch, it was closing the distance.

At least it's stopped shooting at us. As he'd hoped, some lingering maternal instinct meant that the Nightmare wasn't willing to risk harming her own child. As long as Candice held Flash, they were safe from the Nightmare's death-blasts.

He pushed himself even harder, lungs burning in his chest. *We* killed the last one of these, even though it took the whole squad. *If I can just get back to the others...*

Rory! he flung out, but the echo told him that his mental call had gone unheard. They were too far away for him to be able to reach. And if they were out of range for telepathy, they'd be out of range of Callum's senses too. He had a sudden horrible certainty that the Nightmare had been lurking at this location, patiently waiting to spring its trap, for exactly that reason.

It's smart. It's swift. It's strong. His mind raced faster than his hooves, searching for a way out. *But it's not invincible. There has to be something it fears...*

"Wystan!" Candice's knees clenched on his laboring sides as he abruptly switched direction. "What are you doing?"

Trust me! He plunged into the forest, branches whipping past his head. *And hold on!*

The Nightmare had been caught off-guard by his change of course. He clawed back precious distance, recklessly charging between tree trunks at top speed. As he flashed over the ground, he flared his nostrils, tasting the air.

There!

He swerved again, running directly into the wind. His horn cut through smoke. As his hooves devoured the miles, the acrid clouds grew thicker, roiling in his wake in great curling billows.

His breath rasped in his throat. He sucked oxygen out of the air by sheer willpower. If he started choking, they were all dead.

Candice gasped. Physically close like this, he could feel the way her pulse spiked, panic leaping through her veins. "Wystan!"

She wasn't looking back at the Nightmare...but at what lay ahead of them.

The wildfire rose like an orange wall. Whole trees blazed, alight from root to crown. Wind fanned the firestorm, sending it leaping through the canopy with terrifying speed.

In the face of that deadly force, the Nightmare faltered. It pranced to a halt as though an invisible rider had reined it in, neck arching.

Wystan slewed around to face it, horn lowered and ready. Its knife-point feet danced a staccato rhythm, but it didn't advance.

Heat beat against his hindquarters. He could feel Candice shaking like a leaf on his back, face buried in his mane. He held steady, eyes locked on the Nightmare, and waited.

The wind blew a flurry of embers between them. The Nightmare flinched, hissing. It took a quick, darting step backward, and halted, trembling. It seemed to be fighting a battle with itself, torn between equally strong instincts.

With a *crack*, a burning branch dropped from the canopy, landing mere feet away. The Nightmare broke at last. With a final hate-filled glare, it turned tail and fled.

"Run!" Candice kicked frantically at his sides. "Hurry, go, now!"

He shifted instead, catching her as she tumbled off his back. "It's too late for that. I can't outrun the fire, not when I'm already half-exhausted."

Candice clutched the unconscious Flash to her chest, her breathing fast and panicked. He didn't have time to reassure her. Thrusting her aside, he threw off his pack.

He'd picked the clearest spot of ground he could find for his stand. It wasn't ideal, but it would have to do. Dropping to his knees next to his pack, he scraped a shallow pit in the dirt, drawing on all his shifter speed and strength.

"Here." He tugged Candice down as he reached for his pack. In his mind, he showed her exactly how to lie in the dirt, her face turned into small depression. "Like this. No matter what, don't move."

Her eyes were huge in her bloodless face, but she obeyed, hugging Flash tight against her prone body. He was already standing, his hands moving swiftly and surely, knowing what to do without conscious thought thanks to endless drills.

He shook out the fire shelter. It didn't look like much—just a large rectangle of crinkly, reflective material. He'd never before had to deploy one for real. It seemed impossible that the flimsy thing could protect them from the deadliest forces of nature, but he had to trust in the engineers and scientists who'd created the hi-tech fabric.

Despite the furnace heat raging at his back, calm filled him. Somehow he just *knew*, without a shadow of a doubt, that Candice would be safe.

He would protect his mate.

"Don't be afraid," he said to Candice. He pinned the back edge of the shelter under his boot heels, clamping it tightly against the ground. "I'm with you. Trust me. All will be well."

Holding the corners of the fire shelter, he dropped forward, arms spread wide. He covered Candice with his body, the fire shelter settling over them both like a blanket. In the tiny, dark, airless space, he held her tight—in his arms, in his mind, in his heart.

And the wildfire enveloped them.

CHAPTER 20

"Candice," Wystan said from outside the horse stall. He leaned his forearms on the low half-door, exhaustion and concern showing in his dirt-streaked face. "Stop. You have to get some rest."

Candice didn't pause in brushing out Princess's mane. "I just want to get these burrs out. She's been through so much today, she deserves to be comfortable."

"So do you." Wystan unlatched the door, slipping inside. Princess made a soft, sleepy sound of welcome, but didn't lift her head. "Look, she's half-asleep already. All the horses are. There's nothing more you need to do for them."

Candice fixed her eyes on the curry comb, moving it in steady, slow sweeps. The rich, earthy smells of the stable surrounded her—horses and straw, oats and leather.

No hint of smoke. No acrid bite of burning debris choking her throat. No crackle of flames or searing heat. Just the gentle, reassuring sound of Princess's slow breathing, and the soft warmth of her flank.

"Ah." She felt Wystan move to her side. She thought he was going to try to forcibly wrest the brush away from her, but he just ran his own fingers through Princess's grey mane, untangling a stubborn knot. "This is more for you than her, isn't it?"

Candice followed his hand with the brush, so that Princess's mane fell in silky-smooth strands. "You swore that you couldn't read my thoughts, bud."

"I can't. Not unless you show them to me." He picked out a twig from Princess's mane, flicking it away. "But I do have eyes."

Well, he's partly equine. Horses were exquisitely sensitive to body language, Candice knew. It was one of the reasons she liked working with them so much. Horses *made* you be calm and quiet.

Right now, she really needed that.

Wystan didn't make any further attempt to persuade her to stop. He just worked quietly at her side, untangling and grooming, every movement in perfect harmony with her own. Gradually, Candice's tension ebbed away. The deep, companionable silence supported her like a warm bath, gentle and undemanding.

"Okay," she said at last, stepping back to survey their handiwork. Princess's coat gleamed like polished silver in the dim light of the stable. The mare was dozing on her feet, every muscle relaxed. "I'm done now."

Wystan held the door open for her, his face half-hidden in shadow. Only a single flickering bulb illuminated the stable. Soft snorts and rustles drifted from the darkness, horses stirring in their sleep. She paced down the crowded stalls, doing one last check on them all.

She was grateful that none of the horses had come to any harm during their mad flight. With Callum's help, they'd been able to round up the scattered herd without too much difficulty, bringing them all to this safe haven.

Flash lay sleeping in the last stall, snuggled against Fenrir's coal-black body. The hellhound lifted his head as she peered over the door. His tail swept through the straw in a wag of acknowledgement.

Sun Bitch, Fenrir's deep, not-quite-human voice said in her mind. *Am here. Be at ease.*

A spark of red light gleamed deep in his eyes. She remembered her glimpse of his true form, fire dripping from his jaws. He'd seemed huge and invincible...but the Nightmare had taken him out before.

Was surprised, Fenrir growled, and she realized she'd accidentally broadcast her worry to him. *Not again. Go, Sun Bitch. Sleep deep. Pack guards pack.*

"You're sure Rory and the others will spot the Nightmare if it comes back?" she said to Wystan as she flicked the light off.

He nodded, taking her arm to escort her out of the stable. "Even with Callum resting, nothing is going to get past Rory. He can see in the dark better than a lion, and with the acuity of an eagle. He's flying sweeps around the whole ranch. Look."

Candice glanced up as they stepped outside. Even this far from the wildfire, the night sky was still hazed with smoke, shrouding the stars. Nonetheless, she just about made out a broad-winged, black-on-black silhouette sweep silently over their heads. Unlike Happy Hooves, the land around this ranch was all open paddocks. There wasn't any cover that the Nightmare could use to evade the griffin shifter's watchful eyes.

"Guess we're as safe as we can be," she conceded. She rubbed at her face, the long day finally catching up with her. "Where can I crash?"

"The house is all full, I'm afraid," Wystan said, gesturing at the dark building across the stable yard. The ranch had thrown open its doors to evacuees from the wildfire, and now cars and pickup trucks were parked haphazardly all along the drive. "I could set up one of our crew tents for you."

The thought of crawling into yet another small, dark space made Candice shudder. "Thanks, but no thanks."

Wystan's hand tightened for a moment on her elbow; a swift, understanding squeeze. "I thought you might say that. Come with me."

He led her around the side of the stables, where a wooden ladder led up to a small open hatch. Climbing up, Candice found herself in a high-beamed hayloft. Someone—presumably Wystan—had rearranged the stacked bales to make enough room to lie down. A bedroll and blankets lay invitingly across a deep mound of hay, next to a bottle of water.

Wystan's white head appeared in the hatch. "It's not luxurious, but I suspected you might prefer this to a tent tonight."

"It's perfect." The warmth of the stables filled the hayloft. She sank down onto the makeshift bed with a sigh of relief. "Thanks."

He nodded, still perched on the ladder. "If there's anything else you need, I'm just a thought away."

Almost, she let him go. But as he started to disappear back down the ladder, her precarious calm slipped as well. All the things she'd been trying not to think about—the Nightmare, the fire—threatened to burst into her mind.

"Wystan!" She scrabbled on hands and knees to catch his shoulder. "Please. Stay. I...I don't want to be alone."

He hesitated, then pulled himself up. Without a word, he pulled her into his arms, settling her against his chest. She closed her eyes, gratefully listening to the strong, steady beat of his heart. Gradually her own slowed.

When he spoke, his voice was so soft she more felt than heard it. "I'm sorry."

She raised her head enough to see his profile. "What for?"

"Today." He was staring out the open hatch rather than looking down at her. His eyes were haunted, fixed on something other than the horizon. "It didn't occur to me that I was forcing you to relive a traumatic experience. I should never have taken you anywhere near the wildfire. I should have found a different way out."

"Hey." She poked him in the side. "I'm a tough cookie. I can't say it was fun, but I'm okay. And we didn't have a lot of options. Your quick thinking saved us."

"I wasn't thinking at all," he said harshly. "I acted on pure instinct. I felt so sure of myself at the time, but..." He shook his head, jaw clenching. "I took an appalling risk."

She tightened her arms around him. "It worked, though."

"This time." He fell silent for a long moment. His muscles were rock-hard under her cheek, wound tight. "I don't know how to keep you and Flash safe. Not long term. The squad can't guard you both forever."

"Forget forever." She traced a line down his torso. "We're here, now. We're alive. Can't that be enough?"

He caught her hand under his as she sought to go lower, flattening her palm against his taut abdomen. "Candice—"

"We could have died today." She hooked a leg over his. His breath caught as she straddled his lap, pushing herself up so that they were face to face. "The Nightmare could eat us tomorrow. We could get caught in another wildfire. We could just be really unlucky crossing the street. You *can't* ensure that I'm perfectly safe forever, Wystan. Nobody could do that. But we're together now. And I for one would be *really pissed* to get hit by a cement truck before I found out what you look like naked."

His hands fisted, as though he was having to physically hold himself back from touching her. "Candice...you know I can't do casual."

"I know. And I can't promise you forever." She shifted her hips, pressing against him, and he made a low, strangled sound of pure need. "But damn it, there has to be *something* between a one night stand and eternal devotion. Can we...try to find it? Meet each other halfway?"

His hands slid up her thighs. She gasped as he gripped her hips, grinding her yearning core against his hardness. His mouth sought hers in the darkness. Tipping her head back, Candice gratefully surrendered to the wave of pleasure, letting go of everything else.

Then Wystan drew back a little. She let out a small sound of protest, struggling to reclaim his lips, but his arms were like iron bars, holding her away.

"Candice." Her name sounded torn from his chest, his breathing ragged. He leaned his forehead against hers, eyes tight closed as though he wouldn't be able to restrain himself if he looked at her. "You know I'm a virgin."

She had to concede that a sweaty encounter in a prickly hayloft might not have been how he'd pictured his first time. "We don't have to go that far. We could still enjoy each other, even if you don't want to—"

"I do want to." He opened his eyes again, desire clear in their dark depths. His mouth quirked in a pained smile. "But first, I need to tell you something about unicorns."

CHAPTER 21

It took some time.

When he finally wound down, Candice just stared at him.

"I'm sorry," he said yet again. "I'm aware it's...inconvenient."

"*Inconvenient?*" Candice repeated, her voice cracking with incredulity. "Wystan, you just told me that if I have sex with you, I'll kill you!"

"Not me, precisely. Just my animal."

"Oh, well, that's okay then," Candice said, dripping sarcasm. "I'll just rip apart your soul and destroy the core of your identity. I'm sure that won't do you any harm whatsoever."

"You won't hurt me," he said firmly. "Candice. I told you because I couldn't go to your bed with secrets between us. But now you know."

He tried to reach for her again, but she scooted back as though his unicorn might keel over at the slightest touch. "Are you *crazy?* You think you can tell me, tell me that if I don't love you enough then I'll doom you to a fate worse than death, and expect me to just nod my head and carry on? This is *dangerous*, Wystan! We can't risk it!"

His whole body yearned for her, but he forced himself to drop his hand. "I understand your concerns. And I appreciate that you may need some time to reflect, and determine if you are ready for this step. I've waited a long time. I can wait a little longer."

She bit her lip. Her shoulders were hunched, arms hugging her own torso tightly as though she was trying to hide from him. Every line of her body shouted *no, no, no.* "Wystan...you were straight with me, so I want to be straight with you. I need to show you something."

She sat back on her heels, straightening her spine. Her hands went to the top button of her shirt. Her eyes were wide and dark, vulnerable in the dim light.

He drew in a sharp breath as she started undoing her shirt. "Candice, if you're trying to dissuade me, I have to tell you that this is a very poor way to go about it."

She gave him a wavering half-smile, her hands never pausing. "Just stay over there, okay?"

She turned her back on him, letting her shirt slip off her shoulders. Her left was smooth and rounded, faintly tanned. But her right...

He hadn't realized how far her scarring extended. The whole right side of her body was a map of survived pain. The reddened, shiny burn scars ran from her neck to below her waist, a silent testament to her strength and tenacity.

"I was seventeen," Candice said in a low voice. "Seventeen, and so, so dumb. I grew up in care homes, you see. Not good ones. I was so hungry, so desperate for any hint of real affection. And...there was this guy. Of course. The first guy who ever noticed me."

Wystan was instantly seized by an intense need to know the man's name, appearance, and current address, so that he could go beat the bastard to death with a shovel. He could barely form words, his voice twisting into a feral snarl. "He did this to you?"

Candice twisted to cast him a bleakly amused glance over her shoulder. "He's in jail, so you don't need to look quite so homicidal. The last thing I want is for you to end up locked up in the cell next to him for attempted murder."

"It wouldn't be attempted," he growled.

"That's sweet. Psychotic, but also sweet." Candice pulled her shirt up again, though she kept her back to him. "Listen, I didn't show you because I want you to go on some avenging crusade. Or because I want your pity."

He couldn't leave her there like that, so alone and brave. Candice didn't move or look around as he moved to kneel behind her. Very gently, he put both hands on her shoulders, feeling the difference between them through the thin fabric of her shirt. Her breath sighed out, almost too quietly to hear, as he rubbed her tense back in small circles with his thumbs.

"Why did you show me?" he asked softly.

"Because you needed to see how bad the damage is on the outside." Her head was bowed, showing him only the delicate nape of her neck. "So that you'll understand exactly what it means when I say that the damage on the inside is worse."

"You aren't damaged, Candice." How could this incredible, courageous woman think that she was broken? "You're forged in fire, like the finest steel."

She huffed, though it didn't sound *entirely* in annoyance. "Shut up and listen. Like I said, there was a guy. A bit older than me. He was… oh, handsome and charming and all that crap. He made me feel like I was in a fairytale. I was just a stupid, naive kid. I believed everything he told me."

He kept rubbing her back, in slow, soothing strokes. "What did he tell you?"

"Oh, that he could give me everything I'd ever wanted, of course." Her voice softened, turning wistful. "I had…I had this dumb dream. I wanted to have my own ranch, where I could work with rescued horses. And dogs and cats and goats…it was going to be a haven for all animals in need. I had it all planned out. I was going to go to school, get vet qualifications, work my way up until I could afford to buy my own place. And I had a secret stash of money, that I'd been saving since I was seven. Nearly enough for my two years of tuition. You see where this is going now."

"Unfortunately." He concentrated on not letting his growing anger show in his gentle massage. "He found out about your nest egg."

"I was stupid enough to show it to him, can you believe? Because I wanted him to come with me when I finally got free of the care system." Candice's muscles were rock-hard under his palms. "And he hugged me and said he wanted that too, and he couldn't wait until I was eighteen. He said we should go right then and there. Just sneak out of the home and run away together. Because—what an amazing coincidence—he had this elderly aunt in Montana. Who had a horse ranch. She was getting old and needed help and would definitely take us in. She'd probably even leave us the whole place in her will when she died. And I believed him. I was *that* stupid."

"It sounds to me," Wystan said, "more like he was a master of manipulation. And a predator. You were brave enough to open your heart to him, and he took advantage mercilessly."

"Well, whatever. The upshot is, I ran away with him. He took me to this crappy motel room and lit all these candles. He bought wilting gas station flowers and scattered the petals all over the bed as if we were newlyweds. I had this sexy nightdress, all tacky lace and polyester, and when I put it on he looked at me as if I was a goddess. I thought it was all the most romantic thing in the entire world." Candice stopped for a moment, swallowing hard. "And then I woke up in the middle of the night, a few of those candles still burning, and I saw him shoving all my cash into his backpack."

He tightened his hands on her shoulders, holding her, and said nothing.

"He tried to tell me he'd just been packing for the morning, but he had his coat and shoes on and even I wasn't *that* stupid. I threw myself at him, screaming, fighting to grab my life's saving's back. He grabbed the desk lamp and brained me with it." Candice's breathing was going ragged. "I fell down, half-unconscious. And as he bolted for the door, he knocked into the table and one of those oh-so-romantic candles fell down. Onto my cheap fire-hazard nightdress."

She was shaking. He wrapped his arms around her, pulling her tight against his chest. Her spine was rigid as an iron bar.

"Later—a lot later—his lawyer argued that he hadn't seen me go up in flame. That if he had, he would have come back and rescued me. Of course." Candice let out a dry, choked chuckle. "The jury was not impressed. So justice was served, for once. And I learned a really valuable life lesson about trusting people. Especially perfect, romantic men who say they want to sweep me off my feet and fix everything."

"I wish..." He had to stop, his own throat raw. "I wish that I *could* fix everything. Or anything."

"I know. You're a good man, Wystan. I *know* that, up here." Candice tapped her head. "But down here..." She moved her hand to her chest, over her heart. "I was burned, Wystan. Badly, badly burned. In here, where it matters."

"I understand now why you tried so hard to keep me at a distance." He rested his chin on her shoulder, holding her closer. "And how much bravery it must have taken just now to make yourself vulnerable in that way again. You're the strongest person I've ever met, Candice."

"You still don't understand," she said, her voice breaking. "Wystan, you need someone who can offer you her whole heart, you said so yourself. I'm never going to be able to love anyone that way. *He* broke that part of me."

"No." He brushed his hand down her right arm. "You didn't recover the use of this arm all at once, after your injury, did you? But you didn't give up. You exercised and practiced, and every day the scar tissue stretched just a little bit further. Why would your heart be any different?"

She shook her head in a sharp, jerky motion. "No matter how much physio I do, I'm never going to be able to extend my arm above my head. I'm never going to be able to give you what you need. Every time I look in a mirror, I remember what happened to me. I can't help it. No matter how perfect you are, there's always going to be some scared, scarred part of me holding back for fear of getting burned again. And that means when I crack and have sex with you--and I *will*, Wystan, because even this exact second you smell so damn good that it's all I can do not to rip your clothes off here and now—I'll destroy you. I'll kill your unicorn."

"You *won't*," he said firmly. "You're my mate."

"I can't," she whispered. "I can't, Wystan. This isn't going to work."

A sudden storm of wings outside the hatch made them both jump. Wystan spun around, twisting to shield Candice as a huge feathered head blocked the opening. A fierce eye peered in at them—and shrank down to human dimensions.

"Sorry for the interruption," said Rory, crouched at the top of the ladder. "But we've got a visitor."

Wystan tensed, still protecting Candice. "The Nightmare?"

"Nope." The griffin shifter's expression was grim. "It's the Thunderbird."

CHAPTER 22

*J*oe gazed thoughtfully up at the Thunderbird's distant, wheeling silhouette. "I feel we should offer it a cup of coffee."

"Not your coffee," Blaise muttered. She took a long swallow of Joe's special brew and shuddered, straightening a little. "I can't believe you didn't wake us all up, Rory."

Rory shrugged one shoulder. There were dark shadows under his golden eyes. "You were already asleep. And it wasn't doing anything. No sense in all of us being exhausted."

Candice sipped her own drink—which had come from the ranch's communal coffee pot rather than Joe's hip flask—gratefully feeling the caffeine hit. She'd only slept fitfully throughout the night, jolting awake at the slightest noise. Every time she'd opened her eyes, Wystan had been silhouetted against the hatch, watching the sky. She didn't think he'd slept at all.

He'll do anything to protect me. He's a good man. I can trust him.

She *knew* that, without a shadow of a doubt. But when she looked at him, trying to picture herself being able to say *yes* to him, in all the ways that he wanted…her heart flinched.

It was ironic, really. *Fool me once, shame on you.* She'd sworn never to be fooled twice, to never let stupid emotions overrule cold logic again. But now, no matter how much her head insisted that Wystan was kind and honest and true, that scarred part of her soul screamed *no, no, run!*

She'd been burned once. And even the gentlest and most comforting of fires was still flame.

Wystan's gaze, which had been fixed on the circling Thunderbird, flicked to her. Candice realized that she'd been staring at his profile like a teen geek girl crushing hopelessly on the school quarterback. She hastily focused on the sky like everyone else. If she was going to save him from herself, she had to stop giving him any false hopes.

The only way to protect him was to cut him off. No matter how the thought of never seeing him again made her stomach cramp in misery, it was the only way. She couldn't trust herself around him, and he was *too* trusting. She'd never be able to convince him that she was a danger to his unicorn. She had to leave.

But she also *couldn't* leave. Not yet, with Flash still in danger. Candice couldn't walk away from an animal who needed her. And even if she could, she was pretty sure that Flash would just teleport after her. The little unicorn seemed to have imprinted on her. Even now, she was leaning against Candice's legs, idly nibbling at the grass. The unicorn seemed entirely unconcerned about the presence of the circling Thunderbird.

"It hasn't done this before?" she asked Rory.

"Turned up and stayed passive, you mean?" The hotshot squad boss shook his head. "No, this is new behavior. It's been hesitant to attack us before—"

"It flung *lightning bolts* at us," Blaise interjected, scowling. "Multiple times."

Rory turned his hands palm-up, shrugging. "Yes, but not straight away. Remember when it turned up after we killed the snake-demon? It definitely thought for a moment before it torched the area."

Blaise folded her arms. "Guess it takes a while to build up a zillion volts of electricity. I think it's just tired after starting that last forest fire."

"It's a possibility," Rory conceded. "It certainly didn't seem keen to come down and say hello. It just circled higher when I tried to go up to its level. It can fly a lot higher than I can. Callum?"

The pegasus shifter shook his head. "Can't go that high either."

"Well, we can't just sit here and let it recharge," Blaise snapped.

"You volunteering?" Rory said, a note of challenge entering his tone. "If any of us could get up there, it's you."

"Oh, great idea." Blaise rolled her eyes. "Let's replace the giant deathbird with something even worse. Seriously, Rory. There has to be something we can do."

"Well, what we *can't* do is sit here debating it all day," Joe said. "Otherwise we'll have Buck descending on us as well. We're already late reporting back."

"Were you able to get in contact with the chief?" Edith asked Rory.

"I could only get through to Control, at base camp. Buck and the rest of the squad are deployed far out on the front at the moment, out of cellphone contact. I gave them a coded message to relay to him by radio, but it'll take a while to reach him. I could hardly explain why it was urgent." Rory blew out his breath, his brow furrowed with worry. "We're on our own for this one, squad."

"We don't need the chief's orders, though, do we?" Blaise raised her eyebrows, her jaw setting as she looked around at her teammates. "We already know what they would be, after all."

"He'd want us to attack it." Edith's hands fluttered through the air in an agitated gesture that was curiously at odds with her firm stance and focused expression. "But he'd be wrong. He thinks the Thunderbird is pure evil, but maybe we just don't understand it. We're speaking different languages."

"I agree with Edith," Wystan said. "I believe the Thunderbird is here to hunt the Nightmare. Given how the creature backed off when I baited it too close to the wildfire yesterday, I'm now convinced that fire is the snake-demons' fatal weakness. That's the reason the Thunderbird starts the forest fires with its lightning—not out of malice."

"Oh good. It has a reason for burning innocent people," Blaise said. "How comforting."

Candice frowned. Wystan's theory was sound, but something was nagging at her...

It clicked into place at last. "It's not hunting."

The bickering shifters fell silent, blinking at her as though they'd forgotten she was in their midst. "Why do you say that?" Rory asked.

"The flight pattern is all wrong. It's circling as if it's riding a thermal, but there's nothing around to produce that sort of updraft." She gestured around at the flat paddocks surrounding them. "Look how much it's flapping to stay in position."

Joe tilted his head. "So, bro? I'm no expert, but isn't that how flying works?"

"Exactly. Flying like that takes *work*, for a bird that big. It's got the same general shape as a California condor." One the size of a light aircraft, admittedly, but that just made Candice all the more sure that it had to be putting in a heck of a lot of effort into staying in such a small area. "When a condor is looking for carrion, it keeps its wings as still as possible, riding air currents over a broad area. That's the only way they can stay aloft for so long. If the Thunderbird was searching for the Nightmare, it should be flying in wide loops with its wings still, trying to conserve its energy as long as possible, see?"

"I guess so," Rory said, still not looking like he was entirely following. "That's how I'd fly, anyway, if I was searching for something."

"But not if you'd already found it," Wystan breathed, understanding dawning. "You're right, Candice. It's working very hard to stay right above *us*."

"Oh joy," Blaise muttered. "Now there's a cheery thought."

"The Nightmare's not here." Callum sounded utterly certain. "I have its..." He appeared to search for the right word. "Its signature, now. Even with *that*," he jerked his head at the Thunderbird, "looming over us, I'd sense it."

"So if it's not hunting the Nightmare, and it's not here to fight," Joe said slowly. "What *does* it want?"

As if it had heard him, the Thunderbird broke off from its tight circles. Its shadow swept across them. Slowly, wings held motionless, it set an arrow-straight course for the mountains to the north east.

Edith voiced what they were all thinking. "It wants us to follow it."

CHAPTER 23

"This is a terrible idea," Blaise muttered. "This is the *worst* idea."

"I'm not disagreeing," Wystan replied without looking around. Even with shifter reflexes and hotshot training, it took concentration to hike across completely wild terrain. "It does, alas, have a single redeeming quality, though."

Blaise's booted feet crunched through leaf litter behind him. "What's that?"

He shouldered aside a low-hanging branch, holding it back with one arm so that Blaise could duck under it too. "It's the only one we've got."

Blaise shot him a pained look as she passed him, but didn't waste breath arguing further. They'd been hiking for several hours now, since the last tiny dirt road had petered out. Since the Thunderbird had sailed serenely onward, they'd had no choice but to park the squad's truck and follow on foot. Or, in the case of Rory and Callum, wings.

Anything yet? Wystan sent telepathically to Rory. He couldn't see the griffin shifter through the dense forest canopy, but he knew he was circling overhead, keeping track of them.

Nothing, Rory sent back. *The Thunderbird is still making a direct line for nowhere, as far as I can tell. Nothing to see for miles but trees. For all I know it's trying to take us to Nevada. Or Connecticut. Let me know if anyone needs a break, okay?*

Wystan sent a brief, wordless acknowledgement and let the telepathic connection drop. He moved off to one side, pretending to stop to retie his bootlace in order to have an excuse to check on everyone else as they filed past.

Edith was still bright-eyed and bouncy, of course, as fresh as when they'd first started out. Although she didn't have shifter strength, her hard-trained stamina always put the rest of them to shame. Joe, bigger and heavier, was clearly finding the steep, heavily-wooded terrain more challenging, but his stride was still steady even though his usual stream of bad jokes and light-hearted banter had fallen away.

Candice lagged a good ten feet behind Joe. Sweat plastered her hair to her forehead under her hat. She had her head down, her hands gripping onto the straps of her backpack as though she could haul herself up the mountain by her arms. She'd insisted on bringing along her emergency gear from her animal rescue vehicle, with a wide assortment of first aid treatments for just about any species. A telescoping dogcatcher pole was strapped to one side, while a tranquillizer rifle bumped at her hip.

He already knew it would be futile, but he put out a hand to stop her anyway. "Please, Candice. Let one of us take your things."

She shook her head in a tight arc, not looking up from the ground. "I don't need help."

"I assure you, it wouldn't be a burden. We're trained to hike long distances with heavy loads. We're much more used to this than you are."

"I said I'm fine." As if to prove it, Candice ducked around him, picking up her pace. Flash trotted at her heels, every now and then teleporting a dozen yards ahead in a brief sparkle of light. The baby unicorn moved through the tangled forest as easily as a fish through water.

More's the pity. He'd been hoping to use Flash as an excuse to force

Candice to take a break, but the baby unicorn didn't look the slightest bit tired.

"I don't suppose I could persuade you to pretend to have picked up a thorn in your paw?" he murmured to Fenrir, who was bringing up the rearguard.

The hellhound's copper-red eyes gleamed up at him. *Know better than to get involved in a mating fight, Icehorse.*

He was very glad Candice *was* too busy proving how much she didn't need him to glance back and see his expression. "It's not—I'm just concerned. I don't want her to push herself too hard. And we're not fighting."

Hmph. Fenrir sat down and scratched at his neck with one hind leg, looking supremely unconvinced. *Have nose, Icehorse. Can smell. Even able to smell* you, *since Sun Bitch came.*

Wystan blinked, taken aback. "You...couldn't smell me before I met Candice?"

Not in way that matters. Ice walls, all around. Fenrir shook himself in a jingle of harness, and fell into step at his side. *Careful don't freeze again, freeze her out. Need Sun Bitch. Good for Icehorse. Good for pack.*

"She certainly is." Wystan gazed after his mate, longing like a physical weight in his chest. "I do need her, Fenrir. But I don't know how to show her that."

Two-legs, Fenrir muttered, sounding like he was talking to himself. *Amazing you all have any cubs at all.*

"Somehow, we manage." Wystan sighed. "At least, most people do."

Icehorse will get there. Fenrir gave him a friendly nudge that sent him staggering into the undergrowth. *With advice.*

Wystan untangled his sleeve from an over-friendly thorn bush. "And what advice would that be?"

Fenrir gave him another of those thoughtful, penetrating stares. *Don't wait. Sun Bitch won't.*

This seemed rather odd advice to Wystan, given that both Candice's history and his own nature meant that they *had* to take things slowly. But before he could question Fenrir further, a shower of pine needles made them both look up. Rory's broad golden form thrust awkwardly through the canopy. In such dense forest, the big griffin had to tuck his wings against his sides and mostly fall out of the air. Callum followed more gracefully, his red-gold feathers glinting in the afternoon light as his hooves touched down. They both shimmered back into human form.

"Hold it, team," Rory called. "This seems to be where the Thunderbird wants us to go."

"Here?" Blaise asked dubiously as she came back to join them, the others on her heels. She scowled up at the canopy as though she could see the Thunderbird through the close-packed branches. "Are you sure?"

"It's circling again," Callum confirmed. "We're here."

Joe rubbed the back of his neck. "Here doesn't look like much to me."

They all stared around. Wystan had to admit, there didn't seem to be any reason for the Thunderbird to lead them to this particular patch of forest. They were so deep into the wilderness that there wasn't a hint of human presence. No hiking trails or signs of logging; not even a long-discarded drink can. Tiny insects sparkled in the beams of sunlight that managed to cut through the canopy. Bird calls filled the air, vigorous and unworried. It was practically idyllic.

"I don't like it," Blaise muttered. "Maybe it brought us out here so that no one will ever find our bodies."

"There must be something it's trying to show us." Edith crouched down, peering intently through the undergrowth. "Look, is there a very faint path here?"

"You've got sharp eyes." Candice joined Edith, pushing aside some branches. "You're right. It could just be a deer trail…but it seems suspiciously straight. I think this is what we're looking for."

"Let's find out." Rory took the lead, his golden eyes constantly scanning the surroundings for any hint of danger. "Single file behind me, Candice and Flash in the middle. Everyone stay on guard, just in case."

Wystan fell into position behind Candice and Flash, the better to be able to protect them. He summoned his unicorn up from his soul, holding back on the very edge of shift. Energy hummed just under his skin, his muscles tense and ready.

Yet as he walked, it was curiously hard to maintain his state of wariness. The peaceful air of the forest was like a blanket gently draping itself over him. No matter how he tried to focus on staying alert, every step made some of the tension ebb from his shoulders.

Even his unicorn seemed to be affected. He could feel its ears pricking up, nose turning into the wind. Not in alarm—whatever had caught its attention wasn't a threat. His unicorn stood still and quiet, but a strange sensation of *anticipation* shivered through his soul.

The feeling grew until he couldn't hold his tongue any longer. "Can anyone else sense something odd?"

From the way that they all stopped and stared at him, no one did. "Apart from a creeping certainty that we're walking into a trap, you mean?" Blaise asked.

"No, not at all. Exactly the opposite in fact." He spread his hands, struggling to find words for the impression. "A feeling like...coming home?"

"Well, it is a nice forest," Rory said, in a rather irritating got-to-keep-the-team-together tone. "Maybe your unicorn just likes it. The same way my griffin likes high places."

"I don't think it's a unicorn thing," Wystan said, annoyed at the hint of condescension. "Look, it's not affecting Flash in the same way. She seems to be getting *more* agitated, not less."

The little unicorn had been moving closer and closer to Candice as they went down the path. Now Flash was pressed against her leg, shivering. The unicorn's ears flicked constantly as though some predator was lurking just out of sight.

"It's okay, baby," Candice said to the little unicorn. "We won't let anything hurt you." She looked back around at them all. "Callum, can you tell what might be bothering her? Apart from the Thunderbird?"

"No," Callum said. "Nothing bigger than a squirrel for as far as I can sense."

"Actually, I kind of see what you mean about this feeling like home, bronicorn." Joe gazed thoughtfully up at the trees. "I mean, it doesn't feel like *my* home, obviously, but somehow this place does kind of remind me of the woods around your grandfather's place. And your dad's garden, to some extent. Even though the plants are completely different, it's got the same sort of lush wild abundance going on. Maybe that's what's giving you sweet vibes."

Wystan was fairly certain it wasn't, but there didn't seem to be any way of arguing without appearing to be a raving madman. He was forced to let the subject drop, though his instincts still screamed that there had to be something wrong about how *right* he felt.

He was so preoccupied with concern over his own sanity, he almost missed the moment everyone else lost theirs.

One minute, Rory was leading them all down the faint, wandering trail. The next, he'd slowed, hesitating mid-step. Then, for no apparent reason, he turned a complete right angle to the left. The others followed without question as he led them off through the undergrowth.

Wystan had taken several steps after them before his brain caught up with his feet. "Ah, Rory? Where are you going?"

Rory's eyes were fixed on the ground, searching. "I've lost the trail. Maybe if we keep going in a straight line, we'll pick it up again."

It was sound logic...apart from the fact that he'd just literally swerved *off* the trail. "It's right there, Rory. See?"

Rory followed the line of his pointing finger, frowning as he stared directly at the narrow path. "No. Are you sure it turns off in that direction?"

"It didn't turn off. *You* turned off." Wystan looked around at a uniform collection of blank faces. "Is...no one else seeing this?"

Blaise narrowed her eyes at him. "How much sleep did you get last night, exactly?"

"We didn't turn," Callum said, with complete—and completely mistaken—certainty. "We're still going in the same direction."

"You all just turned a literal corner for no reason!" Caught somewhere between aggravation and concern, Wystan pushed past them all, taking a few rapid strides down the trail. "See? It's right—"

"*Wystan!*" Rory shouted.

Wystan whirled, expecting to see the Nightmare leaping out at him—but there was nothing behind him but trees. He turned back to discover the entire squad looking panic-stricken, lunging blindly in every direction except the one he'd actually taken.

"Where'd he go?" Blaise yelled, spinning on the spot. "Cal, where is he?"

"I don't know!" Callum's usual impassive calm had cracked, revealing a degree of alarm that was rather touching, though also unnecessary. "He just disappeared!"

"Wystan?" Alone amidst the group, Candice was looking straight at him. She squinted as though he was backlit by a blinding spotlight. "You *are* still there, right?"

"You can feel him down your mate bond?" Rory pounced on her, seizing her shoulders. Wystan had never seen the griffin shifter look so shaken. "Is he okay? Where is he?"

"I'm right here." Baffled, Wystan rejoined the group. "Everyone calm down—gah!"

From the squad's reaction, one would have thought he'd disappeared for ten months rather than ten seconds. It was all he could do to stay on his feet as they tackled him as one, voices blurring into a chorus of relief.

"All right, all right," he managed to gasp. He extricated himself from the tangle of hugs, and wiped doggy drool off his face. "I'm perfectly fine. I'm beginning to get concerned about the rest of you, though."

"You took two steps and just *vanished*," Blaise said accusingly, as though he'd done it deliberately. "Where did you go?"

"Nowhere, truly." He took her hand. "Look, I'll show you. Follow me."

He led her down the path—or at least, he *tried* to. Between one step and the next, somehow her fingers slipped out of his. He found himself standing alone on the path as yet another hubbub of dismay rose behind him.

"He's there, he's still there!" Candice lifted her voice, shouting down the others. She took a tentative step forward herself. "Wystan, what's going on?"

She could still see him. On impulse, Wystan leaned back, grabbing hold of her wrist. For a second there was a faint, strange sensation, like a soap bubble popping against his entire body—and she was at his side.

"Whoa." Candice shook her head as though she had water in her ears. "That was weird. Where are we?"

"Exactly where we were, but now none of the others can perceive us," Wystan said, watching as the rest of the group thrashed through the undergrowth behind them. He leaned back far enough to shout out, "We're fine! Wait there for a moment while we investigate, please."

He drew back before any of them—especially Rory—could argue. He put out a hand, concentrating. Now that he was looking for it, he could sense a very faint difference in the air, a kind of tingling against his palm.

"Can you feel that?" he asked Candice. "Evidently there's some kind of magical barrier concealing this part of the forest."

"Magic," Candice muttered, sounded faintly disgusted. She patted vaguely at nothing, then shook her head. "I'll have to take your word for it. I can't tell that there's anything there. Is this a shifter thing? Like, do you have whole towns hidden away?"

"Some of us have ways of protecting our territories." He frowned at the invisible barrier. "There's something a little like this around my own ancestral lands, in fact. But our one doesn't stop people from seeing through it."

"Huh." Candice shot him a sharp look. "Wait, what do you mean, ancestral lands?"

"Er. Long story." This did not seem the time to mention that he was technically heir to an Earldom. "Tell you later. In any event, this must be why the Thunderbird led us here. Perhaps it can't cross through itself. Though why only you and I seem to be able to penetrate the barrier when the others can't, I have no idea."

"You, me, and Flash," Candice corrected, as the little unicorn sparkled into being next to them. "Clever baby, whatever this is didn't fool you, did it?"

The whites showed around the edges of Flash's amethyst eyes. She danced between the two of them, jabbing at their calves with her tiny horn as though trying to urge them to go back.

"Whatever this place is, she doesn't want us to be here." Wystan tried to send a telepathic sense of reassurance and comfort to the baby unicorn, but she just grew more agitated. He could feel her trembling. "What is it, little one? What's wrong?"

Abruptly, Flash froze. For a second she just stood there, ears focused forward, every muscle tense under her white fur. Then, like a shy child hiding behind her mother's skirts, she darted behind him. Her soft warmth pressed against the backs of his legs.

"Wystan." Candice was staring past him. He'd never seen that expression on her face before. "Look."

CHAPTER 24

The unicorns shimmered through the forest like sculpted moonbeams.

They appeared so softly and silently that it seemed like they'd always been there, and she somehow hadn't noticed. Three, five, nine—Candice lost count after a dozen, her brain overloaded with wonder. Everywhere she looked were shining white coats and jeweled eyes; sea-foam manes and starlight horns.

And every sharp, gleaming point was aimed right at her.

Or rather, right at Wystan. He'd moved like the unicorns, so fast and fluid that she hadn't even been aware of it. Now he stood between her and the unicorn herd, tense and ready, shielding both herself and Flash.

"It's all right," Wystan said—not to her, but to the unicorns. Despite the bristling wall of spearpoints threatening him, his voice was soft and steady, totally calm. "She's my mate, and I'm like you. Look."

A ripple went through the unicorn herd as he shifted. Although they were the same basic shape as Wystan, he dwarfed them like a racehorse amongst ponies. The other unicorns shied in alarm, backing away from his powerful form—but they didn't break and run. One by one, they crept forward again, ears pricking up tentatively.

That's right. Candice heard Wystan's voice inside her head, warm and gentle. He stood still, head and tail relaxed in a non-threatening posture. *We're friends.*

One of the unicorns noticed Flash peeping out from behind Wystan's legs. The adult unicorn let out a distinctly undignified squawk, rushing forward. On pure instinct, Candice snatched up the baby unicorn, holding her protectively out of reach.

The adult unicorn—a stallion, she realized—checked his charge, skittering sideways. He pawed at the ground in indecision, eying her. Then he wheeled on Wystan. He was barely half Wystan's size, but he set his hooves in an attitude of challenge.

Wystan shifted back into human form. A wondering, delighted smile dawned across his face. "It's all right, Candice. That's Flash's father."

Candice tightened her grip on the baby unicorn. "Doesn't necessarily mean we can trust him. If this is Flash's family, why doesn't she look pleased to see them?"

"Because she ran away from home." Wystan put a hand on her shoulder in reassurance, dipping his head to address Flash. "Everyone's been worried about you, little one. I promise, you aren't in trouble. Please, go to your father."

Flash blew out her breath, sounding an awful lot like a sulky teenager. She wiggled free of Candice's arms, jumping to the ground. Head hanging guiltily, the little unicorn went to her dad, who instantly started nosing her from head to tail, snorting and blowing. Candice didn't need telepathy to interpret the clear outburst of relief and concern: *Are you hurt? Are you hungry? Where have you been, we've been worried sick!*

Wystan chuckled as more unicorns crowded around the pair. "It's a little hard to interpret their mental speech, but I gather that Flash went missing some days ago. They're all delighted and grateful to have her back."

A few other unicorns sidled up to Wystan as he spoke, stretching out their necks to nose curiously at his jacket and hands. Candice found herself surrounded as well, though her audience stayed well out of arm's reach.

All the unicorns were white, but not all of them had plain silver horns like Wystan. A handful—Flash's father included—had a narrow band of gold spiraling up their horns from base to tip. She wondered if it was natural color variation, or if they'd somehow decorated themselves.

Has to be natural, she decided. *It's not like they have hands.*

Flash wasn't the only youngster in the group. There were a number of fascinated young colts and fillies mixed in amongst the adults, although they were being kept well back by their parents. A small unicorn—bigger than Flash, but clearly only half-grown—started to skip toward Candice, only to be herded away again by an adult mare that she presumed was his mother.

"They're not entirely sure about you," Wystan said to her. More unicorns were mobbing him now, sniffing at everything from his shoelaces to his backpack. "None of them have ever seen a human being before."

Candice crouched down, keeping her eyes downcast submissively and her body language relaxed. "You're smart to be wary, gang," she said to the nervous crowd. "Humans *are* dangerous. But I promise, you can trust me. I only want to help."

Flash's father broke off from his careful examination of his errant offspring. He took a cautious step forward, nostrils widening. A tentative sense of gratitude and wonder unfolded in Candice's mind's eye like a blossoming rose.

"You're welcome, buddy," Candice replied. "I'm Candice, and this is Wystan. You got a name?"

The unicorn tilted his head to one side. He had the look of someone attempting to follow a foreign movie in a language he didn't speak, but Candice thought he'd grasped the basic thrust of her question. He sent her a mental image of himself, which blurred into a startlingly vivid impression of rain falling softly onto dry, parched ground, plants turning thirstily to the sky…

"Uh…" Candice flung an entreating look at Wystan. "I can't possibly call a unicorn 'Wet Leaf Smell.'"

"Petrichor," Wystan suggested, the corner of his mouth quirking up. "The scent of rain after drought."

"Much better. Thanks." Candice held out her hand to the stallion. "Hi, Petrichor. Your daughter is a strong, special little girl. I'm so glad we could help bring her back to you."

Petrichor's warm breath blew across her fingertips. But before he quite touched her hand, a sharp call rang out. The stallion leaped back as though he'd been caught with his muzzle in a cookie jar. There was abruptly a lot more space around Wystan and Candice, the unicorns backing away as one.

A mare cut through the herd, unicorns drawing aside respectfully to let her pass. Her coat was more silver than white, and there was a certain deliberate care to the way that she moved that made Candice certain she was much older than the rest of the herd. Nonetheless, the mare's horn gleamed bright, while her dark grey eyes were sharp and canny.

Lead mare, Candice thought, recognizing the way the rest of the herd deferred to the matriarch. *She's the boss here.*

Wystan must have had much the same realization. He actually bowed to the mare, as if being presented to a foreign queen. "Madam alpha. Our apologies for intruding uninvited. We mean you and your herd no harm."

The lead mare's eyes narrowed a little. Her gaze flicked to Flash, then to Candice, and finally back to Wystan. Her ears flattened.

Wystan winced. "She's not happy with you being here. They've kept themselves utterly hidden for centuries. She's worried you're going to lead other humans to this haven."

"I won't," Candice said to the lead mare. She opened her hands, trying to open her mind as well. "Look inside my head. I've devoted my whole life to rescuing animals and fighting human cruelty. I swear I will protect your home."

The lead mare hesitated, then paced forward. Candice made herself hold still as the needle-sharp point of her horn descended on her. The tip touched the middle of her forehead, light as a butterfly. Light flared, forcing her to close her eyes.

When she opened them again, she found herself staring into the lead mare's storm cloud gaze. There was still wariness there, but also a grudging respect.

You protected one of my herd. The lead mare's telepathic communication was startlingly precise—not Flash's swirl of imagery and emotion, but actual words. *I am...grateful.*

"You talk," Candice blurted out.

The lead mare's long eyelashes lowered in acknowledgement. *I have walked in the dreams of your kind, and learned your speech. It is not a gift I relish, but it has helped me to protect my herd. I send my mind out to cloud the perceptions of any who approach, so that they turn aside even before they reach our border.*

"You created the barrier?" Wystan asked.

The lead mare shook her head. *No. That defense was set generations ago, with talents that are now lost to us. It prevents those who are not of our kind from entering. It is also strong enough to turn aside fire, flood, any physical thing that might threaten us. But If humans ever discovered our land, I fear that even our ancient ward would not hold against their machines and wickedness. So I use the talent of my bloodline to hide us as well.*

"We'll keep your secret. You have my word." Wystan bowed again, one hand on his heart. "How should we address you, madam?"

The mare's long tail swished from side to side. *My name is...* A brief impression of small, white wings silently flitting through moonbeams. *Your language is inadequate, but you may call me Moth.*

"We are honored, Moth. My name is Wystan, and this is Candice." Wystan hesitated. "There are others who accompanied us, members of my firefighting squad. They are shifters like myself, and I can personally vouch for their integrity and honor. May they also enter your territory?"

No! Moth tossed her head angrily, her horn glinting like a sword blade. *No outsiders! Bad enough that you have been able to cross our wards, half-blood, you and this human who shares your scent. I may not be able to keep you out, but I shall not allow any others to defile our lands. I must keep my herd safe!*

Wystan held up his hands in surrender. "I understand. Would you step outside with me to meet them, then?"

The watching herd snorted and shied, as though he'd suddenly shouted out an obscenity. The lead mare stamped a front hoof, and they settled down again.

We do not leave our sanctuary. Moth's telepathic tone rang with iron finality. *Not even I. That is the law.*

"But Flash broke it," Candice pointed out. "She went outside."

The mare turned a cold stare on Flash, who edged behind her father. *The law has been broken recently, true. And the consequences of that were catastrophic. I will not allow any to break it again. Not for any reason.*

Wystan drew in a sharp breath, as though something had fallen into place in his head. "Flash isn't the only one who left, was she. Her mother disappeared first. And you forbade anyone to go look for her. Not even her father."

Petrichor's head drooped, the point of his silver horn touching the ground in shame. Flash nuzzled her dad, love and forgiveness clear in the gesture.

The lead mare huffed. *That is herd business. It is no concern of yours.*

"Forgive me, but it is." Wystan's tone was mild and respectful, but there was a dangerous glint in his eyes that showed he wouldn't allow himself to be deflected. "We have encountered Flash's mother. Or at least, what is left of her."

Petrichor's head jerked up. He pushed his way through the herd, ears swiveling from Moth to Wystan. Candice had an impression of urgent query and worry.

"You don't know," she breathed, pity rising as she deciphered the stallion's wordless telepathic message. "You don't know what happened to her."

We do not speak of Sunrise! Moth crowded her shoulder against

Petrichor, driving him back with sheer willpower despite his greater size. *She left the herd, she broke the law! She is dead to us!*

"She is worse than dead." Wystan spoke directly to Flash's father, his voice firm and clear. Candice could sense him broadcasting mental images to accompany his words, so that they could all understand his meaning. "But she is not yet lost. She is possessed by a dark creature, which has corrupted her body and overridden her will."

Whinnies of distress rose on all sides as the unicorns saw his telepathic picture of what their friend had become. Some of the stallions wheeled and lowered their heads as though to defend the herd from the threat. Their horns brightened, driving back shadows in a wash of rainbow-edged light.

Only Moth stood firm and unmoved. *I grieve for Sunrise. But what is done is done. We cannot help her.*

"With respect, you can." Wystan turned to Petrichor. "Or rather, *you* can. Earlier in the summer, a similar creature possessed one of my friends. But his mate was able to drive it out of him. Once it had been forced to take physical form, my team killed it. I think that we can do the same here. You can save your mate."

Moth snapped at Petrichor, but this time he bared his teeth right back at her, holding his ground. A ripple of shock went through the herd at the show of defiance. The lead mare shrieked in outrage, rearing to lash out at Petrichor with hooves and horn. For a second Candice thought that the stallion would fight, but it seemed his equine instinct to submit to female authority was too strong. Petrichor backed down, tail lowering in submission.

Moth stared him down for a long moment before turning back to Wystan. *Sunrise is beyond saving. Even before she broke the laws and left our territory, there was darkness in her heart. She brought this evil fate upon herself.*

The herd's agitation grew. Some of them were arching their necks and snorting in assent, while others flattened their ears and tails at though they didn't agree with this assessment of Sunrise's character. A few of the older mares nipped at a group of younger fillies who were looking particularly rebellious.

"Not everyone seems to agree with you there," Candice said. "What did she do that you think was so bad?"

She defied my authority, our sacred laws! She abandoned the herd! Moth stamped a hoof. *She was dissatisfied with our way of life here. She had a foolish idea that we should leave our beloved home and seek out a new territory.*

A young mare with deep brown eyes tossed her mane, the set of her ears defiant. A rapid flurry of images tumbled across Candice's mind: streams choked with slimy grey-green scum, trees dead and leafless, a dead rabbit with patchy fur and staring eyes.

"Sounds like Sunrise had reasons for suggesting a move," she said to Moth. "Things haven't been perfect here, have they?"

It is true that our talents are not what they once were, the lead mare admitted, sounding reluctant. *It grows harder to preserve our home, with humans encroaching ever closer. But the answer is not to abandon our land! I have seen the minds of your kind. You have polluted the entire world. This is our last sanctuary. There is no other place where we can flee. Even if there was, we have lost the skills to set up new wards. We would be defenseless! No. Our only hope is to hold fast to what we have now. I will do whatever it takes to protect our land.*

"We will help you in any way we can. I understand your reasons for caution. My kind, shifters, also struggle to find space to live in an increasingly human world." Wystan's jaw set. "But regardless of Sunrise's views, no one deserves to suffer as she is suffering."

It cannot be helped. Moth's mental tone was as unyielding as iron. *The safety of the herd outweighs the needs of one member.*

"You can't just abandon her!" Candice shot to her feet, fists clenching. "Even if she *was* a piece of garbage—which she isn't—she's still a living being. You have to help her!"

"Yes. You must." Wystan matched Moth stare for stare, his green eyes equally uncompromising. "Even if you will not be moved by ethics, you have no choice."

Moth's horn lit with an ominous, eerie glow. She levelled it directly at Wystan's heart. *You dare to threaten us, half-blood?*

"No. I only tell you the truth." Wystan didn't flinch. "You call me *half-blood*, yet I was able to break your wards. Even Candice could enter against your will, although we are not yet fully mated. How do you think you will be able to keep the Nightmare out? No matter that she is possessed, she is still one of your own. Your defenses are powerless to stop her."

For the first time, Moth looked less than utterly certain of herself. *It...it will not come here.*

"It *will*," Candice said fiercely. "Because *Flash* is here. It's attacked us multiple times, trying to snatch her away. We don't know why, but the Nightmare is obsessed with her. And it seems to be able to follow her trail. It could already be here within your wards!"

The herd crowded closer together, mothers pulling their foals close to their sides. The unicorns' growing agitation hung over the clearing like a looming thundercloud. Candice could sense sharp crackles of wordless dread and fear leaping from mind to mind.

I tell you, we are safe here! Moth arched her neck in a show of bravado, but her nostrils flared nervously, betraying her own worry. *Even if the creature does come, the herd is strong. The herd protects its own. We will keep Flash—"

Petrichor's cry interrupted the lead mare. The stallion spun on his hocks, ears swiveling frantically in every direction. He lifted his head and called out again, the sound filled with heart-twisting terror.

Candice scanned the clearing herself. Her stomach lurched. "Wait. Where *is* Flash?"

CHAPTER 25

No one else was going to rescue Mama. It was up to her. Again.

Flash darted minnow-quick through the forest. Mama and Papa had always said that she'd been born running. She was fast, faster than any of the other foals, faster even than most of the mares and stallions. Certainly faster than stick-in-the-mud Moth.

Stupid Moth, who always said *no*. The old mare was like a frog with a one-note song. When Mama had wanted to talk to the herd about the bad thing: *No.* When Papa had wanted to go look for Mama: *No.*

Well, no point asking a question when you already knew what the answer would be. Flash hadn't asked last time. She hadn't asked this time, either.

While Moth was arguing with Strong Guard and Bright Heart, Flash had taken a crafty-quiet step backward. And another, and another, so snail-slow that not even Papa had noticed that she was no longer at his side. And then she'd just *gone*.

They'd noticed now, she knew. She could hear Papa calling for her in her head, distant and scared. It gave her a bad hurting feeling in her chest, but she closed her mind to the herd-bond and ran on.

She'd do what he couldn't. Papa wanted to help Mama, she knew he did, but he was just a stallion. Stallions had to obey the lead mare, that was just the way things were. Even Strong Guard—the biggest, boldest, toughest stallion *ever*—followed Bright Heart without hesitation.

If only Bright Heart had hooves and a horn! Then she could have knocked that snapping-turtle Moth off her high rock, *crash*! But strong and stubborn as Bright Heart was, she couldn't challenge Moth. She couldn't be lead mare.

No. Flash couldn't rely on Strong Guard and Bright Heart, not any longer. She'd thought they were on her side, but they'd tricked her. They'd brought her back to the herd, back to mean old *Moth!* Turned out they were just like any other grown-up—so certain they knew what was best, so blind to what needed to be done.

Not Flash. *She* was brave and bold, just like Mama. Papa said so.

She was going to make Papa proud, so that he could stop being sad. She was going to find Mama, and get rid of the bad thing. And then they would go home and Mama would challenge Moth and the trees would stop getting sick and everything would be right again.

Gathering up her strength, she squeezed her eyes shut. It was hard to *go* again so soon, but she forced her power up and out. She concentrated with all her heart on *Mama.*

The tip of her horn caught in the fabric of the world, making a gap for her. She wriggled through, dropping out into a different place. Where, she didn't know, or care. It was closer to where Mama was, and that was good enough for her.

Mama! she called out, now that she was far enough away from the herd that they wouldn't be able to hear her. *Mama! I'm here! I'm coming for you!*

And Mama was there.

Mama! Happiness sparkled through her from horn to tail. She bounded forward eagerly—but Mama faded back among the trees, as if they were playing hide-and-seek. Flash checked herself mid-leap, prancing to an uncertain halt. *Mama? It's me, it's Flash!*

Flash had thought that Mama would rush forward to fuss over her just like Papa had done, but to her surprise and hurt Mama backed away instead. Not all at once, as though she was *really* trying to run away, but in funny stop-start rushes. When Flash moved, so did Mama; when she stopped, Mama stopped.

Is it a game? Flash was getting a not-nice feeling in her stomach, like the time she'd eaten all the blackberries. No matter how she tried to reach Mama, Mama wouldn't stay still. *Mama, stop it, I don't want to play! I want you!*

Mama didn't reply. There was a big black cloud hiding her mind. Flash was certain that she *wanted* to talk, but the bad thing wouldn't let her. The bad thing was inside Mama, making her look funny and act strange...but she was still *Mama*, underneath, where it counted.

Mama jerked to a stop again, as though she'd gotten tangled up in invisible vines. She was shaking all over, twitching her hide like bugs were biting at her—but there weren't any bugs. The not-nice feeling got worse in Flash's middle.

It was the bad thing. Mama wanted to come and take care of her—of course she did—but the bad thing wouldn't let her. The bad thing was trying to pull Mama away. It didn't want to let Flash anywhere near. It knew that everything would be fixed once she and Mama were back together.

It was *scared* of her.

Flash took a deep breath, setting her hooves.

It's okay, Mama, she said, whisper-quiet, bear-strong. *I'm coming to save you.*

She was tired enough to fall down and sleep for a whole moon, but she forced the last of her strength into her horn. The bad thing tried to make Mama jump away again, but Flash was already *there*, right in front of it.

The bad thing shrieked and reared, blotting out the sun. Its ice-cold shadow fell across her, red eyes staring down. Flash didn't flinch. She looked up, up, at those wolf-fang hooves and gaping foam-flecked jaws, and she wasn't afraid.

Mama would never hurt her.

"Flash!"

One second Flash was reaching up to Mama to make it all better. The next, Mama was knocked away by a blur of white. Flash cried out, throwing herself forward—and bounced off a leg like a tree trunk, hard enough to make her ears ring.

Strong Guard was there, blocking her way. His horn blazed so bright it hurt Flash's eyes. She couldn't see past him, couldn't see where Mama had gone.

Let me go! she shouted at him, furious and frightened for Mama. *I want Mama! She needs me!*

"Stay down, baby!" Bright Heart slid down from Strong Guard's back, landing right next to her. She had something in her front paws, a long shiny stick. She raised it to her shoulder, sighting down it as though it was strange kind of detachable horn. "*Now*, Wystan!"

Strong Guard leaped aside. Flash had a single, shining glimpse of Mama charging toward them, coming for *her*, coming to her at last—

Bright Heart moved. Just one finger, tightening just a little. There was a tiny *pfft* noise.

Mama stumbled. There was something in her neck, something like a giant bee stinger. She staggered sideways, still fighting, still trying to come to her.

Flash shrieked again as Mama crashed to her knees and lay still. She started to run over to her, but Bright Heart's arms wrapped around her neck, holding her back.

"It's okay, baby, it's okay." Bright Heart held her tight, refusing to let go no matter how Flash struggled. "It's over."

CHAPTER 26

Joe prodded cautiously at the Nightmare with a fallen branch. "How long do you think the sedative will last?"

Blaise slapped at his hand. "Longer if you stop poking it with a stick, idiot."

"It's okay." Candice was crouched by the Nightmare's head. It gave Wystan the crawling horrors to see her putting her hands so close to those fang-filled jaws, but Candice had insisted on making sure that the creature's windpipe was clear. "If she so much as twitches, I'll stick her again. I have enough drugs packed to keep her sedated for a week, if we have to. Not that it would be a good idea, medically speaking."

"Let's hope it doesn't come to that." Wystan finished lashing branches together into a makeshift stretcher. "This should help us move her. Rory, give me a hand."

"Hurry," Callum said, staring upward with unfocussed eyes. "We've got company."

Thunder rumbled, underscoring his words. The afternoon light abruptly darkened, clouds gathering out of nowhere.

"Don't you dare!" Blaise yelled up at the unseen Thunderbird. "If you so much as think about setting fire to us, I swear I will come up there and smack you one!"

Thunder growled in response, as though the distant creature had somehow heard her words. A light scatter of raindrops pattered down around them, but no lightning followed.

"Quickly." Wystan rolled the Nightmare onto the stretcher, unable to restrain a shudder at the feel of its greasy, scaled hide. "Before our unpredictable friend up there changes its mind."

He took one end of the stretcher, while Rory took the other. Candice scooped up Flash. The little unicorn had gone so berserk when she'd seen her mother fall, they'd had no choice but to sedate her too. As fast as they could, they hastened through the woods.

"Petrichor!" Wystan called out as they once again approached the edge of the unicorns' territory. He sent out his mind as well, trying to reach the stallion. "We have Sunrise! Quickly, she needs you!"

A pale shape stepped out of the shadows—not Petrichor, but Moth. The lead mare halted right at the edge of the invisible boundary. She stared at the Nightmare's limp form, going utterly motionless herself.

"It's all right, Moth." Wystan stopped before he crossed the ward, not wanting to disappear from the others' sight. The rest of the squad was already looking a little befuddled, their minds struggling against Moth's obfuscating magic. "We caught the Nightmare. She can't harm your herd. Please, send Petrichor out. I know it's against your rules, but we need to him to drive the demon out of his mate."

Moth's back hooves shifted uneasily. *You said that would make it manifest?*

"Yes. I will not lie to you, there is some risk. The last time we did this, the demon's true form was very large, and very dangerous." Wystan gestured at the rest of the squad. "But my colleagues and I were able to defeat it. That's why we need to do this outside your territory. Unless you will allow them in?"

Moth flattened her ears in instant refusal. *No.* She looked again at the unconscious Nightmare, her grey eyes troubled. *I don't...I cannot simply allow Petrichor to cross the border. Not yet. I must think on this.*

"You don't have *time* to think on it." Wystan jerked his head at the darkened sky. "If we don't do something about the demon quickly, I'm certain that the Thunderbird will. It led us here to you, but we cannot truly communicate with it. This uneasy truce we seem to have forged could break at any time."

"Hang on," Joe said. "I can only follow half of what's going on here, but that did not sound good."

"She's hesitating," Candice relayed to the group. "She doesn't want to let us in, and she doesn't seem to want to let Petrichor out, either. It's against their rules."

"What?" Edith looked shocked. "This is one of her own kind! She can't be that inflexible, surely?"

I am the lead mare! My first duty is to the whole herd! Moth said hotly, even though her concealing magic meant the squad couldn't hear her. *Sometimes leadership requires difficult decisions.*

"You're planning to keep this a secret from Petrichor, aren't you?" Candice pushed her way to the front, glaring at Moth. "Because *he* isn't going to think that keeping some stupid rule is more important than saving his mate."

Our sacred traditions keep us safe! Moth's horn lit with her anger. *Our young colts and fillies are already beginning to harbor dangerous thoughts, thanks to Flash's transgressions. I cannot let Petrichor set them another bad example! Worse yet, endorse it! No. I will not be rushed into an action that could doom us all.*

A crack of thunder sounded, right over their heads.

"Then," Wystan said, as the echoes died away, "I believe you have about thirty seconds to come up with an alternative, before things start getting uncomfortable down here."

Moth eyed the gathering storm, and tossed her mane scornfully. *We do not fear that one. It has tested our borders before. Let it send its lightning again. Our ancestors set their wards well. No wildfire can touch our lands.*

"That's all very nice for them," Candice muttered to Wystan. "But *we're* out here."

Wystan clenched his jaw. He briefly contemplated asking Rory to try using his commanding power on the lead mare, but even if the griffin *could* use it against someone he couldn't see, Moth was probably too alpha herself to be affected.

"Rory," he said, coming to a decision. "Let go."

Rory's eyebrows rose, but he dropped his end of the stretcher. Wystan adjusted his own grip, taking up the extra weight. Then he strode forward.

Moth danced back, shying. *What are you—no! It cannot come back here! I forbid it!*

"Too late," Wystan grunted, hauling the unwieldy load across the border. As he'd thought, the mystic barrier did nothing to stop the Nightmare from entering. He let go of the stretcher handles, letting it fall to the ground with a defiant *thud*. "If this is the one place where the Thunderbird can't reach her, then this is where she's going to stay."

Candice joined him, Flash in her arms. It seemed that she too could freely cross the wards now, having been helped through once. "I told the others what's going on," she said to him. "Rory and Callum are ready to drive the Thunderbird off if it throws a fit at losing its prey."

"I don't believe that will be necessary," Wystan replied, hoping that his intuition was correct. "It's an intelligent creature. And I don't think it's vicious. If it already knows its wildfires can't get through the barrier, it has no reason to start one."

Sure enough, a rather sullen roll of thunder shook the air. The light began to brighten, storm clouds thinning once more.

Moth had moved to stare down at the unconscious Nightmare. She bowed her head, her horn not quite touching the black, twisted form. It was difficult to read her equine face, but the lead mare looked weary, burdened by sorrow.

She was supposed to take my place one day. Moth's mental voice was quieter than before, heavy with regret. *That thought gave me comfort, once. To know that someone would be able to protect the herd after I was gone. Ah, Sunrise. If only you'd listened.* Moth raised her head once more, shaking off her momentary melancholy and returning to her usual brisk, certain self. *Very well. I will allow the creature to remain, for now. But I will not tell Petrichor his mate has been captured. Not yet. I must consider what is the best course of action for the herd.*

Candice looked like she was about to argue, but Wystan put a hand on her shoulder, forestalling her. "It's the best we can do for now, Candice. We hardly want Petrichor charging in here and releasing the demon when the rest of the squad is stuck on the other side of the barrier. The last demon was as big as Joe, once it took its native form."

Candice blew out her breath. "Yeah, I don't think my tranquillizer gun would work on that." She looked across at Moth, her expression distinctly unfriendly. "I'll have to keep sedating her, you realize."

You will not, Moth replied, in equally chilly tones. *My power will keep her locked in dreams far more effectively than your human toys. You will not be required further.*

Wystan's unicorn bristled at the lead mare's rudeness to their mate. With effort, he held himself in check. "Candice brought down the Nightmare with her 'toy', Moth. Gratitude would be appropriate. If you cannot manage that, you will at least show her respect."

Moth sniffed. *Stallions. It's almost endearing, the way you all believe you can handle mares. Almost.*

"It's okay, Wystan." Candice touched his arm, making him realize that his hands had balled into fists. "Fine by me if she doesn't want any more help from us. It's going to be freaking hilarious to watch her try to move that stretcher without opposable thumbs."

Moth huffed again. *We have our own means, human. Watch.*

Turning away, the lead mare let out a long, clear call. Distant whinnies rose in answer. Within moments, a pair of unicorns glimmered through the trees to join them. They were both mature mares, so identical in every detail that Wystan couldn't tell them apart. Their mauve eyes went very wide when they saw the Nightmare, but they went over to Moth without hesitation, ducking their heads in respect.

A brief flurry of silent communication passed between the three unicorns, too fast and foreign for Wystan to even begin to follow. The two mares bowed again, as if something had been decided. One went to stand next to the stretcher, while the other approached Candice.

Candice yelped a swearword, leaping back as the unicorns' horns lit up. "What the hell?"

Peace, human. They will not harm you. Moth tilted her head, indicating Flash, still sleeping in Candice's arms. *They are here to take the little one back to her father, and her mother to a place where she may be kept safe and secure until I decide what is to be done about her.*

The unicorn standing next to the stretcher bowed her head, touching her horn to one end of it. Pink-purple light—the exact same shade as the mare's eyes—ran over the Nightmare's black hide.

Candice swore again as both the stretcher and the Nightmare rose silently into the air. "Wystan, are you seeing this?"

"Telekinesis," Wystan breathed, equally stunned as the unicorn disappeared back into the woods, the stretcher levitating behind her. "I've heard of shifters who have similar abilities, but I've never seen it before. Let Flash go, Candice. She should be with her father when she wakes up."

The other mare was waiting patiently, horn glowing. Candice hesitated, then reluctantly held Flash out to her. At a touch of the mare's horn, the baby unicorn floated into the air, cradled by light. Flash didn't so much as twitch an ear as the mare carefully carried her away.

Wystan turned back to Moth, shaking his head in amazement. "You seem to have many extraordinary talents amongst your herd."

Generations of lead mares have striven to keep our bloodlines flowing, Moth said, sounding rather proud. *There are only a handful of families that have withered without issue, taking their unique abilities with them.*

"Talents are genetic?" Candice asked, looking interested.

Moth hesitated, as though she was having to sift the meaning of the word out of their minds. *Yes. They are passed down by blood, parent to offspring. We strive to mate like to like, to ensure the lines breed true.*

"That explains why I've never heard of any of these other unicorn abilities before," Wystan said. "My family are the only unicorn shifters, as far as I know, and we're all descended from a common ancestor. We're all from the same bloodline, so we're all healers."

Healers? Moth sounded startled. She took a few steps toward him, peering up at his face. *You and your bloodline are healers?*

"All of us, as far back as our family records go. Which is quite some time," he said, startled by her sudden interest. "Why? Do you not have healers here?"

A few. Sunrise was one. She was staring into his eyes as intently as if she'd just discovered he was *her* true mate. *I wished her to mate another healer, to ensure the bloodline continued, but she chose Petrichor instead. That is why Flash is a sport, a wild talent. Such things occur when the bloodlines are not carefully managed. I thought...you are certain your own bloodline is pure?*

"Okay lady, stop eying him up like he's a prize bull." Candice looped an arm possessively through his, to Wystan's secret delight. "I don't care how much you want more healers, some things are *not* gonna happen. Let's go, Wystan. The others will be tearing their hair out wondering what's taking us so long."

Moth shook herself, seeming to snap out of her peculiar fascination. *Yes. Go back to your own herd for now. I must retreat to our sacred heartland, and...seek guidance. Return tomorrow, at dawn, and we shall speak further.*

"We will." Wystan bowed to her as she turned away. "I know this is a difficult situation for you, Moth. I hope you will come to accept what must be done."

Moth paused at the edge of the glade. Her head lowered a little. She didn't look back.

Yes. Her voice was the barest whisper in his mind, old and weary. *I will.*

CHAPTER 27

"I come bearing wondrous news!" Joe announced as he returned to the clearing where the squad was setting up camp.

Wystan paused in setting up Candice's tent long enough to raise an eyebrow at the sea dragon. "You appear to come bearing firewood."

"That too." Joe dumped his armload of dry branches next to the fire circle Edith was constructing out of rocks. "But also wondrous news. I have found...*a stream.*"

Blaise dropped the hammer she'd been using to pound down her own tent pegs. "Joe, you are a god among men."

"A stream," Edith breathed, clasping her hands together. "A *clean* stream?"

Joe kissed his fingertips like a French chef praising a culinary masterpiece. "As pure as a newborn baby. Of course, it's probably been filtered through three dozen unicorns before it gets this far, but let's not dwell on that."

Candice stared around at them all, looking distinctly perplexed. "You all seem unreasonably excited about the existence of water."

"If you routinely went weeks without showers, you would too,"

Rory told her, grinning. "And sadly, wildfires are rarely considerate enough to occur near bodies of water. We've learned to seize on any opportunity for a wash."

Candice plucked at the front of her sweaty shirt, making a wry face. "Gotta admit, this stream *is* starting to sound pretty wondrous."

"I've got soap," Blaise said, digging into her pack. She pulled out the wrapped bar, brandishing it aloft like a trophy. "You coming, Candice? Or, uh," her eyes flicked to Wystan, "on second thought, maybe you'd prefer to be private."

Candice shook her head, slinging her own pack onto her back. "Nah, I'll come with you. I didn't think to bring soap."

Blaise tried again. "I'm sure Wystan has soap he could share. Better soap. Don't you, Wystan?"

"It's okay," Candice said before he could even open his mouth. She didn't even glance in his direction. "I'd rather borrow yours. Which way to this stream, Joe?"

Sorry, Blaise sent telepathically to Wystan, as Joe gave Candice directions. *I tried.*

I appreciate the effort, Wystan sent back. He pressed his lips closed, smothering a sigh. *Even though it was about as successful as my own attempts.*

Blaise gave him a sympathetic punch on the shoulder as she went past. *Don't worry. I've got plenty more embarrassing stories about you I can tell her while we're drying our hair.*

He winced, but didn't bother to ask her not to. It was futile to try to change Blaise's mind about anything...and in any event, it wasn't like she could say anything that would make his relationship with Candice *worse*.

He morosely watched Candice gather up her things and leave with Blaise. She didn't look back once. Ever since they'd stepped out of the unicorn lands and rejoined the rest of the squad, she'd seemed determined to pretend he didn't exist.

If only the Nightmare was still free, he thought with bleak humor. *What I need now is another crisis.*

When they'd realized Flash was in danger, it had been like they'd briefly become a single mind in two bodies. They hadn't needed to exchange a single word. Candice had just leaped onto his back the instant he shifted, clinging tight to his mane as he'd raced through the forest. For a brief, shining moment, they'd been one.

But now, with the Nightmare contained and Flash safe with her father once more, he could feel Candice retreating from him. That had been the common purpose binding them together, after all—and now, it was nearly at an end.

And then she wouldn't need him.

"Yo, bronicorn." Joe's shadow fell across him. "Looks like it's just you and me. You coming?"

Wystan glanced around. Rory and Edith were slipping away from camp hand in hand, their own intentions clear. Fenrir lay sprawled in a patch of sunlight, paws in the air. The hellhound held very firm opinions on baths, namely that they should happen to other people. In some ways, he truly was more dog than man.

Wystan was pleased to see that Callum was also electing to nap rather than wash. The pegasus shifter had been driving himself to the edge of exhaustion over the past few days. He was already asleep, his curly auburn head propped up on Fenrir's dark flank.

His own bedroll beckoned to him enticingly, but Wystan forced himself to his feet. His chances of persuading Candice to risk intimacy would not be improved by smelling of day-old horse. Grabbing his pack, he followed Joe.

"Sooooo…" the sea dragon began, eying him. "You and Candice."

Wystan winced again. He rubbed at his forehead, where a headache was starting to gather. "I would really prefer to discuss another subject, if you don't mind."

"Tough. I do." Joe draped an arm across Wystan's shoulders, sparking another pulse of pain through his temples. "You, my horny friend, are in serious need of advice."

"With all due respect, I sincerely doubt that you are an expert in persuading a woman to say yes to a life-long commitment," Wystan snapped, discomfort fraying his patience. "As far as I'm aware, you've never had a relationship that lasted longer than twelve hours."

Joe dismissed this criticism with an airy wave, unoffended. "Every single one of my relationships has lasted exactly as long as I intended, bro. And more importantly, exactly as long as the lady wanted. I have a one hundred per cent success rate of unbroken hearts. And in terms of absolute hours, I've racked up enough time in relationships to qualify as a bona fide love doctor. Go on. Hit me."

"Don't tempt me," Wystan muttered. His headache was threatening to turn into a full-blown migraine. "Joe, would you *please* stand further away?"

Joe held up his hands, backing off. "Sorry, bro. I didn't realize your unicorn sensitivity thing was still playing up."

"It wasn't, until a moment ago." He groaned, squeezing his eyes shut as he realized the problem. "It's Candice. This happens whenever she's out of my sight. I have no idea why."

Joe cocked his head to one side. "Isn't that obvious? It's because you need her."

"I do, but that doesn't explain why I feel like I'm being torn apart whenever I leave her side. I thought it might be because she was awakening my unicorn's powers. But so far there's no sign of any progress on that front." He smiled savagely, in black humor, as pain beat through his head. "It's ironic, really. If I could mate Candice, I could heal. If I could heal, I could mate. And so we're stuck."

"Whoa." Joe shook his head, frowning. "I think you missed a few steps there. I know you hope that finally claiming your mate will unblock your unicorn's mojo, but what in the sea does that have to do with winning her in the first place?"

They'd reached the stream, which was just as clear and inviting as Joe had promised. Crystal water ran smoothly between steep, overhanging banks. Wystan forced back an involuntarily—and arresting—mental vision of how Candice would look, rising from the waist-deep water like a nymph out of legend. Clearing his throat, he shrugged off his pack.

"Don't you see?" He knelt to unlace his boots. "If I could unlock my power, I could help Candice. I could heal her scars."

Joe's frown deepened. "Why would you want to do that? She looks bad-ass."

Wystan would have gone with 'breathtakingly stunning', or perhaps 'maddeningly attractive', but he had to concede that Joe's choice of adjective was also apt.

"She does indeed. And she knows it. That's not the issue." He pulled off his boots, lining them up neatly before standing up to pull his shirt over his head. "It's nothing about how she looks. It's about what she sees."

Joe folded his arms. "Vague, much?"

Wystan gazed down at his own reflection, distorted in the rippling water. He picked his words carefully, not wanting to reveal too much of what Candice had told him in confidence. "She was hurt, Joe. Terribly hurt. And she has to face it every day. She said herself, every time she looks in a mirror, she's reminded of what happened to her. She's afraid that she'll never be able to get over that trauma. That it will be a barrier between us forever."

Joe came to stand next to him, staring down into the water himself. "And what do you think?"

Wystan massaged his aching temples. "I think that if she didn't have to see those scars, she'd be able to let go of her fears. If I could heal, if I could take away that constant reminder…it would solve everything. She would be able to forget the pain in her past. If I healed her, she would love me."

Joe looked at him, his face uncharacteristically solemn. The sea dragon reached out, placing one large hand on his shoulder in a silent gesture of understanding and sympathy.

Then Joe pushed him into the stream.

It was indeed very clear, very clean, and very, *very* cold.

Wystan resurfaced, spluttering. "*Joe!* What the devil? Why did you do that?"

"Because you," Joe said, folding his arms again, "need to go soak your head. For the love of sweet little fishes, will you stop thinking with your horn?"

Wystan managed to get his feet underneath him, the water-smoothed rocks slippery under his bare soles. "That's rich, coming from a man who rarely has a thought that originates above his belt."

Joe's sea-blue eyes flashed. Wystan had never seen him genuinely angry before. "You think I can't understand you? You think *I* don't know what it's like to have impossibly awesome parents? My mother is the *Pearl Empress*! You think you're the only person who wrestles with the guilt and pain of being a disappointment? At least *you* don't have to do it in public, with an entire council of courtiers and politicians just waiting for you to finally screw up permanently. You think I like having half the entire population of sea shifters whispering about me behind my back, and the other half sneering at me to my face? If you think I can't understand you, Wystan, then you don't know me. You don't know me at all."

Wystan sloshed his way to the bank. He held out his hand. "I'm sorry. I know you have your own burdens. I may not understand or agree with all your lifestyle choices, but I don't truly think that you're shallow."

Joe's uncharacteristic anger evaporated as quickly as it had appeared. He leaned down to clasp Wystan's wrist, hauling him out of the water. "Eh, to be fair, you're supposed to. Not sorry for pushing you into the stream, by the way."

Wystan looked down ruefully at his dripping pants. "Well, at least you didn't ruin my boots. But you may consider my head thoroughly soaked, along with the rest of me. Though I'm not entirely sure why you felt that would be beneficial."

Joe let out his breath in a long sigh. "Look, Wystan. How do you think I please so many women?"

"I try very hard not to think on it at all. And I would honestly rather not know, thank you."

"I give them what they need," Joe said forcefully, ignoring this objection. "Not what *I* want, or even what I want them to need from me. What. They. *Need*."

Wystan digested this for a moment. "You're saying...I'm the one who wants Candice to need me to heal her."

"Right. That's what you want." Joe raised his eyebrows at him, his expression challenging. "But is it what *Candice* needs? Really?"

Wystan tipped his head back, staring at the sky. He pictured Candice: Her fierce strength, her boundless compassion, her hidden fears.

What does *she need?*

"Joe," he said slowly, "you are as shallow as the Atlantic Ocean."

"Hey." Joe gave him a playful shove. "Keep your voice down, or I'll have to knock you into the stream again. Can't have you ruining my reputation."

Wystan jammed his feet into his boots, not bothering to bend to do up the laces. "I have to find Candice. Right now."

Joe beamed. "There, see? Now aren't you glad I dunked you? Thanks to me, you've come to your senses *and* you don't stink."

"Thank you. On both accounts." Wystan hesitated, looking back at him curiously. "Joe? Why do you do that?"

"Do what?" Joe put a hand to his chest, striking a pose. "I can't help being this effortlessly awesome, bronicorn."

Wystan made an exasperated gesture at him. "Do *that*. You truly aren't as frivolous as you try to appear. And you just said you don't enjoy the way other sea shifters sneer you for your playboy ways. Why do you work so hard to cultivate a reputation for foolishness and hedonism?"

Joe shrugged, his smile free and easy as always. "Isn't that obvious? Who wouldn't want to bed a different beautiful woman every night?"

Wystan cocked an eyebrow at him. "That's different to saying that it's what *you* want."

Joe's cocky grin flickered, just a fraction. "Why would I do it, if it wasn't what I wanted?"

"I don't know. And you're still not saying that it's what you want."

Joe pushed him again, this time in the direction of the trees. "Go to your mate, bronicorn. You need each other. Don't let anything come between you."

Wystan gave up, allowing Joe to shoo him away. "Well, I just hope that you meet *your* mate one day. And that she isn't put off by your past."

Joe's smile didn't waver, but something changed in his eyes. For the briefest moment, Wystan saw straight through that light, dazzling surface, into the fathomless depths below.

"I don't," Joe said quietly, not sounding at all like his usual self. "That's the whole point."

CHAPTER 28

Candice's nerves wound tighter with every step. She hoped that Blaise's supernatural shifter senses couldn't pick up on how much her palms were sweating.

"Uh, hey, Blaise?" she said when she couldn't last another second. "Um, actually I've changed my mind. I'm gonna go find Wystan. I need to...share his soap after all."

Blaise swung around, a wide grin breaking across her face. "Thanks. That's saved us both from a very awkward conversation. I was prepared to wrestle you to the ground and put you in an armlock in order to force you to hear me out."

Candice was pretty sure Blaise wasn't joking. "You were going to tell me more childhood stories about Wystan?"

"Nah, I was going to yell at you to leap on him like a sex-starved cougar," Blaise said matter-of-factly. "I love Wystan, but that man does *not* know how to open up. He'll never show it, but I know all this has been killing him."

Candice fidgeted uncomfortably. "He said he would wait as long as I needed."

"Yeah. He would. Doesn't mean that he wouldn't be dying inside the whole time. I'm glad you're going to put him out of his misery."

Blaise's smile faded. "Assuming you aren't going to destroy him, that is."

"I'm not." Candice swallowed the lump in her throat. "Ever."

"Good." Blaise's white teeth flashed again. "Because I like you. I would hate to have to kill you."

Candice forced a matching smile. "Enjoy your bath. Do me a favor and take your time, okay? Otherwise it's going to be obvious to everyone that Wystan and I have snuck away together. It may sound dumb, but I'd rather not have the rest of the squad speculating about what we're doing while we're actually doing it, y'know?"

Blaise stretched her jaw in an exaggerated yawn. "Such a nice afternoon. I might take a nap by the stream. A *long* nap."

With a parting wink, Blaise sauntered off. Candice waited until she was out of sight before pulling out her compass. Settling her pack on her shoulders, she started walking—not in the direction of camp, but back down the mountain.

Sorry, Blaise. She hated to have to mislead the hotshot, who—death threats aside—had been nothing but friendly to her. *But it wasn't really a lie. I'm* not *going to destroy Wystan.*

Even if it meant breaking his heart.

She blinked hard, fighting back the moisture threatening to blur her vision. She forced herself to pick up her pace, pushing through undergrowth. She couldn't waste this chance. She didn't know how far Callum could sense people. Her only hope was to put as much distance between herself and the camp before he woke up and alerted the squad that she was gone. With enough of a head start, she could get back to her truck before they caught up with her.

And then she could disappear.

She'd miss working with Bethany, but there was nothing else tying her to California. Her crappy one-room apartment was just a place to sleep. She didn't have any family to miss her. She could just pick a direction and go. Wherever she went, there would be animals who needed her.

She wished that she could have said goodbye to the squad properly. She wished she could have hugged Flash one last time. She wished she could have told Wystan...

Candice pressed her lips together, squashing the useless regrets back down. Everything was going to be fine. Flash was safely back with her herd. Soon the baby unicorn would be reunited with her mother as well as her father. The squad didn't need her help to drive out the demon.

And Wystan...Wystan would be better off without her.

Eventually, he'd realize that. His unicorn was everything to him. She couldn't let him risk losing his animal, his magic, his very identity. Not for her.

"Candice! Wait!"

Oh no. No, no, no. Her heart seized at Wystan's shout. Why had he come after her?

There was no point trying to pretend she hadn't heard. She set her shoulders, steeling herself. She'd selfishly hoped to save herself this pain by sneaking away, but she had to do this. It was for his own good.

"Don't try to stop me, Wystan," she started, turning. "I—"

All her carefully-marshalled objections flew out of her head.

He halted in front of her, bare chest heaving. He must have been running flat out to catch up. "You're leaving."

"You're half-naked and dripping wet," she blurted out.

"Joe pushed me into the stream." He pushed his hair back from his face, water-darkened spikes sticking out in all directions in wild disarray. "Thankfully. Where are you going?"

"Away. Somewhere. Anywhere." Hard enough to do this to his face. It was practically impossible to do it when he was shirtless, soaking, and disheveled. She scrunched her eyes shut. "Just let me go, Wystan. This isn't going to work. I can't be what you need."

"You *are* what I need, Candice. You're my mate." She heard him take a step closer. "But that's not the most important thing."

She risked a peek at him, trying to work out what he was talking about. "It's not?"

"No." He was very close now, close enough that she could see droplets of water clinging to the damp curve of his bare neck. "I've been going about this all backwards, Candice. I've only been thinking of what *I* want, what *I* need. I've been so fixated on what I can't do that I've ignored what I *can* do."

Her mouth had gone dry. "What's that?"

"Ask you." His green eyes were deep and clear and certain. "What do *you* want, Candice?"

She looked down at her boots. "To be a different person," she muttered.

"No." He touched her chin, gently making her raise her head once more. "That's what you think I need. And it's not. Try again."

He was barely touching her, but his presence wrapped around her like strong, comforting arms. In that safe, quiet space, she could only speak the truth. "I want you."

"Good," he said, very softly. "Because I want you too, desperately. And what do you need?"

"I need..." She hesitated, searching her own heart. "I need to take this one day at a time, Wystan."

He was holding very still, as though she was a wild animal who might run away if he made the slightest motion. "I can do that."

"No, you can't," she said bleakly. "You told me yourself, you need someone who can promise you forever. I'm never going to be able to do that. I can't—"

"Candice." He laid his thumb across her mouth, silencing her protests. "That's all forever is. One day at a time, one after another. Every day, choosing to stay. One day at a time."

"But that's not how it works for you," she said, lips brushing against his warm skin. Just that light friction made her tremble with desire. "That's not the kind of love you need."

He traced the shape of her mouth, and her knees buckled. "That's the only kind there is."

Slowly, holding her gaze the entire time, he leaned closer. His mouth touched hers—lightly at first, then deeper as she opened to him. He kissed her unhurriedly, but with utter confidence, savoring and lingering as if they had all the time in the world.

As if they had all eternity.

Her backpack dropped to the ground with a thud. She wound her arms around his neck, the slow, certain strokes of his tongue setting her on fire. She pulled him deeper, consumed with the need for more. He made a deliciously feral sound deep in his throat, his kisses becoming wilder, hungrier. Her own desire leaped as he matched her stroke for stroke, nipping and biting.

His hands found her waist. He pulled her tight against his body, swinging around to back her up against the nearest tree. Heat shot through her as he pinned her between the hard trunk and his even harder body.

"Wait," she managed to gasp into his mouth. Dizzying need pulsed between her legs, but she wrenched her face to one side, breaking the kiss. "We can't—"

"Stay with me." Wystan's hips pressed against hers. He kissed down her neck, open-mouthed and fierce, over scars and skin alike. "Be with me. Not forever. Now. One day at a time. One *breath* at a time. Just choose me, with every beat of your heart, as I choose you. That's enough. That's everything. Oh Candice, my mate, *Candice.*"

One breath at a time. She let go of all her fears, letting them fly away like lost balloons. She didn't need to worry about forever. She could love him *now*, completely, with all her soul.

And that was enough.

"Yes." She tipped her head back, giving him her throat, giving him everything. Just for this breath, and this one, and this one… "Wystan. Yes."

She'd imagined that Wystan would be a sensitive, gentle lover. She'd pictured those sensitive hands exploring her body shyly, sweetly, that endearing flush staining his cheeks as she showed him how to please her.

She hadn't pictured *this*.

He was about as hesitant as a stallion scenting a mare in heat. She yelped as he tore her shirt right off her body, seams ripping under his inhuman strength. His hands scooped her up effortlessly, lifting her so that he could plunge his face into her breasts. Her surprise was washed away in a blaze of pleasure as his mouth found her nipple.

Yes, oh yes, there. But harder, with teeth. She hadn't realized she'd been sending him her thoughts until she felt his deep chuckle echo through her chest. He obliged, passionately following her every half-formed desire until she wasn't sure he *was* following. She couldn't tell what was her idea or his; who led and who followed; his pleasure from hers. It all blurred into one mounting wave of ecstasy, both of them swept up together, one.

He only paused once, for one moment. Though her body trembled around his, though his breath came harsh and ragged, though she dug her heels into the backs of his thighs to urge him on—he held himself back, right at the brink. His eyes sought hers.

"Now?" he whispered.

"Yes." She pulled him in, welcoming him, claiming him for her own. For this breath, and the next, and the next… "Now."

CHAPTER 29

He awoke remade.

The mate bond burned in his heart like the sun. He was filled with light, radiant with it, strength coursing through his veins. Candice's love shone in his soul, illuminating the darkness at last.

Oh. Wystan lay there with his eyes closed, holding very still, adjusting. Magic trembled within him, overflowing, ready to spill out at the slightest thought. *Oh. So that's what it feels like.*

A soft breath ruffled his hair. *So this is your dream.*

He opened his eyes at last, looking up into Moth's enigmatic grey ones. There was something odd about that, but the thought fled as he tried to grasp it. Nothing could be wrong. Not when he felt so perfectly, utterly right.

The lead mare nosed him again with her velvet muzzle, nostrils flaring as though perplexed by his scent. *This is your heart's desire. Your deepest wish. To be a healer?*

"Yes." He lifted one hand in front of his face, mildly surprised his fingers were still flesh and blood. From the raging potential vibrating through his bones, he'd half expected his skin to have turned transparent as crystal, glowing with the power within. "This is everything I've ever wanted."

Moth tilted her ears at him. *And what would you do with this power?*

Candice lay curled against his side, face turned into his bare chest and one arm flung possessively around his waist. Carefully, moving slowly so as not to wake her, he eased out from underneath her. She mumbled in sleepy protest as he sat up, then sighed and fell still once more.

"I can help her now," he said softly, gazing down in wonder at his mate. He brushed her hair back from her peaceful face, tucking the short strands behind her ear. "I'll be at her side, always. When she rescues animals who are sick or hurt, I'll be able to help them. She'll never have to feel the agony of losing any of them, ever again. If she's ever hurt, I can heal her. I'll take away her pain."

Moth's equine face was unreadable. *You would give up your life for her. You would abandon your work, your friends, to follow her without a thought. Would she do the same for you? Follow you into any peril?*

He breathed in Candice's presence, her fierce courage filling every corner of his soul. "Yes. Oh, yes."

Moth's tail flicked from side to side, very slightly. *And...she is the source of your power.*

"She is my mate," he said, simply.

Moth looked at him for a long moment. Then she shook her mane as though coming to a decision. *You said you would use this power to take away her pain. You are strong now. Strong enough to heal* all *her pain.*

He followed the line of her pointing horn to the vivid scars on Candice's face. "No, Moth. It's true, her scars do remind her of her past trauma sometimes. But they show her strength, too. I wouldn't want to take that away from her. I don't think she'd want me to either."

She is suffering, Moth insisted. *Look, even now she hurts.*

Candice's face twisted in sudden pain. She cried out in her sleep, curling into a tight ball as though trying to hide.

"Candice!" He tried to shake her, but she didn't respond. No matter how he tried, he couldn't wake her. She was trapped in a nightmare.

So are we, a voice whispered in his soul, almost too faint to hear. Despite the power blazing in his hands, there was a strange absence where his unicorn should be. He had an impression of it struggling to reach him, held back by grasping grey fog. *This is wrong. This is not real.*

But it *was* real. Every hair on Moth's hide stood out sharp and vivid. He could *feel* Candice, her skin cold and clammy as she fought her memories. He'd never felt so alive and awake in his entire life. How could it not be real?

All you have ever wanted is to be able to heal. Moth's harsh, certain voice drowned out his unicorn. **Now you can. Will you leave her wounded and in pain?**

Light gathered easily in his fingers. So simple, so straightforward, like flying in a dream. He couldn't understand why he'd never been able to do this before. It was so *easy*.

All he had to do was touch her face.

Candice sighed, all the pain draining out of her body as her scars faded away. She opened her eyes. Love shone there, and gratitude, and worship. She smiled up at him, the right side of her face a perfect mirror of the left.

"Wystan." She touched her unmarred skin, then laid her palm against his own cheek. "You healed me."

Remember, Moth said in his mind as pride filled his chest. **Remember how this feels.**

Moth stepped back, fading away. Everything else faded as well— Candice, the forest, his power, his own sense of self. All that was left was Moth's lingering whisper as darkness closed over his head.

Remember, Moth said again. **Now wake up.**

CHAPTER 30

Candice jolted out of sleep all at once, heart hammering as though she'd just fallen. Shreds of her dream clung to her mind like cobwebs—something about stumbling through darkness, desperately trying to follow the distant, distressed sounds of a trapped animal calling for help?

The confused, unsettling feelings quickly faded, thankfully. She relaxed again, dropping her head back down onto Wystan's bare chest. Heat pulsed through her as she breathed in his rain-and-smoke scent. She ran her hand over his smooth, muscled side, the last of her dream slipping out of her mind.

"Hey." The relaxed curve of his mouth was almost unbearably tempting. With heroic effort, she restrained from kissing him. "Hey. Wake up."

He didn't stir. She grinned, feeling a little smug at having reached the limits of even his supernatural stamina. Of course, given the satisfied tenderness between her thighs, he'd more than earned his nap.

But it would have to wait. Dusk was falling, the cooling breeze raising goosebumps on her bare back. They'd been away from camp for hours. No doubt everyone was wondering where they'd gone.

"Wystan." She dug her nails into Wystan's hip. "Wake up. We gotta get back before the rest of the squad send out a search party."

He mumbled something that might have been her name. His eyes flickered behind his closed eyelids. He flinched suddenly, but didn't wake up.

"Wystan?" Starting to get worried, she shook his shoulder, without effect. She could *feel* his agitation and distress, gathering at the back of her mind like a thunderstorm. She tried to reach him down that strange new connection. "Wystan, wake up. It's just a dream."

His features relaxed again, all at once. He drew in a deep, calm breath, a smile tugging at his mouth. There was something odd about it, a kind of smug satisfaction she'd never seen in his face before.

His eyes opened, meeting hers. His mouth curved further, into his real smile, the one that never failed to send butterflies flurrying through her stomach. His deep, quiet delight shone down the mate bond like moonbeams.

"Hello," he said softly.

"Hi." She couldn't help an answering smile spreading across her face, like the worst kind of lovesick idiot. "You okay? You looked like you were having a bad dream."

"It was a dream?" He sat up swiftly, spilling her off his chest. He stared around at the forest glade as though searching for someone. "She's not here?"

"Who?"

"Moth. She was…" He trailed off, his breath catching. He stared down at his hands as though he'd never seen them before. "It wasn't a dream."

"Uh, you were definitely asleep." Her heart was suddenly racing. It took her a second to realize it was *his* mounting excitement. It was unnerving to have someone else's emotions echoing in her own body. "It was actually kinda hard to wake you up. Wystan, what's going on?"

"It wasn't a dream!" He rounded on her, hands outstretched. "Candice, I can feel my unicorn!"

Guilt punched her in the gut. She'd been so caught up in how right everything felt that she hadn't even worried about the possibility that he might lose his animal. Clearly *he* must have been worrying about it.

But he said *he wasn't afraid.* She couldn't help feeling a little betrayed. She'd *trusted* him. He'd seemed so sincere when he'd reassured that her love would be enough…

She reached for her pack, pulling out her spare shirt. "Well, I guess that must be a relief."

"No, you don't understand." He grabbed her shoulders, swinging her around to face him. "Candice, I can do it now, I can feel it!"

His emotions blazed down the mate bond like wildfire. She flinched, clinging to her own confusion and irritation as a flimsy shield against his all-consuming presence. "Bud, slow your roll. You're blasting me out of my own head. This is too much, too fast. I need you to back off and explain what's going on."

He let go of her, taking a step back, but his half-mad, wild grin didn't flicker. "I'll do better than that. I'll show you. Everything's going to be fine now, Candice. I can fix everything."

His form blurred into light. There was something different about that radiance, a sunlight-gold tint rippling through the cooler moonlight tones.

Her breath left her as the unicorn appeared. He stood proudly, head and tail carried high, every line of his body proclaiming confident strength. His horn was no longer pure silver. A bright gold spiral twined up the gleaming length.

His horn lit, summer sunlight and moonbeams intermingling in an ever-shifting dance. She held still as the sharp point dipped toward her face—not out of fear, but pure wonder. His horn brushed her cheek like a kiss.

Light wrapped her. She was bathed in love, cradled in protective strength. She closed her eyes, but tears leaked out anyway as some frozen part of her heart melted in that gentle warmth. A part of her that had always been tense and on guard, ready for attack, finally sighed and relaxed.

The light faded, but the feeling didn't. She kept her eyes closed, holding her breath, not wanting to do anything that might break the moment.

She was loved. She was cherished.

For the first time in her life, she knew that she was perfectly safe.

"No." Wystan's whisper shattered the silence. His dismay flooded through her, a black tide obliterating her calm joy.

Her eyes flew open. Wystan was back in human form, desperate denial written across his face. He put his palm flat against her right cheek. For a moment, he kept it there, jaw clenching as though he was struggling to lift a tremendous weight—and then he snatched his hand away again.

"Why isn't it working?" He stared at his own fingers as though all the flesh had fallen off his bones. His voice rose, bleak with utter despair. "I'm supposed to be able to heal now. *Why can't I heal you?*"

His words echoed through her like a thunderclap. For a second, she could only stare at him, breathless with betrayal.

Then rage overwhelmed her. She welcomed it, opened her arms out to it, embraced it. Anything was better than that cold void of grief.

"That's what this was about?" she snarled. "All those fancy words, all that sweet talk—it was never about me, was it? You just thought a mate would unlock your powers."

He dropped his hands, eyes widening. "No. No. Candice, that's not true."

"It *is!*" She shoved him, hard, sending him staggering back a step. "Don't try to lie to me! I can feel what you feel, thanks to your stupid mate bond. I know *exactly* what you're feeling!"

He drew in a sharp breath. His expression locked down, bitter grief disappearing behind a smooth, impenetrable mask. Her sense of his emotions cut off abruptly. The mate bond went numb, as though he'd retreated behind an icy wall.

He picked up his discarded clothes, starting to get dressed. When he spoke again, his voice was back under control, all reserved courtesy. "I'm sorry for losing control and upsetting you. I was just…a bit disappointed."

The ludicrous understatement tore a bark of laughter out of her.

She turned away, savagely pulling on her pants. "Whatever, bud. It doesn't matter. The others will be waiting for us."

"Candice." He tried to touch her shoulder, but she jerked out of his reach. "I can't deny that I was hoping that mating you would unblock my abilities. I didn't tell you because I didn't want to put any more pressure on you. I didn't want you to get your hopes up—"

"What, that you would be able to magically heal my scars?" She shoved her head through her shirt to glare at him. "I never hoped for that, though apparently *you* did. What, you think I'm not pretty enough for you?"

He recoiled as though she'd shoved him again. "No! That's not it at all! I just—I thought, if I could heal them, it would make things easier for us. Make it easier for you to trust me. You said yourself that they reminded you of your past."

"Yeah. They do." Finishing getting dressed, she swung around to confront him head on. "And clearly I should have looked in the mirror more. Maybe then I wouldn't have been so dumb as to fall for another smooth-talking liar. You know what, Wystan? You're *worse* than him. At least he just tried to rip me off. Not rip me apart."

He seemed to have stopped breathing. "Candice—"

She cut him off, savagely. "We're done here." She slung her pack over one shoulder, setting off without looking back. "Let's go."

CHAPTER 31

I've ruined everything.

Candice wasn't speaking to him. She was trying to hide her mind from him too, but he could still feel her anger and hurt with every beat of his heart. He kept his side of the mate bond shielded, iron control stopping his own emotions from leaking back in return. He'd already caused her enough grief without adding his own to it.

Go to her, his unicorn insisted. His beast tugged at his awareness, repeatedly drawing him back to the bond he was trying to ignore. *She is hurting. Only we can heal her.*

It was ironic, really. Now that it was absolutely, utterly clear that he couldn't heal, would never be able to heal...his unicorn was convinced that it could.

No matter how much he tried to shove his animal back into his subconscious, he couldn't keep it caged. Ironically, the cursed creature was stronger now, more certain of itself. Its calm confidence shone in the black depths of his soul like the full moon sailing through midnight skies.

Go to her. Drop your shields. Go to our mate.

He kept his distance. He threw himself into the mundane tasks of breaking camp, trying to keep as much out of Candice's sight as possible. Though it tore his heart in half, he left her alone. It was the best he could do for her. It was the only thing he could do for her.

He'd hurt his mate. And he couldn't heal her pain.

The rest of the squad could tell that something was amiss, of course. It was a strained, awkward morning, everyone edging around the two of them as though they might explode at any second. Edith, in her typical endearingly direct manner, had started to ask him what was wrong, only to be gently drawn away by Rory.

"Give them space," Wystan had overheard the griffin shifter murmuring to his mate. "They need to work this out on their own. Like we did." Rory had glanced over Edith's head at him, catching his eyes for a moment. "It'll be okay. They're true mates. They'll get through this."

Rory didn't know what Wystan had done. He'd hurt Candice, betrayed her utterly. How could he ask her to forgive him? When he'd never forgive himself?

He'd hurt his mate.

"So." Joe broke the uncomfortable silence, clearing his throat. "Who's up for fighting a giant demonic snake monster today?"

"*Please*," Blaise muttered into her coffee mug. "Anything but this."

Pack shouldn't fight, Fenrir growled. His tail was tucked unhappily between his back legs. *Not like this. Not yet.*

"Unfortunately, I don't think we've got much of a choice." Rory cocked an eyebrow at Callum. "Our big feathered friend still up there?"

Callum made a circling motion with one finger, pointing at the sky. "Staying high. Waiting."

"Let's hope it will hold back a while longer. The last thing we need is a forest fire on top of everything else." Rory turned to Wystan. "I think we're as ready as we'll ever be. Want to go see if the unicorn alpha has come to her senses?"

Wystan nodded. Shouldering his pack, he set off for the border—and was surprised to find Candice falling into step behind him.

"You don't have to—" he started.

"I do," she said curtly. "I need to make sure that Flash is safe. I don't trust that snooty so-called lead mare. I bet she doesn't even turn up."

But Moth was waiting for them as promised, in the small clearing just beyond the border. What was more, she wasn't alone.

"Flash!" Candice rushed forward, flinging herself down next to the small, twitching form. She flung a glare up at Moth. "What did you do to her?"

Peace, human, Moth said coolly. *I am merely keeping her entranced in dreams. She is determined to go to her mother. She does not understand the danger. I have tried to explain to her in dream, but she is too young to understand. She thinks that we are trying to hurt Sunrise, not save her.*

Relief rose in him. "So you are willing to let Petrichor attempt to drive out the demon?"

Yes. Moth looked down at Flash. *But I am concerned that the little one will interfere. With her power, we cannot stop her from teleporting into the middle of the fight. I cannot keep her trapped in dreams for much longer. Already she fights me, attempting to awaken.*

"I can't sedate her again," Candice said. "She's too tiny, it wouldn't be safe."

Then our only choice is to remove her. Moth's ears tilted at Candice. *You cared for her before. She seems to respect you, certainly more than she does me. Take her away from this place. Far enough that she will not sense what is occurring, and teleport back. You must keep her safe until the danger has passed.*

"Wait," Wystan said. "Candice isn't going anywhere."

Candice bristled at him. "Candice can speak for herself, bud."

Moth's grey eyes met his. He had a sense of her telepathy narrowing, speaking into his mind alone. *She must go, for her own sake as well as Flash's. She is only human. She has no powers. Do you want her to be nearby when we release the demon? The creature will sense her weakness. She will be in danger.*

His heart lurched as he envisioned Candice facing off against a towering monstrosity. "Actually, Moth has a point, Candice. You can't fight the demon alongside the rest of the squad. The best way for you to help is to make sure that Flash is safe."

Candice hesitated, her mouth tightening. "You're right. Flash has to be our first priority." She threw an unpleasant look at Moth. "And I definitely don't want to leave her *here*."

He couldn't help feeling a tiny glimmer of hope. They were working together again, side by side...he turned back to Moth. "Very well. We'll take Flash to safety. One of my squad can come find us once the demon has been slain and it's safe for us to return."

No, Moth said swiftly, once more broadcasting to both of them. **The human must go alone. We will need you here, in case anyone is injured in the fight with the demon.**

He shook his head firmly. "I'm not leaving my mate. And I'm of more use helping her with Flash than I would be here. I may be descended from healers, but I don't have any powers myself."

That is not true. Moth sounded utterly certain. **Your talent is strong, stronger than any I have ever sensed. And it is even greater now than when we last spoke.**

His pulse spiked. He stared at her, hardly daring to breathe. "You can sense power in me?"

Candice's eyes narrowed. "Why didn't you say anything about this before?"

I did not know that his talent was blocked. Moth rippled her hide in an equine shrug. **It is a rare thing, but not unheard of. The most powerful of our kind are sometimes the last to fully bloom. Occasionally they require assistance to release their potential.**

"What sort of assistance?" Wystan took an eager step forward. "Can you help me?"

I can. Moth turned her head, pointing with her horn. **I will allow you into our heartland, our most sacred grove. There, you will find your destiny.**

"Wystan." Candice caught his sleeve. "I smell bullshit. Or unicorn shit. This is too convenient."

He hesitated...but his half-remembered dream pulled at him. He'd felt so *right*, so powerful and strong...

"If there's a chance that Moth can unlock my healing ability, I have to take it. Especially if she can do it before we fight the demon."

Almost, he confessed his deepest fear—that someone he loved would get hurt, and he'd be powerless to help—but he bit back the words. Candice didn't need to be burdened with his weaknesses. "Go back to the squad and tell them the plan. Callum can fly you and Flash back to where we left the cars. You'll have to drive fast so that you're well away from here before Flash wakes up."

Candice shook her head stubbornly. "Don't stay here alone. I've got a bad feeling about this. I don't trust this bedazzled cow any further than I could throw her."

He put a hand on hers. "Moth has been honest with us, Candice. I know you find it difficult to trust anyone, but—"

"Oh, you did *not* just go there," she breathed. She dropped his arm as though it had abruptly become red-hot. "Fine. Have it your way, since power is the only thing that matters to you. See if I care."

"Candice," he started, but she was already turning away. She scooped up Flash, cradling the little unicorn. Her face was pale with anger, scars standing out vividly. Without looking back, she strode away.

Go! His unicorn reared in his mind. *Go to our mate!*

He shook his head, pushing his unicorn back down. This was one of the times cold human logic had to override animal instinct. Better for Candice to be safely away and angry at him than to run after her now. He'd fix things with her later.

He turned back to Moth. "Show me what I have to do."

∼

He'd never imagined anything like the unicorn homeland.

The sense of peace he'd felt at the edge of the forest was nothing compared to the deep tranquility that fell over him as he followed Moth deeper into the forest. Plants grew in wild abundance, untouched by human hands and yet exquisitely in harmony with each other as though every leaf had been planned by generations of gardeners.

It was like walking through Eden, the morning after the world was made. Birds sang in the trees, pouring out pure joy. Squirrels came out to watch him go by, their bright button eyes curious and unafraid. At one point, he had to pause to let a glorious flame-red fox drift unhurriedly across his path on some mysterious errand of its own, trailing its tail like a knight's banner. Everywhere he looked, there were wild creatures going about their lives. In this one place, it was as if humans had never existed.

I wish Candice could see this.

Her absence was an ache in his chest. He'd been able to tell when she left, the connection between them stretching painfully as she drove further away. The mate bond was still there—nothing could ever change that—but he couldn't sense her thoughts anymore.

She is out of our reach. His unicorn paced in his soul, round and round, like a zoo animal trapped in a cage. *She is too far away. We cannot protect her.*

His shoulders twitched with his animal's agitation. He forced his knotted muscles to relax. Candice didn't need his protection. The Nightmare was safely contained, no threat to her or Flash. She would be perfectly safe without him.

"How long will this take?" he asked Moth. "The rest of the squad will grow concerned if I'm gone too long."

It will take as long as it takes. Moth drifted between the trees like a ghost, never looking back. *And your companions have no choice but to wait. I could not allow them through our wards even if I wished to. Come. This way.*

The forest grew darker, older, as she led him onward. Ancient trees blocked out the sun, their branches gnarled like old men. The birds grew scarcer, songs dying away, until they were walking through cathedral-like hush. Deep, crisscrossed layers of fallen twigs crunched under his boots like tiny bones. A feeling he couldn't quite name prickled the back of his neck. He found himself walking closer to Moth, every sense on high alert.

"Where is the rest of your herd?" His voice sounded too loud, too human, unnatural in the eerie silence. "I haven't seen any other unicorns."

This is a sacred place. She paced on, her hooves making no sound on the dry, brittle leaf-litter. *They do not come here. I have forbidden it. I have not allowed any to set hoof here for years, save...* She hesitated for a moment. *Save for Sunrise. I brought her to the heartland when I chose her as my successor. I wish that I had not.*

A dead tree caught his eye, the first thing he'd seen in the entire forest that wasn't lush and thriving. As he followed Moth deeper into the forest, he noticed more dry, leafless snags, skeletons amidst the living trees.

"What's happened here?" he asked Moth. "Some kind of disease?"

A sickness, she replied. A deep abyss of grief lay under her mental words. *One even our magic cannot fight.*

He touched one desiccated trunk as they passed. Though the bark was dry, it felt oddly repulsive, like putting his hand into moldy garbage. It made his unicorn shy away, ears flattening.

"This is why Sunrise wanted to leave, isn't it." He pulled his hand away again, restraining a shudder. "Is it spreading?"

It was. But I have contained it. Sunrise was wrong. Moth halted. *We are here.*

A circle of trees ringed a small glade. Every single one was dead, bark peeling away to reveal bleached wood pale as bone. Brown husks that must once have been verdant wildflowers lay flat against bare, powdery earth.

His skin crawled. He stepped past Moth, drawn out by horrified fascination. Dust puffed up under his boots. The ground was cracked and crazed, as though rain hadn't fallen here for decades.

At the very center of the clearing, a wider chasm yawned—a deep, black split big enough to swallow a man.

"Here?" He stopped on the edge of that gaping mouth. He looked down into the abyss, and a vertiginous sense of *wrongness* made his head swim. He retreated hastily, turning back to Moth. "But this is—"

Moth's blazing horn struck his forehead like lightning, and blackness claimed him.

CHAPTER 32

"Stupid idiot," Candice muttered, hands clenching on the steering wheel hard enough to turn her knuckles white. She took the twisting mountain bends at unwise speed, as much through rage as necessity. "Arrogant overgrown ass! Serve him right if, if he walks right into that evil mare's trap. Whatever it is."

She knew Moth had to be planning something. She just couldn't work out *what*. Why had Moth suddenly taken such an interest in Wystan's theoretical powers? Had the lead mare somehow known that was the one bait he couldn't resist? What could she possibly hope to gain by luring him into the unicorn lands?

It didn't make any *sense*.

Maybe she wants exactly what she said, she thought bleakly. *Maybe it's just that healers are rare, and she wants to help him so that he'll be able to help the herd in return. Maybe I* am *being paranoid.*

Flash stirred on the passenger seat next to her. The baby unicorn made a small, questioning sound, lifting her head to peer around groggily.

"Hey, baby." Worried that Flash might try to teleport away, Candice pulled over to the side of the road, cutting the engine. She could only hope that they were already far enough away from the unicorns' territory. "It's okay. I'm here."

A little fire burst of purple sparks swirled in her mind's eye. She had the impression Flash was happy to see her, but confused as well. The little unicorn climbed shakily to her hooves, peering out through the windscreen. She made a startled, flute-like squeak.

"Yeah, I know. It's not your home." Candice stroked Flash's mane, trying to broadcast reassurance to her. "I have to take you away for a little bit. Your daddy's going to make your mom better, I promise. But they need to be private and alone for a while. Moth asked me to look after you."

Flash's ears flattened at the sound of Moth's name. She turned her head as though searching for something. Candice received a clear mental picture of a towering, gleaming shape...

Her heart tightened. "No, Wystan's not here. He's...busy. Moth needs his help to heal your mom."

Flash shifted uneasily, her ears clamping down even further. The flurry of images she sent were very definitely referring to Moth, and not at all flattering to the lead mare.

"Yeah, I don't trust her either." Candice bit her lip. "But you know, Wystan can take care of himself. He's three times Moth's size, after all. Even if she called in the whole herd, he could kick the entire pack of them into next week. He'll be fine."

Flash treated her to a deeply dubious look.

"Hey. He's a grown-ass man. And a giant magic stallion. He's big and strong and..." Candice trailed off. "And he needs me."

Flash nickered, bobbing her head in enthusiastic assent.

"You're right." Candice threw the Jeep into reverse. "We're going back."

She did a tricky three-point turn on the narrow road. The anxious tightness in her chest eased as she gunned the Jeep back up the mountain. Even though she was still mad at Wystan, he needed her.

She wasn't going to abandon her mate.

Flash's ears pricked up. She whinnied, high and urgent.

"You're worried too, aren't you?" Somehow, she *knew* Wystan was in trouble, with bone-deep certainty. Candice glanced at Flash, taking her attention off the road just long enough to give the unicorn a reassuring pat. "It's okay, baby. Just hang on. This is going to get bumpy."

She looked back through the windscreen—and slammed on the brake.

Because the Nightmare was standing in the middle of the road.

CHAPTER 33

Do we have a bargain?

The sharp telepathic voice cut through his confused, fog-filled dreams. A vast grey weight pressed down on his mind, trying to keep him still, but he fought against it. The faint sense of Moth's presence was a tenuous mental link to the outside world. He clung to it in the darkness, struggling towards consciousness as if hauling himself hand-over-hand up a rope.

These two, and no more, Moth continued, talking to someone he couldn't sense. *This shall be the end of it, understand? I will not give you more!*

Wystan's eyelids felt as if they had rusted shut. Slowly, painfully, he managed to drag them open, and found himself staring at a pale shape. Not Moth.

"Petrichor," he said, his tongue thick and clumsy in his mouth. His head pounded as though Moth had struck him with a sledgehammer rather than her horn. "Is that you?"

The stallion whinnied in miserable assent. Twisting branches caged him, twining so closely around his flanks and neck that the unicorn couldn't move an inch.

His own arms were wrenched up and behind at a painful angle.

Wystan tried to turn his head, and discovered that branches wrapped around him as well. Bark pressed against his back and chest.

"What...?" Living wood creaked as he tried to move his limbs. It was as if he'd been unconscious for years, turned to stone as saplings sprang up and grew around him. "Petrichor, what is this? It can't be Moth's magic."

Petrichor shook his head, as much as his cage allowed. He sent Wystan a mental image of a mare with her horn alight, plants writhing and growing at impossible speed under her direction. Wystan recognized the unicorn—the brown-eyed one who'd seemed to speak up angrily against Moth, in defense of Sunrise. In Petrichor's vision, the mare seemed to be sleep-walking, glassy-eyed and stumbling. Moth stood next to her, horn touching her flank as though goading her on.

"I see. Moth can hypnotize the others, and make them use their powers as she directs." *Candice was right. I shouldn't have trusted her.* "Do you know what she wants with us?"

The whites showed around the edges of Petrichor's pale grey eyes. He didn't answer, instead going back to struggling against the twining tree trunks binding his legs. Cruel stripes across his white coat showed how hard he'd been throwing himself against his prison, but the saplings held firm.

Deep in his soul, Wystan's own unicorn raged, desperate to break free. He took a deep breath, forcing himself to relax. If he tried to shift, he'd tear himself apart.

At least Candice is safe. It might have played right into Moth's hooves, but he couldn't regret sending her away. He only hoped that she hadn't sensed his own peril down the mate bond. Or if she had, that she was angry enough to ignore it.

Don't come back, he silently begged her. If she did, she'd fall straight into Moth's trap as well. The rest of the squad couldn't cross the barrier surrounding the unicorn lands. She'd be alone and unsupported.

Don't come back, Candice. Stay away. Live.

It didn't matter what happened to him, as long as his mate was safe.

"Moth!" Wystan called. Twisting his head as far as he could, he just managed to catch sight of the lead mare's silver form. She was facing away from them, apparently talking to someone hidden from his view. "Moth, whatever you are planning, please rethink. I am not your enemy. I only want to help you."

I know. Moth's mental voice was heavy with regret. She turned, revealing a glimpse of that strange, blackened clearing with its ominous crack. *For what it is worth, I am sorry. But this is the only way.*

Wystan kept his voice very calm and soothing, though his heart hammered against his ribs. "The only way to do what?"

To keep my herd safe. Moth took a few paces back. *If it comforts you, know that your sacrifice will protect other innocent lives. You are a great prize. They promised that if I gave you to them, they would be satisfied at last. They will retreat, leaving us in peace once more.*

Wystan stared past Moth at that gaping, bottomless cleft in the earth. Ice ran down his spine. "Who, Moth? Who will leave you alone?"

Moth's head dropped low. The light from her horn faded to nothing.

Her voice whispered in his mind, low and ashamed. *The demons.*

The ground beyond her heaved. A new crack splintered off from the first, zig-zagging across the clearing. The very earth seemed to draw back in revulsion as a blunt-nosed, serpentine head thrust into the air. Soil sloughed from curving black horns.

I am sorry, Moth said again. *I tried everything, when the corruption first appeared. But I could not stop them from rising. I could only strike a bargain.*

Tree branches bit into his wrists. "Moth. Moth, no. I don't know much about these creatures, but I do know that they are evil. You cannot trust them."

I gave them Sunrise, and they left the rest of us alone. Moth backed away as the snake-like creature fought its way out of the ground. *They will do the same again. Your sacrifice will keep my herd safe.*

The horned serpent slid free at last. It was much smaller than the one Wystan had fought with the squad before, barely six feet from nose to tail-tip. It thrashed, clumsy and awkward as a newborn fawn, until it managed to roll onto its belly. It drew itself up, forked tongue tasting the air. Its head turned.

"No!" Wystan threw himself against his prison as the demon started to wriggle toward Petrichor. "Moth! Tell them to leave him alone, it's me they want! Give *me* to them!"

Moth's horn jabbed into his hip, sharp enough to penetrate his protective gear and draw blood. A grey fog smothered his mind, cutting him off from his body. Paralyzed, he could only watch as the demon opened its mouth wide.

I will, Moth said, her magic gripping him like iron bands. *But they want him as well. They fear him. You were right, he* could *free Sunrise.*

Petrichor screamed as the demon's fangs sank deep into his foreleg. The horned serpent seemed to pour itself into the wound, its sinuous body disappearing. Black streaks raced under the stallion's skin. Petrichor's cry choked off abruptly. He fell still, all at once.

When he looked up again, a blood-red mist hazed his grey eyes.

But no longer, Moth said. *Now they are both trapped.*

The possessed unicorn bared teeth that were already noticeably sharper. It jerked its head, the motion almost casual. The branch wrapped around its neck splintered and fell away.

Moth's mental voice faded to a whisper. *They wanted Flash too. But I saved her. Her, at least, I could save.*

With hideous strength, the demon broke free of the trees. It stepped delicately free, every movement somehow *wrong*, muscles flexing in alien ways.

Moth stood firm as the cold red eyes turned to her. *Remember our bargain. Hunt as you please. But do not touch my herd.*

The demon wrinkled its muzzle again, showing its fangs. A hissing telepathic voice slithered through Wystan's mind, raising goosebumps on his arms. *But the other prey? The griffin, the dragon, all the fighters of fire who wait at your border—those are ours?*

No. Horror gripped him, but he couldn't so much as move his lips. Moth's magic held him motionless, helpless.

What do I care for humans and half-humans? Moth replied, her own lip curling in distaste. *Take them. If you dare. I warn you, they have faced your kind before.*

The possessed unicorn hissed. *We know.* The crimson stare fell on Wystan. *But with this one's strength, we will take them easily. Revenge shall be sweet. Hold him still.*

Behind the demon, the ground began to heave.

CHAPTER 34

The Nightmare leaped out of the way as the Jeep slewed past it in a spray of gravel. Candice spun the steering wheel madly, fighting to keep the vehicle on the road.

"Brace yourself, baby!" she yelled to Flash as she wrestled the vehicle back under control. She floored the accelerator, praying that the engine wouldn't stall.

It didn't. It exploded.

A bolt of black lanced through the hood, gutting the car. The steering wheel and pedals went dead. The Jeep shuddered to a halt, thick black smoke pouring past the windows.

Candice tore off her seat belt, hurling herself across Flash. The little unicorn squeaked and struggled, but Candice held her tight.

"Baby, baby, listen to me," she said rapidly, over the *pings* of cooling metal and the hammering of her heart. "I know that's your mom out there. I know you want to go to her. But you can't, not now. I need you to take us to Wystan. Take us both to Wystan, baby."

Flash stared out the side window, quivering. Outside, smoke swirled around a darker shape.

"*Please*, Flash," Candice begged, as the Nightmare stalked toward them in jerky, start-stop steps. "He needs our help. I need your help."

Flash stretched her muzzle out toward the looming Nightmare. She called out to her mother, soft and anguished, every muscle trembling with yearning.

Then she closed her eyes.

The unicorn's horn flared.

"Candice!"

The ground hit her hands and knees. Her ears rang as though she'd been walloped by a golf club. Completely disorientated, Candice stared wildly around. Trees, unicorns, *Wystan—*

"Get away from him!" She flung herself at Moth, who had her horn pressed into Wystan's side. Moth reared, kicking out, but Candice knew how to handle horses. She grabbed the unicorn's upper lip, twisting hard. "Get away from my mate!"

Moth squealed, instinctively going limp like a cat held by the scruff of the neck. Candice dragged the unicorn around in a circle, shoving her away from Wystan. Moth staggered back, shaking her head, dazed.

"Candice!" Wystan shouted again. He was somehow caught, impossibly, in the grip of three saplings that twined around him like a cage. *"Look out!"*

His fear for her screamed down the mate bond. It physically yanked her back, her body moving without her own volition. A gold-and-silver horn cut through the space where her head had just been.

"Petrichor?" Candice hurled herself away as the stallion stabbed at her again. "What the-?"

"It's not Petrichor!" Wystan's pinned hands opened, fingers straining futilely for her. "Get Flash, get out of here, *go!*"

Terror twisted her gut as she recognized the evil red light burning in the stallion's eyes. She threw herself into a diving roll as the possessed unicorn struck at her again, razor-sharp hooves whistling past her ear.

She snatched up Flash, hugging her tight. The baby unicorn was unconscious. She must have strained her power to the limit to teleport them both so far. Candice could only shield the baby with her own body as demon-Petrichor reared above them.

The possessed unicorn's maddened red gaze fell on Flash. Demon-Petrichor suddenly twisted, as though someone had grabbed its ear and wrenched its head away. Candice scrabbled back as its hooves slammed into the ground, barely missing her. The demon hissed and bared its teeth, but didn't attack. It seemed to be wrestling with itself, starting forward and then jerking back as though thinking better of it.

Petrichor's still in there, she realized in a flash of inspiration. *He's stopping the demon from hurting his baby. Just like the Nightmare.*

Tucking Flash awkwardly under one arm, she ran to Wystan. She scrabbled at the tree trunks wrapping him, breaking her nails on unyielding bark.

"Candice! No!" The mate bond pushed at her, trying to force her away. "Run!"

She set her feet stubbornly, twisting at a branch with all her strength. "I'm not leaving you!"

"You have to!" Wystan's voice cracked and broke, raw with desperation. *"There's another one!"*

Something hissed, right behind her. Freezing cold blew across the back of her neck.

She spun around. A horned, serpentine head rose above her, swaying like a cobra. She looked up into hellfire eyes and dripping fangs.

The demon struck.

CHAPTER 35

"*No!*" His unicorn surged up from his soul...but not to shift. It was nothing like his dream. Not gentle, healing light filling his body, gathering soft and warm in his palms.

This power seared through his blood with the force of a supernova. A shockwave of incandescent energy burst from his straining fingers. He struck the demon threatening Candice with a lifetime of pent-up, righteous fury.

The serpent wailed in fear and anger, writhing helplessly as it was blasted back. Moth and the possessed Petrichor went flying too, swept off their feet and hurled away by his power.

His overwhelming need to protect his mate pulsed through his body. A glowing, swirling dome of energy sprang up, completely shielding both Candice and himself.

Lit by sparkling, ever-shifting light, Candice stared at him, Flash still in her arms. "Are you doing that?"

Power burned in his spread fingers. "Apparently?"

Candice flinched as a dark shape struck at the shield from the far side. "How long can you keep it up?"

He clenched his jaw, concentrating on channeling his strength outward. "No idea!"

The horned serpent attacked his shield, silver sparks flaring from its gaping fangs. Wystan felt each bite echo through his body—just a stinging pinch of pain, but enough to warn him that he wouldn't be able to hold the shield indefinitely.

Candice had gone back to tearing at his wooden prison. No matter how she tried, she couldn't bend any of the interwoven branches far enough to let him get free.

"Damn it!" Candice whirled around, glaring through the glittering barrier. "Moth! Whatever you've done, let him go!"

The lead mare was only just regaining her hooves, stunned by the force of his power hitting her. She lifted her head, and her grey eyes widened as she took in the sight of his glowing shield.

I knew it, her voice whispered in his mind. Awe filled the word, and relief, and a deep, bitter triumph. *You were never a healer. Not with those eyes. You are the bloodline we lost—the ones who created our wards, the ones who kept us safe. You are a Guardian.*

"And you're gonna be a throw rug if you don't move these damn trees!" Candice yelled back. "Let him go right now!"

Moth hesitated. She took a limping, hobbling step toward them—and a scaled black shape struck her in the neck.

Wystan threw himself into his shield, straining to push it far enough to cover the lead mare—but it was too late. The demon disappeared into Moth's body, her eyes glowing red as it took possession of her soul.

"Well, that's just wonderful," Candice muttered, as the possessed mare began attacking the shield as well. She dropped to her knees, gently shaking Flash's limp form. "Come on, baby. You have to wake up. You're our only hope now. You have to wake up and get us out of here. We need you."

"Perhaps she's not the only one who could help us." Wystan reached out with his mind as he spoke. "I don't much like the thought of drawing any of the other unicorns into the fight, but we're running short on options. If I can reach them, perhaps they can…"

"What?" Candice said as he trailed off. "Wystan, what is it?"

"The barrier," he whispered. "Not my one. The *other* one."

He could *feel* it, like a crystal dome set over the top of the mountain. Moth had said that it had been created by unicorns like himself. Now, with his power running freely through him at last, he could sense what they'd done.

He closed his eyes, tracing the shape of those ancient wards. The energies wove together like intricate chain mail armor, looped and interlinked. He could feel how it worked, how every part fitted together in exquisite harmony.

And he knew how to undo it.

He took a deep breath. "Candice, help me. I can't do this without you."

She didn't ask what was going on. She didn't so much as hesitate. She simply nodded, mouth setting in a determined line. Leaving Flash lying on the ground, she stretched up to him. Her reaching fingers interlaced through his.

The mate bond roared as their bare skin met. He opened fully to her, showing her what he needed, no shields between them now. In return, she sent him all her fierce love and furious compassion; her boundless drive to save and help and protect. Her soul flooded through him, powerful as the sun. Her strength filled his hands.

Together, they reached out.

And brought down the barrier.

CHAPTER 36

Wystan let out a long, relieved sigh. He opened his eyes, smiling at her. "There. We did it. Everything will be fine now."

Since he was still stuck in a tree while two demon-possessed unicorns poked furiously at his magic whatever-it-was, this seemed wildly optimistic to Candice. Nonetheless, she found herself grinning back at him. She *couldn't* be worried. Not with his calm certainty shimmering down the mate bond, filling her heart with light.

"Cool." She stretched up to kiss him, just about able to reach his mouth. "Uh. What did we just do?"

His lips curved under hers. "Let in help."

An eagle's scream split the air. A huge golden shape swooped down from the sky, striking at the possessed Petrichor with razor-sharp talons. The demon danced back, hissing in fear. The griffin landed in front of it with a thump, wings spread wide.

Edith and Blaise scrambled from Rory's back as he squared off against the possessed unicorn. The two firefighters ran up to Wystan's shield. Edith had a chainsaw over her shoulder, while Blaise clutched a hand axe.

"Wystan!" Edith called as Callum also swooped out of the sky to attack the other possessed unicorn. She struck the barrier with a fist, making sparks fly. "Let us in!"

From the way Wystan's face twisted into a grimace, Candice guessed that he wasn't entirely sure *how* to let them in. "I don't think I can. Not without dropping the whole thing, anyway."

"Do it," Candice urged. Rory and Callum were holding the two demons at bay with bared talons and teeth. Joe had slid off Callum's back and was circling the fight. Candice guessed he was trying to find a clear enough space to shift in the dense forest. "The others have it under control. We have to get you out."

Wystan relaxed his splayed fingers, letting his hands fall again. The glowing shield faded, leaving spots dancing in Candice's vision. She stepped aside to give Edith and Blaise access to her mate.

Edith's eyes swept over Wystan, taking in his predicament. With one smooth, practiced motion, she unshipped her chainsaw, yanking on the cord. The blade roared to life.

"Stay very, *very* still," she advised Wystan.

Candice watched anxiously as they attacked the trees. Catching her eye, Wystan gave her a reassuring smile. He looked remarkable composed for a man having a power tool wielded around his neck.

Something bumped into Candice's ankles. She swallowed a scream, leaping back—but it was only Flash. The baby unicorn was stirring at last, hooves pawing weakly at the air.

"Oh, baby, my brave baby." Candice dropped to her knees, cradling the little unicorn. "Don't try to get up. Everything's okay. You did good, you saved us all. Just stay still and rest."

Flash snorted in denial, still trying to get her legs underneath her. With great effort, she lifted her head an inch from the ground. She made that heart-rending, lost-child call once more.

"I know, you're worried for your daddy." Candice cuddled Flash closer, trying to block the fight from the unicorn's view. She bit her lip as the possessed Petrichor lunged at Rory, forcing the griffin to slash at his flank in defense. "It's going to be okay. They won't hurt him."

"*Rory!*" Wystan shouted. He was only half free of the trees, but he thrust one arm forward, his fingers splaying in the griffin's direction. "Look out!"

A shimmering shield flashed over the griffin just in time. A black bolt of energy hit the swirling silver barrier, shattering into harmless sparks.

"It's the Nightmare!" Joe shouted. He ducked as another blast of dark power cracked past his head. "It's found us!"

"I can only make one shield at a time. I think." Wystan's teeth were clenched, his shield disappearing and reappearing in a frantic dance of light as he tried to protect his friends. "Joe, don't shift, you'll be too big a target! Remember, they can possess you if they bite you!"

Candice squashed back against the tree trunk, giving Wystan a clear view so that he could see where to deploy his shield. Chips of wood showered down around her as Edith and Blaise continued to hack at Wystan's prison.

The battle devolved into a mad scrum of fur and claws and horns. Fenrir joined the fray, appearing out of nowhere—literally—to face off against the Nightmare. He breathed out short blasts of flame, forcing the creature back.

Rory and Callum were also holding their own, but they were handicapped by their desire to not hurt the possessed unicorns. The demons took full advantage, hurling themselves at the shifters with suicidal ferocity. Candice noticed that they were particularly targeting Joe. All it would take was one lucky bite, and they would all have a *really* big problem.

A sparkle of light shimmered in the midst of the melee, catching her eye. Not Wystan's shield, but a brighter, briefer flare.

Her heart turned to ice as she realized Flash was no longer at her side.

"*Flash!*" she screamed as the little unicorn's white form appeared in the middle of the fight. "Wystan, protect her!"

Blaise nearly took Wystan's hand off at the wrist as he twisted around. He was almost free now, but Flash was directly behind his prison. He couldn't see where she was, couldn't get a shield over her in time—

Flash stood between the Nightmare and the possessed Petrichor, tiny and frail. She looked up at the monsters that her parents had become. She called out to them.

The two demons stilled. They turned to Flash, muscles moving jerkily, as if they were puppets on strings. Flash called out again, with the imperious confidence of a beloved child. Crimson eyes narrowed and fang-filled mouths snarled, but the demon bent their heads as though forced to do so by some external force. Softly, gently, Flash touched noses first with her mother, then her father.

The two possessed unicorns collapsed, convulsing. Thick, oily smoke poured from their mouths and nostrils. Darkness drained away from the Nightmare's twisted form, scales rippling into white fur. The red glow faded from their eyes.

Petrichor and Sunrise struggled back to their hooves. Flash danced around them in mad joy as her restored parents leaned on each other, gold-banded horns touching, blue eyes gazing into grey.

"She did it," Wystan breathed, free from his prison at last. "She drove out the demons. We were wrong, it didn't take a true mate. Just love."

Candice clasped his hand, mutual understanding dawning in both their minds. "The demon was never trying to force Sunrise to hunt Flash. It was trying to *stop* Sunrise from going to Flash. All along, she was just trying to get to her baby."

The rancid smoke that had come out of Sunrise and Petrichor was still writhing across the ground. It separated into two long, coiling shapes. Scales and horns solidified. Red eyes opened, burning with hatred. Back in their own true forms, the two demons reared back to strike at their previous hosts.

Wystan surged forward, hand outstretched to throw a shield—but there was no need. In perfect unison, Sunrise and Petrichor leapt past each other, synchronized as ballet dancers. Their horns stabbed down.

Wystan dropped his hand as the light faded from the demons' eyes for good. "Well. I suspect they both found that tremendously cathartic."

"Yep," Candice agreed, as the two unicorns went back to nuzzling at each other and Flash. "Now, what the heck do we do about *her?*"

Demon-Moth was backing away, rolling its eyes frantically as Rory, Callum, and Fenrir closed on it. The possessed unicorn seemed to be searching for a way to flee. Fenrir breathed out a burst of fire, cutting off its escape route.

"Don't hurt her!" Wystan called to his friends. "She's possessed too."

"You really think we can find someone who loves *her?*" Candice muttered as the possessed unicorn hissed like a poisonous snake. "After all she's done?"

Wystan grimaced. "Well, we can't just kill her in cold blood. Have you got your tranquillizer rifle?"

"It's back at my Jeep." Candice looked doubtfully at the angry demon. "I don't think she's gonna wait nicely while I go and fetch it."

"Eh, we can handle one emo pony, bro," Joe said, overhearing. He flashed a cocky grin as though he was personally holding off the demon single-handed rather than standing back at a safe distance. "There's only one of her, after all. What's she going to do?"

Demon-Moth's horn lit up with a sickly, eerie light.

"Joe," Blaise groaned. "Why did you have to say that?"

Callum shied, spinning around on his back hooves, wings half-spreading. His ears swiveled in all directions. He let out a fierce, urgent call, somewhere between a neigh and a hawk's shriek.

"*Back!*" Wystan shouted, grabbing Candice and thrusting her behind him. "Everyone, to me! Quickly!"

The squad obeyed without question, falling back from the demon and clustering around Wystan. Candice pressed herself against him, Rory's golden feathers hemming her in on her other side. Wystan's shield dropped around them all in a shimmer of light.

She'd expected the demon to take the opportunity to flee, but instead it held its ground. Its lips wrinkled back in a freakily human grin. The glow from its horn brightened.

"What's it doing?" she asked Wystan. "What's did Callum sense?"

Wystan had his arms outstretched to either side, fingers spread wide to keep his shield over the whole squad. He jerked his head, gesturing with his chin. *"Them."*

Pale shapes appeared between the trees. Two, four, a dozen, more—what looked like the whole unicorn herd closed in on them, eyes blank. They moved like zombies, lurching and staggering, all grace ripped away. Mindless as moths drawn to light, they began battering at Wystan's shield.

"It's Moth's power." Wystan's expression was grim, his jaw tight with pain as he fought to resist the mass onslaught. "The demon's controlling the whole herd with her magic."

"Wys, I'm sorry, but we've *got* to kill her." Blaise readied her axe in both hands, holding it like a baseball bat. "We haven't got a choice. Drop the shield."

"With the My Little Pony remake of the Walking Dead going on?" Joe yelped. "Bronicorn stops doing his thing, we're all shish-kebabs!"

Drop it just long enough to let me out, Rory's voice spoke in Candice's head, making her jump. The griffin crouched down, powerful haunches gathering. **I'll deal with her.**

"Rory, no!" Edith grabbed her mate's wing, holding him back. "You can't, not alone! Look behind her!"

Candice squinted through the sparkling shield. Her heart lurched as she saw what Edith had spotted. The ground in the clearing was humping and cracking again. More horned heads thrust out of the dirt.

"Oh no," Candice breathed, as the newly-hatched demons squirmed free. "They'll go after the unicorns!"

Pack must protect, Fenrir growled. **Pull down the prey together. Only hope.**

Rory's beak clenched. **All together, then. On three. One. Two—**

A deafening thunderclap drowned his words. Incandescent light lanced down into the clearing.

"Yes!" Blaise punched the air as the lightning bolt hit the heart of the demons' nest dead on. She threw her head back, aiming her words at the sky. "I could *kiss* you!"

Thunder rumbled in answer. The Thunderbird's vast silhouette swept over their heads, half-hidden by the forest canopy. Candice caught a glimpse of a white, blank eye, alien and impenetrable, staring down at them through the leaves. Then it was gone, the huge creature soaring silently away once more.

The hatching demons had disappeared, blasted apart instantly by the Thunderbird's wrath. The entire clearing was burning, bone-dry trees going up in flames like lit matches.

The demon possessing Moth screeched in terror, backlit by fire. Its muscles twitched and trembled as though it was desperate to flee, yet its hooves stayed glued to the ground. It tossed its head, plunging and writhing, seeming to be fighting with itself. Its eyes met Candice's.

The red glow flickered, revealing grey. Just for an instant, Moth looked back at her.

Take care of them, the lead mare whispered in her mind.

The demon fought, but Moth's will was stronger. Candice's last sight of Moth was the mare standing perfectly still as the flames engulfed her.

The other unicorns' eyes cleared, all at once. They shook their heads as though waking up from a dream—and shrieked in fear as they saw the forest fire sweeping toward them.

"No, don't run!" Wystan shouted. His shield flickered and faded. "In here!"

Sunrise arched her neck, calling out to the panicked unicorns in clear, firm command. Instinctively, the herd obeyed their new lead mare. They gathered around her, white bodies packing tight.

Wystan drew in a deep breath. His hand sought hers, gripping tight. She squeezed his fingers in return in silent assent and reassurance.

Wystan squared his shoulders. His shield reappeared, much larger this time, protecting the entire herd. Candice could feel him shaking with the effort. She wrapped her arms around him, bracing him with her mind as much as her body.

His love wrapped around her in return. She opened her heart to him, as he opened to her, holding nothing back.

The firestorm swept around them, powerless in the face of their united strength. She couldn't have said how long it lasted. It could have been five minutes. It could have been eternity. She just held onto her mate, supporting him. Heartbeat to heartbeat, moment to moment.

One breath at a time.

CHAPTER 37

"Fifty-seven deer," Bethany repeated, her voice going high with disbelief. *"Fifty-seven deer?"*

Candice leaned her elbows on the rail fence, gazing at the field of unicorns. "More or less."

Most of the herd were sleeping, exhausted after the long, hard trek down from the mountain. Princess and the other rescued horses grazed peacefully alongside the slumbering unicorns, not at all disconcerted by their strange new paddock-mates. Which was more than Candice could say for the humans. Even now, half a dozen ranch-hands and volunteers were hanging around the edges of the field, gawping at the latest animal refugees to arrive at the emergency shelter.

If only they knew what they were really looking at, Candice thought in amusement. *Then they'd* really *be staring.*

"Only you would rescue an entire herd of deer from a forest fire." The vet shook her head, her expression caught somewhere between admiration and utter despair. "An entire herd of *albino* deer, at that. How on earth did that happen?"

Candice shrugged. "Guess they've just been an isolated for a long time. Mutated genes in a small population, you know."

"Maybe," Bethany said, sounding doubtful. "Though from my examinations, they're all in perfect health, without any signs of inbreeding. And ridiculously tame. Even so, I can't imagine how you persuaded them all to follow your Jeep all the way back to this ranch."

Candice gestured at Sunrise, who was nuzzling Flash. "Oh, it wasn't hard. I just had to get the lead mare on my side."

Bethany narrowed her eyes at her. "You mean the alpha doe."

"Do I?" Candice said innocently.

Bethany continued to glare at her for a long moment. "I get the feeling there's a lot of this story that you're not telling me."

"Sorry." Candice grinned at her friend. "There's a lot of stuff I had to promise to keep secret. Keep watching the herd. Maybe you'll figure some of it out."

Leaving Bethany staring at the field of unicorns with a perplexed frown, she headed back toward the barns. She wondered if Bethany *would* see through the unicorns' concealing illusion. She'd had to promise to Sunrise that she wouldn't outright *tell* anyone the truth about the herd, but that didn't mean she couldn't drop a few hints.

I really hope she does *work it out.* Fifty-seven displaced, homeless unicorns were a *big* responsibility. She needed all the help she could get.

Not that she didn't already have a lot of help. Her heart lifted as she spotted A-squad's battered yellow truck parked outside the main ranch house, along with a couple of other Thunder Mountain Hotshot crew transports. The firefighters had returned at last. She could still see smoke rising from the distant peak of the unicorn mountain, but the crew must have managed to contain the worst of the blaze.

She hastened her steps, more than her own anticipation thrilling down the mate bond. Sure enough, Wystan jumped down from his squad's vehicle, his face lighting up as he saw her. She could sense the exhaustion weighing down his limbs, but he still caught her up in his arms, her feet coming clear off the ground as he kissed her.

"Blough." Candice made a face, even as she enthusiastically kissed him back. "You're filthy."

The soot ingrained into his skin cracked as he smiled ruefully. His hair was more grey than white, flecked with ash. "It's quite a mess up there. The old barrier did its job a little *too* well. If the unicorns had let the occasional little forest fire sweep through to clean out the worst of the dead undergrowth every few years, the whole place wouldn't have gone up the way it did."

"And maybe the demons would never have emerged. I got the impression they aren't big fans of fire." Candice slid back down his body to the ground. "Is it all under control now?"

"Yes. There are still a few other crews up there, tackling the last few hotspots, but there's no danger of the fire spreading any further." His smile faded. "But we couldn't do anything to save the unicorn homeland. There isn't anything left for the herd to return to, I'm afraid."

From what she'd seen of the fire in her rearview mirror as she'd led the unicorn herd away, she'd suspected that would be the case. She kissed him again. "I'm just glad you're safe."

"Of course he was," Rory said, appearing around the side of the truck. He slapped Wystan on the back, grinning broadly. "With this man on the team, the whole squad doesn't have anything to fear. His shield trick came in handy more than once while we were mopping up."

"Well, I don't care how essential he is, I'm not going to let you work him into the ground." Candice wound a possessive arm around her mate's waist. "Come on, Wystan. I have something for you."

A loud wolf-whistle came from inside the truck. "Go, bronicorn!"

"A *shower*," Candice clarified.

"A shower?" Blaise stuck her head out the side window, fixing her with entreating, puppy-dog eyes. "Candice, I love you. Ditch Wystan. Run away with me instead. Have my gloriously clean, soapy babies."

Candice laughed, already steering Wystan away. "Sorry. Gonna stick with this one. He's a genuine unicorn, after all."

"What *am* I going to do with fifty-seven unicorns?" she said to Wystan, much later.

They were back in the hayloft. Moonlight shone soft through the half-open hatch. Small white moths fluttered through the beams, drawn by the warm glow of Wystan's flashlight. In the barn below them, horses dreamed, bedded down into stalls for the night. The occasional stamp of a hoof or soft, contented snort drifted up.

Wystan's bare chest moved under her cheek as he chuckled. "Fifty-eight unicorns," he corrected her.

She trailed kisses down his throat. "Oh, I know exactly what to do with you."

His fingertips traced patterns over her shoulder, raising a delicious shiver across her naked skin. "You certainly do."

She hooked a leg over his hip, snuggling closer to him—and winced as something hard and stiff jabbed her thigh.

"One of these days, we're gonna have sex in an actual bed," she said, fishing out the stray stalk of straw and flicking it away.

Wystan chuckled again. "The end of fire season can't come too soon, as far as I'm concerned."

She propped herself up on one elbow, gazing down at him. "But you love it really, don't you?"

"Firefighting?" He let out his breath, staring up at the moths dancing in the beam from their flashlight. "Yes. I do. But it's not exactly a nine-til-five sort of job. If you wanted me to find something else—"

She pressed a finger to his mouth, silencing him. "I don't. Your crew needs you, and you need them. We'll work something out."

His lips curved. He kissed her fingertip. "One day at a time?"

"Exactly." She drew her hand down his chest, still hardly able to believe that all this perfect male was *hers*. "One day at a time."

One of the moths dove down, battering its soft grey wings against the front of the flashlight. Wystan flicked his fingers. His shield sparkled into life, protecting the moth from hurting itself.

She watched as his shield gently chivvied the insect away from the light. "You're getting good at that."

"Mmm. I think it's more that I've finally worked out how to *stop* doing it." Wystan's expression turned thoughtful as he guided the moth out the hatch again with brief nudges of his power. "I think...I think I was always doing it, before. I thought that my unicorn just wasn't sensitive to sexual energy, but now I think I must have been shielding myself without knowing I was doing it, all the time. I always used to get so tired around crowds..." He looked back at her, eyes softening. "Until you came along. And I stopped shielding myself. You remember the first time the Nightmare attacked us? The fire?"

"I didn't get burned," Candice said, realizing what he meant. "Even when I ran into the trailer with sparks flying all around, my clothes didn't get so much as singed. *Yours* did, though. You reckon you were subconsciously shielding me instead of protecting yourself?"

"Exactly." He touched her chest, above her heart. "Whenever we were apart, I felt like part of me was still back with you. And it was."

"Huh." She lay back down again, on top of him, though she kept her chin propped up on one fist so she could still see his face. "I found out how Moth knew you weren't a healer, by the way. Sunrise told me. She couldn't believe we hadn't already worked it out. Your dad's got blue eyes, hasn't he?"

His eyebrows rose. "He does indeed. How did you guess?"

"Because so does Sunrise." She traced the line of his cheekbone. "Remember how Moth going on about bloodlines? Unicorn powers *are* genetic. They're linked to eye color. All healers have blue eyes. But yours are green."

"Like my mother's. She's a wyvern shifter." Wystan's face broke into a wondering, startled smile. "Moth did say that wild talents cropped up when different bloodlines mix. And I'm certainly a little more mixed than most. So there aren't any green-eyed unicorns in the herd?"

"Not for generations." She made a face. "Seriously, Wystan, what *am* I going to do with fifty-seven unicorns? Sunrise is going to make a kick-ass lead mare, but she doesn't know anything about the wider world. She's depending on me to find a new home for them all."

"I...might have an idea about that." He hesitated, eying her.

"There's a lot of unused land around our hotshot base back in Montana. Superintendent Buck basically owns most of Thunder Mountain. We keep the forest maintained, but other than that it's been left to go wild. It's quiet, out of the way, unspoiled…"

"And perfect," she finished for him. She caught her breath, delight rising. "Wystan, that's perfect! Do you think I could get a job nearby? I could be close to you and still help out the herd!"

"I haven't told you all of it, yet." She could sense his nervousness down the mate bond, as though he wasn't quite sure how she was going to react. "There's a ranch."

She stared down at him. "A…ranch?"

"A small horse ranch, on Buck's land, right at the foot of the mountain. We sometimes hike past it when we're training. It's old. Fallen into disrepair. I don't think Buck's even been down there for years." Wystan frowned a little. "He went a little quiet when I asked him about it, which isn't like him. But to cut a long story short, he's willing to let us have it. You could start up your own animal refuge. If you wanted."

Her mouth had gone dry. "But…I don't have any money."

"Er." He looked slightly embarrassed. "That's not an issue. My family owns a fair chunk of England. And my mother actually runs her own charity, for orphaned shifter kids. I'm sure she'd be delighted to help you get started with the business side of things." He trailed off, anxiously scrutinizing her face. "If you want to."

She flung her arms around his neck, kissing every part of him she could reach. "Yes! Oh, yes!"

He laughed out loud, his arms coming up to hold her tight. "Don't get too excited just yet. I have to warn you, the ranch is pretty derelict. The stables and barns are still standing, but the house apparently burned to the ground years ago. We'll be living out of a trailer for a while. It's going to be a lot of hard work."

"But we'll do it together." She hugged him back, feeling his deep, quiet joy rising to meet hers, shimmering down the mate bond. "One day at a time."

EPILOGUE

*V*ery few brides were escorted down the aisle by unicorns. Flash went first, proudly bearing the rings aloft on her tiny horn. Joe grinned at the ripple that went through the crowd as the young unicorn pranced between the flower-decked rows of seats.

"Good thing everyone here is either a shifter or knows about us," he murmured to Blaise, who was sitting next to him. "Otherwise we'd have a *lot* of explaining to do."

Blaise elbowed him in the ribs. "Shut up. Here they come."

Sunrise and Bethany were next, the human bridesmaid bearing both a bouquet and a distinct *how-is-this-my-life* expression. The vet had been in on the secret of the unicorns for months now, but still hadn't fully adjusted to her expanded reality.

Sunrise, of course, was as serene as ever, luminous as the full moon. White roses and forget-me-nots were woven into her rippling mane. A hint of roundness to her flanks showed that Flash would soon have a new baby brother or sister. Sunrise paced solemnly at Bethany's side, but her blue eyes danced with delight.

And last, but by no means least, came Candice.

Her dress was as perfectly white as the unicorns' coats, brilliant in the warm May sunshine. Her smile shone brighter than their horns.

Joe turned to look at Wystan, waiting for his bride at the front of the gathering under an arch of white roses. Rory stood by his side in his role of best man, magnificent in full kilt, grinning from ear to ear. And Wystan...

The pure joy filling Wystan's face sent a stab of pain through Joe's heart. Happy as he was for his friend, it was abruptly too much.

"Joe!" Blaise hissed as he sidled away from his seat. "Where are you going?"

"Usher duties," he improvised. "Got to check everything's ready for the reception after the ceremony. Be back in a sec."

It was generally hard to escape unobtrusively when you were nearly seven feet tall. Fortunately, everyone else was too enraptured with the bride to pay him any attention. Grateful that Candice and Wystan had decided to hold their wedding outside at their new ranch, he fled.

The music faded behind him as he ducked into one of the barns. The inside of the freshly-restored building was draped in silk and flower garlands, the plank floor polished and gleaming, ready for the dancing later. Trestle tables laden with refreshments lined the walls, awaiting the guests.

He snagged the nearest bottle of wine, popping the cork off with his thumb. Leaning back against the wall, he raised the bottle to his mouth, already anticipating the comforting numbness.

Someone said his name. Not his human name. His *real* name. All thirty-eight rolling, liquid syllables.

There was only one person who called him *that*.

Joe sighed, letting the bottle fall back, untouched. "Hi, Dad."

Light gleamed from polished steel armor as his father moved out of the shadows. Deep blue eyes fixed on him in a familiar expression of disappointment. "You are supposed to be at the ceremony."

Joe gave the bottle of wine one last longing look, and returned it to the table. "So are you."

"*I* am the Imperial Consort, Champion of the Pearl Throne, Guardian of the Empress." His father touched the hilt of his sword, slung as ever across his shoulders. "It is my duty to stay on guard, ready to meet any threat that might dare to attack your mother."

Joe raised a skeptical eyebrow. "At a party?"

The pearl set into the pommel of the sword winked at him as his father shifted his shoulders, looking a little rueful. "Also, weddings make me cry. Which is not entirely befitting the dignity of the Pearl Throne. Why are *you* not witnessing your companion's hour of triumph?"

Bitter jealousy rose in his throat. He swallowed it back, pasting a carefree grin onto his face instead. "Oh, you know. Not big on true love and eternal commitment, me."

"Yes," his father said, distinct disapproval darkening his tone. "I know. I hope that you are not planning to do anything that might dishonor your name."

"Well, at least you don't need to fear catching me with one of the bridesmaids." Joe started to duck out the door again. "Great talk, Dad. We must do this again next year. Bye."

"Wait." Something in his father's voice made him pause, though he didn't look back. "I wish to speak with you further."

Joe sighed again. "How have I brought shame upon the ocean *this* time?"

"You have not." His father cleared his throat. "Your mother and I are...proud of you, son."

That *did* make him turn. "Who are you and what have you done with my father?"

His father looked down at his gauntleted hands. "I am aware that we have not enjoyed the easiest of relationships. I must admit, when I coerced you to join Rory's firefighting squad, I did not have high hopes that you would rise to the challenge."

That sounded a lot more like the father he knew. Joe relaxed a little, no longer looking for the tell-tale signs of demonic possession. "I'm happy that I once again failed to meet your expectations."

His father blew out his breath, looking annoyed. "Please drop your foolishness for one minute. I am trying to say that I was wrong. I thought to punish you for your frivolous ways, force you to experience true hardship. I secretly hoped that you would end up begging me to allow you to return to the sea and finally take up your duties as the Heir to the Pearl Throne. But...you have won a true place for yourself here. You have fought with honor, guarded your companions against a foe that none of us knew existed. You have more than proven yourself."

Joe stared at him, still half-expecting some kind of trap. "I'm still not coming back to the sea, if that's what you're getting at. It may not have been my idea to join the squad, but they're my family now. They need me here."

"Yes," his father agreed quietly. "They do. Now more than ever, with these strange demonic forces threatening the land. I am glad that you are staying. But I am also worried. As is your mother. You are our only son. More than that, you are the Heir. You will be the next Pearl Emperor. The sea cannot afford to lose you."

"So I'll be careful," Joe said, shrugging. "Is that all?"

"No." His father drew himself up to his full height. "Your mother and I spoke on this matter, before we came here. We agreed to let you stay, but only on one condition."

"What?" Joe said warily.

His father moved to one side, turning. "That you agree to accept a bodyguard."

Someone stepped out of the shadows. Someone pale and slight, clad from head to foot in form-fitting armor. Her fierce, guarded eyes met his—

∽

"Joe! *Joe!*"

Joe jerked upright, heart hammering. Wystan let go of his shoulder, backing off with upraised hands.

"You were having a nightmare," his friend said. "You were yelling loudly enough that I heard you all the way up in the hayloft."

Joe stared around, sweat clammy on his skin. He was tangled up in his bedroll. He remembered laying it out against the side of the barn.

In the distance, he could make out the gleaming white forms of the unicorn herd, napping together in a field. The ranch lay still and peaceful under the stars.

Not Wystan and Candice's ranch. Not yet.

That hadn't happened yet.

"I can't come to your wedding," he blurted out.

Wystan stared at him as though he'd just announced he couldn't go to Mars. "Candice and I only just got together. We haven't exactly started discussing dates yet."

"You're getting married next May. Pick the eighteenth. The weather will be good." Joe scrubbed his hands over his face, still fighting free from the too-real vision. "But I can't come. Sorry."

Wystan patted his shoulder tentatively. "All…right. That's fine, Joe. You just lie down. Go back to sleep."

"Yeah," Joe muttered, letting his friend pull his blanket back over him. "Okay."

He stared up at the stars, head whirling with his unwanted power.

The power that he'd never told anyone about.

"May," he muttered to himself. He closed his eyes. "A lot can happen before then. It'll be okay. I'll find a way out. I always do."

He had until May to work out how to avoid meeting his mate.

Or else she would die.

~

Joe meets his doom in Wildfire Sea Dragon
- coming soon!
To be notified when it's out, join my mailing list.

Have you read the first Fire & Rescue Shifters series, featuring the parents of the Wildfire Crew?
If not, binge the complete series starting with Firefighter Dragon

ALSO BY ZOE CHANT

Fire & Rescue Shifters

Firefighter Dragon
Firefighter Pegasus
Firefighter Griffin
Firefighter Sea Dragon
The Master Shark's Mate
Firefighter Unicorn
Firefighter Phoenix

Fire & Rescue Shifters Collection 1

Fire & Rescue Shifters: Wildfire Crew

Wildfire Griffin
Wildfire Unicorn
Wildfire Sea Dragon (coming in Fall 2019)

… and many more! See the complete list at www.zoechant.com

WRITING AS HELEN KEEBLE

Author's Note: These are YA paranormal comedies, not adult romances. No sex, no swearing, lots of laughs!

Fang Girl

No Angel

"Keeble's entertaining plot contains action and suspense coupled with a witty protagonist and a great cast of secondary characters. A funny, refreshing novel." (School Library Journal)

"Quirky and fun. The authentic teen dialogue is refreshing and reminiscent of Louise Rennison's Confessions of Georgia Nicolson series." (Voice of Youth Advocates (VOYA))

"Likable voice, well-drawn characters and dead-on humor."--Kirkus Reviews

Printed in Great Britain
by Amazon